1

CW00848347

THE CONTINENT OF LIES

By

GEOFFREY SEED

First published in 2014 by CreateSpace Independent
Publishing Platform

ISBN : 978-1499146042

www.geoffreyseed.com

Geoffrey Seed is a former newspaper and TV journalist. After leaving the Daily Mail, he worked for every leading current affairs programme - Granada's World in Action, BBC Panorama and the ITV series, Real Crime, which critically re-examined controversial murder cases.

He specialised in producing major TV investigations - from cocaine smuggling in Colombia and political repression in the Soviet Union to torture in southern Africa and the British army's covert involvement in terrorism in Northern Ireland.

He is married with three grown up children and lives in mid Wales.

The Convenience of Lies is a follow-up to his acclaimed debut novel, A Place of Strangers.

4

Praise for **A Place Of Strangers**

"Geoffrey Seed certainly has a place in the line of successors to le Carré while at the same time being completely unique. Highly recommended for all spy novel lovers." Karen Bryant Doering, US book reviewer

"...one of my all-time favourite books, gripping, dark and haunting, too. Several days after finishing, I am still thinking about it and the dilemmas it poses." Anne Loader, ex-newspaper editor and independent publisher

"Nothing is what it seems in this beautifully written spy story. Morally complex, multi-layered and intelligent. A book to be savoured and enjoyed." Alan P. Wilson, law lecturer

"Astonishingly well written and a fascinating read... full of twists and turns right to the very end." Audrey Johns, landscape artist

"Seed is a brilliant writer." Valerie Byron, author, Los Angeles

Dedicated to the memory of my mother, Joan Ruleman

*

As for certain truth,
no man has known it... for all is
but a woven web of guesses.

Xenophon
435-354BC

Prologue

On the day little Ruby Ross disappeared and her mother became so consumed by fears of death she could barely speak or breathe, it was hot enough for a television weather man to go into the street and fry an egg on a car. He cracked it into a pool of cooking oil spitting on the bonnet then prodded away with a wooden spatula till the egg was round and sunny and good enough to eat.

Ruby thought this silly. Eggs must only be fried in a frying pan, never on a car and she would have shouted this at the TV but something different came on. Army men were firing guns at people running across a sandy beach towards the sea. Then a helicopter flew low over the building where the picture-maker was hiding by a window. There was lots of swirling black smoke and really loud bangs. Some children screamed and the grown-ups were yelling in a language Ruby did not know for this was happening in a far away place where palm trees grew.

She was sure this wasn't make-believe. It was on the news and they only put grown-up things like wars on the news. Violence frightened Ruby. She jumped up from the settee and pushed through the beaded curtain to the kitchen then out into the safety of the communal yard with its bins and bikes and cars with no wheels, all simmering in the summer heat.

Ruby felt happier here. Mum would be too busy to wonder where she might be or what she was up to. She was still with the man who often came to their flat for a reading. He had pink eyes and a mark like strawberry jam on his neck. Mum called him *Mr Ginger* because of his hair.

Ruby always registered those who materialised in the landscape of her closed and very private life. The art was in the seeing. The camera of her mind's eye ensured those she did not like couldn't ever cross into her world - the one beyond the casual cruelties of this.

'You go and watch television or do your drawing,' Mum said. 'I've got work to do.'

Then she'd led Mr Ginger into her bedroom. Ruby heard the key turn and a cassette of wave and waterfall music click on. Mum always took her regulars in there. She would close the velvet curtains then light candles scented like peaches which glowed behind lumps of amethyst in front of the dressing table mirror.

So now Ruby could play as she pleased and make herself invisible to the other neighbourhood children. She was glad they didn't want her at school any more. It only upset her there and gave her angry tempers. They said she was bad so she knew there must be a naughty part of her brain which made her different. It was best for everyone for Ruby to be on her own.

She left Linden House and turned into Woodberry Street, lined with poplar trees where she'd seen spiky green caterpillars crawling in the leaves. The air tasted gritty and smelled like disinfectant from the melting road tar being squeezed into folds beneath the wheels of the rat-run traffic.

It took only a moment for Ruby to be absorbed into a blur of strangers - women in saris pushing prams, men with skullcaps carrying food for Shabbes in blue plastic bags. Few would later recall such a waif of a girl, ghosting between the bleaching sunlight and the dusty shadows.

Here was a child hiding in plain sight, eyes averted and hugging the wall. Those who might have noticed her couldn't be sure if they had when police came to question them later.

For now, Ruby considered going to Café Leila where they gave her milk and biscuits because she weighed no more than a doll and needed nourishing. But she didn't and that was a tragedy as Leila would tell the policeman who called.

'Such evil in the world you wouldn't believe,' she said. 'We're all as the leaves in autumn. We come, we go, we blow away - but not to vanish like this.'

Ruby made instead for her favourite place in all her world - the reservoir. It would be cool there. She could climb her magic tree and watch for her unicorn and be safe from all she didn't understand. So Ruby skipped her oblivious way down Park Street, by the carousels of fast drying washing on lawns of beaten earth and as she did, she sang to herself for who at all the open windows would bother to listen?

Six little mice sat down to spin, Pussy passed by and she peeped in.

What are you doing, my little men? Weaving coats for gentlemen.

Never once did she step on a crack or a sweet wrapper so Ruby's special rules allowed her passage to the most secret of paths without having to start all over again. But first, she must spin round twice on one leg then bow three times to the guards of the bushes so they might raise their swords and let her through.

Then Ruby was free to run into the tunnel of darkness ahead. Yet she must be quick for there was danger within. The overhanging laurel twigs caught in her wiry brown hair like the claws of bats and that scared her. But at the far end was the wooden fence where it took only a second to be up and over and into the promised land beyond.

On the far bank of the reservoir was the yellow castle - *her* castle, reflected on the placid sheen of water, all turrets and towers and bigger than a hundred houses. Here was where the unicorn lived and Ruby reigned, a princess worshipped by each of her subjects and all their animals for they thought her the most beautiful and wise ruler they could ever have.

Ruby never needed to actually go inside the yellow castle to know where each log-smoked fireplace was placed, where every brocaded curtain hung and each foot-worn corridor led. These were her hidden places where only Princess Ruby could go for the key to the castle's iron-studded door was in her head… and no one knew how to get in there.

So she made for her great horse chestnut tree and its cruck of high branches from where she could gaze across to the battlements of her fortress haven and act out her engagements for another royal day.

Shall I come in and cut off your threads?
No, no, Mistress Pussy, you'd bite off our heads.

But something dark moved across her path between the tumps of marsh grass and the snagging brambles alongside. It was only a small shadow, no bigger than a man's and would soon vanish as the massing thunderheads smothered the sun.

Ruby stopped singing. Later that night, her mother's cries would echo back from the sheer cliff face of the castle walls and slip unanswered beneath the inky black waters far below.

One

McCall never wanted to be in Oxford that morning, shouldn't have let himself be bounced into seeing a psychiatrist when all he wished for was to be left alone. The session was the mistake he feared so he'd walked out.

Three heretics were once chained to stakes and burned like witches near to where he now stood. The martyrs' sculpted images stared blindly from the whittled stone spire commemorating their tortured passage to heaven. People still held what others charged were false beliefs but they were tethered to couches now, consumed only by their own despair.

In his heart and in his bones, McCall knew he and his career were fast falling to earth and he'd lost the means to save himself. One is what one does. If there is no purpose to it any more, what fills the void or banishes the shame of that which cannot be put right?

McCall never truly signed up for the interrogation he'd just quit. He had neither the desire nor the courage to submit to the artful little man in the brown corduroy suit and lemon bow tie who feigned insight into a world of which he could know nothing.

'Why have you stopped being a journalist, Mr McCall?'

'I haven't, not really.'

'So when did you last write for a newspaper or research a television programme?'

'A while back.'

'Why might that be?'

'I've needed some time out.'

'What about Iraq invading Kuwait only this week? That's your sort of story, isn't it?'

'Not any more.'

'Is that because your wife worries about the risks you take?'

'I'm not married.'

'And you've no girlfriend or a partner?'

'No one who goes the distance, no.'

'Do you find commitment difficult, then?'

'No... sometimes.'

'Right, well we can come back to that. Now, the note from your GP says your last assignment was in Africa. I don't know that part of the world, so where were you?'

'In the north of Namibia, near the border with Angola.'

'That's a pretty dangerous place, isn't it? Always a war going on.'

'It's called the liberation struggle.'

'Or what the South African government calls terrorism?'

'It's a cliché but don't they say one man's terrorist is another man's freedom fighter?'

'I suppose so but what was the story you were after?'

McCall broke off eye contact then to stare instead at the diorama of tawny-coloured colleges beyond the window, each patinated by age and learning and set beneath the turrets and towers of churches demanding obeisance to an all-powerful God.

'Did something happen out in Africa, Mr McCall... happen to you, I mean?'

It wasn't the shrink's fault - and it was arrogant to entertain the thought - but what direct experience had he of the unquiet world outside his consulting room? Neither his words nor his drugs could ever erase the blurred little cave paintings of memory McCall saw in the dark or absolve him from all the occluded guilt of years spent whoring through the misery of others.

This was his problem... that and the face of the Namibian boy staring up from the bloody earth at a white man in a blue sky getting darker with every click of a camera. The image drew McCall back again and again to a tiny kraal in a wilderness of thorn bushes. The child's lips move though he has nothing to say any more. His eyelids flutter, moths at a flame, then are still. All is quiet but for the gathering of flies and the shrieks of scavenging birds circling on a thermal high above.

How pink human tissue is, how like ivory our bones. And in the sand and amid the shit of animals, the brass casings of bullets glint like golden splinters.

The boy hadn't fallen alone that day. But unlike them, McCall was spirited to safety. Those whose eviscerated lives had little value but to enrich his own were left to bloat in the pitiless heat.

Yet here was a crime scene. His fingerprints were everywhere should anyone care to look. The proof was in each of his pictures. More powerfully, it was in his head and in the eyes of a child with no name who may haunt him for ever.

But under the psychiatrist's questioning, McCall knew he was being opened up, slowly and slyly as he himself had done so often as a hack to get inside whoever he'd needed to befriend or suborn.

'Look, no offence but I feel a real fraud for coming to see you.'

'Believe me, you shouldn't, not for a moment.'

'No, but I do. You must have far needier patients than me.'

'Possibly, but you require my help, too... and you're here now.'

'But only because I fancied a drive through the Cotswolds.'

'Why do you make so light of what's affecting you, Mr McCall?'

'Because I don't want the black dog barking at me.'

'Should I take that as a tacit acknowledgement of your depression?'

McCall had admitted too much already. It wasn't just political lives which were doomed to end in failure. He rose and moved towards the door.

'Leave if you must but talk to someone, Mr McCall. Anyone, doesn't have to be me.'

He went without another word and made no new appointment. Outside, he shielded his eyes against the fierce August sun. He thought of crossing the street for no other purpose than to look more closely at the Martyrs' Memorial or to see the ancient gate charred by the very flames which were the winding sheets of the heretics.

But there seemed no point - not to this or much else. His Morgan was parked near the station. He would head home to the Welsh border country, foot hard down as if nothing really mattered.

Being in Oxford somehow made everything worse. Its cleverness and urbanity were mortared between the stones, cut and dressed and perfectly appointed. Those who studied here had that look of brahminical entitlement to succeed where he had long since failed. It was no longer possible for McCall to be the person he pretended to be. Africa had finally robbed him of artifice and condemned him to wander his own little asphodel meadow.

He turned by the haughtily gothic Randolph Hotel but was stopped from going any further by a line of metal barriers. Beaumont Street was closed off for the filming of a new episode of *Inspector Morse.*

McCall scanned the TV production crew with a casual interest. He'd worked with the sound recordist fitting a radio mic inside Morse's jacket and got a surprised but friendly wave. Then his gaze fell on someone else he knew yet whose coincidental presence in that street at that moment defied all logic.

On the hotel steps stood Lexie Nadin, his personal Lorelei whose treacherous song he once followed to near destruction. Her hair was no longer the colour of straw but a salty, driftwood grey. Yet that odd conjunction of a child's smile in a courtesan's face had barely altered.

Almost a quarter century had passed since he last woke beside her and saw in those sea-green eyes all the promises she was to break.

And now the once stage-struck hopeful who needed drama every day, was an extra preparing to shoot a scene in "Inspector Morse".

What confronted McCall was surreal… life conflating with art. How could any of this *be*? Hurt and bitterness were supposed to fade in time because there is no grave over which grass will not eventually grow. For an instant, he felt again that gravitational pull he'd once been powerless to resist. But that was then. Fragile as he might be, McCall still retained some instinct for self-preservation. He took a couple of steps back into the anonymous crowd of autograph hunters and tourists then vanished before he could be seen. At least, that's what he thought.

Two

At home next morning, McCall re-read the letter from his adoptive mother's solicitor and knew a melancholy duty could be put off no longer.

Dear Mac

I write to say that all the legal formalities conveying Mrs Beatrice Wrenn's estate to you as sole beneficiary viz Garth Hall near Ludlow, Shropshire, all contents, land, shares etc, are almost complete. I also enclose a note she wrote for you and which has just been forwarded to my office from the care home in Israel where she died.

It would have been my wish to have accompanied you when her ashes are scattered on Long Mynd as per her instructions. Alas, I must plead old age and infirmity but I will think of you when, in due course, you do so - albeit that I shall have a heavy heart. Beatrice was a most remarkable woman and it was an honour for me to have been both friend and adviser to her and to her late husband.

Bea's writing was barely legible. Her sight had almost gone by the end. The multiple strokes she had suffered impaired the ability of this once cinematically captivating woman to walk or talk.

Yet she had managed to scrawl a final message to the man she helped to mould - however imperfectly - from the mutely damaged little boy whose birth parents died in tragic circumstances.

Think only of our happy days, Mac. Forgive my failings, please, but I tried my best, poor though it was. I was cursed to live in interesting times.

There is a line in the Talmud which I once heard, something about life being a passing shadow, the shadow of a bird in its flight so take heed of this, dearest boy. My most fervent wish is for you to find the peace of mind you have always sought.

Later that day, McCall paused amid the heather and curlew calls of Long Mynd, a thousand feet and more up its rocky breastbone. He looked over towards the wooded Welsh hills where Bea's roots were deep laid.

She'd known the misty flounces of the Mynd, places of myth and legend, battles and sorcery, of bronze-age burial sites and the still-used pathways of Neolithic traders. Bea played games in these ice-gouged valleys as a child, made camp fires, feasted on sweet wimberries and ran herself ragged in a breeze which blew from all the counties at her feet and the world beyond.

Of the woman she became, of her guile and alluring beauty, only crushed traceries of fluted bone remained, white and brittle like fossils from a desert and held in a cardboard box.

But it was time to part so McCall let her go, let her fly into the wind that whispered her home and into the ancient earth once more.

When it was done, when he was finished, McCall turned and walked away, her dust on his hands and her face in his head.

*

He drove through oak woods and hill farms on his way back to Garth Hall. Here was his refuge, a place of genteel decay where he began his bewildered childhood, journeying through the remains of other lives in rooms no one used anymore and nothing was properly understood. This was his own subconscious border country, the poet's land of lost content where all was safe.

Yet however hard McCall searched for the place to cross back into what he once had, he was never able to find the path. There was no right of return.

He parked the Morgan in the stable yard and heard Hester shout a welcome from the open kitchen window.

'I've made some elderflower cordial,' she said. 'You want some?'

'Please, yes.'

He made for the deck chairs in the shaded cool beneath the great copper beech on Garth's meadow of a back lawn.

Hester came through the slanting sunshine in a saffron kaftan she'd made herself, wayward grey hair held in a peasant scarf.

She'd arrived at Garth in a psychedelically-daubed camper van five years before, an American earth mother on the wrong side of sixty seeking out her family's Celtic ancestry.

'My, what a magical old house,' she'd said. 'Feels like in that poem... you know, that one about Wales having no present, only the past... all wind-bitten towers and castles.'

Bea hadn't long since gone to see out her widowed days with an ex-lover in Israel, leaving Garth to its ghosts and McCall to cope alone. So Hester took one of the guest rooms and lived rent-free in return for gardening and keeping house.

She placed McCall's drink on the wicker table between them.

'So, you did it, Mac... scattered her ashes?'

'Yes, not easy... had to be done, though.'

'Sure it did, but you know she's at peace. It's your turn now.'

She'd not known if McCall's withdrawal into himself was due to grief over Bea's death or something which happened in Africa. His refusal to say why no story about the assignment ran in any of the Sunday colour supplements or on television, only added to her concern.

She tried to coax him into her confessional, to admit to what was causing him pain. But he'd a politician's way of evading difficult questions.

'Mac, when a sculptor is working a great piece of stone, every blow from the chisel might seem like an injury but in the end, something of beauty can be achieved because that's what was in the artist's mind all along.'

McCall sipped his cordial and said nothing. For him, the matter was closed. He'd grown fond of Hester, even allowed her to badger him into seeing the shrink. But she didn't know the half of anything in his world.

The gentlest wind soughed through the tree above them. He looked across at Garth and thought yet again how like a once-beautiful woman it was, sustained by prayers and potions and nursed along by those who knew little more could be done.

But when the sun shone, when they remembered how she had been, so the diamonds of crinkly yellow glass sparkled in the windows, its raspberry-red bricks glowed and all the coupled chimneys stood proud above the many gables of the mossy green roof.

It was all of a piece, organic, as if it had grown from the earth without any architected symmetry. And as always with the old, there were secrets and stories within.

Hester was sure she'd once seen a lady in a long pale skirt pass through the panelled walls of the drawing room. McCall hadn't the heart to say it'd just be a trick of the light filtering through the trees.

She refilled his glass without being asked.

'Mac, don't you think it's time you got stuck into a project or some journalism?'

For all her clairvoyant tendencies, Hester couldn't read his mind.

'Yeah, maybe. Give it a while.'

'The world has plenty of wickedness for you to choose from.'

'All your usual suspects, Hester?'

'Too right, my friend. The military, big business, all their spies and lackeys, they're the ones with the real power who manipulate events to suit their own purpose.'

Before she could set off on another of her conspiracy theories, a blue Volvo estate drew into the yard. An elegant woman in dark glasses and a chic designer dress got out carrying a large leather shoulder bag. She peered around like an insouciant model posing on a photo-shoot.

Then she saw McCall and began sashaying towards him through the coltsfoot and clover, smiling with private satisfaction as only Lexie Nadin knew how.

Three

The swallows dipping through the flower-scented air of Garth Hall's gardens were much as Lexie herself - creatures of iridescent grace and exuberance, instinctive and beyond the wit of man to catch or tame and gone the moment autumn beckons.

McCall watched her approach, superficially annoyed he'd been spotted in Oxford but intrigued that she'd wanted to see him again. He was also conscious of how unprepared he felt for whatever drama was about to unfold. He knew only that Lexie would cast herself in the central role and have the camera on her throughout. McCall was predestined to play his part, however demanding, whatever the hurt.

This much was written and had been since the unforgettable accident of their first meeting on that bitter winter's day in 1965.

*

A wind of Baltic iciness sheers across the black fens and gusts into the cloistered reaches of Cambridge, burning the face and watering the eye.

Some of those huddled on the pavement outside Miller & Sons, television and music dealers, are close to tears anyway - women in headscarves and thick woollen coats, stiff ex-servicemen who'd survived to count the cost of war.

They brave the chill of January to mourn Winston Churchill, their leader throughout it all and watch from afar as he is borne through the sooty streets of London on a gun carriage.

A line of dockside cranes bow their jibs in unison as a barge carries his coffin along the iron grey Thames beneath. It is making for Waterloo Station, to the place of departure which railwaymen call the platform of laughing and crying. From here, a train of Pullman coaches will deliver him home to the earth of Oxfordshire and the bones of his ancestors.

A high angle camera slowly widens out from the gleaming, steaming engine as it picks up speed and passes through wreaths of its own smoke then is lost in the gloom of a winter's day.

McCall turns a corner into Sidney Street and registers the little crowd by Miller's window. He still feels fragile from the boozy midwifery required to get another issue of Varsity to press and is poorly kitted out for such weather. Beneath his borrowed parka he wears only an incongruous white dress shirt, jeans and tennis pumps.

He is in urgent need of tea and toast and a place to sit and feel better - physically, if nothing else. It isn't just his hangover which weighs heavy. It is Cambridge itself. His dread of tutorials is becoming phobic. Each week's essay crisis is worse than the last. He is fast being exposed for the chancer he is, trying to bluff his way through the oral-formulaic theory of Anglo Saxon poetry or the structural unity of Beowulf.

His grades had been borderline. Only his shmoozer's charm at interview – and some Wrenn family string-pulling – won him a place. Barely into his second term and McCall knows the end is nigh.

A man and woman hold hands outside the television shop. Side-on, he seems in his early thirties, studious and intense and wearing a Gannex overcoat like the Prime Minister's.

McCall cannot see the female's face yet but she appears younger with hair the shade of ripened wheat and cut to the shoulder. She has a dancer's legs in stockings with a Beatles motif and is very svelte, even in a sack-like duffle coat.

He is less than three yards away. For no apparent reason, she turns her head. She looks directly at him. It is as if he has been expected but is late.

She gives him the slightest hint of a smile and appears almost relieved. She need worry no longer. He has arrived. Her eyes say it all - and more - in that primitive, wordless way only those who are to be lovers understand.

For McCall, it is exactly the same. He has known this stranger all his nineteen years. He stands by her side. Neither notices anyone else. He could kiss her – and she him. It would be the most natural response either could make.

'Look, I'm going for breakfast,' McCall says. 'Please, you must both come with me.'

It feels weirder than a rag week stunt, a command based on an assumption. Yet the couple grin at each other and agree. Something strange has just happened, something uniquely particular to them and within their subconscious selves, each recognises the significance of the moment.

The girl suggests they go to The Welcome, a café near the Arts Theatre where she works. McCall's depression has already swung into a mood of elation. His hangover is a memory. He is volubly at ease - politically radical about growing US imperialism in Vietnam or lampooning the drunken cabinet minister in Harold Wilson's government he'd interviewed for Varsity.

The girl laughs and is captivated. The man laughs but not as much for he has eyes to see. Then it's lunchtime and she and he have to be somewhere else. McCall sits where they leave him, suddenly aware he's no idea of their names – or they of his.

He runs into the street but it's empty so he chases down to the Arts Theatre stage door in St Edward's Passage. The theatre is deserted except for a man sticking up posters for next week's production of Loot. McCall feels breathless with anxiety. Something of his has just been taken from him and he must get it back.

*

Perceptive, protective Hester didn't need telling Lexie and McCall had history. Yet even she would struggle to understand its complexity, how torn the curtain between love and loathing had become, if only for McCall.

He tried not to appear too fazed by Lexie's unscripted arrival and introduced the two women. They exchanged notional smiles. Hester admired her dress, bud-green silk, plain and minimal yet sensual.

'It's a Dries van Noten. He's getting quite well known.'

'Is that a fact? Well, I guess I should look out for his stuff.'

'Do that darling but I'm not so sure he goes up to your size.'

Very little rattled Hester yet she knew it wiser to retreat. She got up and walked back across the yard to the embrasured safety of the kitchen.

A wheelbarrow full of onions needed plaiting to dry with the herbs she'd already gathered. The long farmhouse table by the Aga was already heaped with pears for bottling and courgettes and runner beans to cut and freeze for winter soup.

She always understood why a sixth century holy man thought gardening virtuous and godly. The rhythm of life at Garth gave Hester a sense of contentment and well-being, brought her closer to the scheme and order of things which she'd sought in the collectives of California but failed to find.

Yet Lexie's arrival had put Hester strangely at odds with herself in this most gentle of seasons. Her karma was upset, maybe even the feng shui of the old house itself. Hester knew intuitively Lexie was trouble. Yet McCall was under her malign spell. That much was obvious. Too bad for him there were none so blind as those who will not see.

Hester paused to dead-head one of the old English roses in the bed by the kitchen window. They were fading now but a few still managed to raise their defiant colours like the flags of a routed army.

*

'Please don't tell me you're sleeping with that dumpy old matron,' Lexie said.

'She keeps house while I'm away. I like her. She has insight and real spirit.'

'If you say so. Now listen, you saw me filming in Oxford. Why didn't you wait?'

'I could ask why you didn't wait for me all those years ago.'

'Yes, I suppose you could... but what would be the point?'

McCall studied the face he'd once so adored. She was right, there wasn't any point. Whatever she answered would change nothing.

'Then tell me why you're here.'

'Because I need your help. You're still a reporter, aren't you?'

'In theory.'

'Well, something awful has happened in my family and it's like it's all become mixed up with the script for the "Inspector Morse" I've just done.'

'I don't understand. Acting is entertainment, not real life... remember?'

'Sure, but a kid disappears in Morse and it turns out she's been murdered and you'll never believe it but my sister's little girl has just vanished, too.'

'I'm sorry to hear that but it doesn't mean she's been murdered.'

'No, but I've got this terrible premonition that something wicked's happened to her.'

'That's just your vivid imagination, Lexie.'

'You're not taking me seriously. I've got this terrible feeling. I'm worried sick.'

McCall knew how Lexie could make a production out of nothing but thought it best not to remind her.

'I take it the police are involved.'

'Yes, they're out looking for her.'

'Then I don't see what I can do to help.'

'Let me see if I can change your mind,' Lexie said. 'But can we get out of this pollen stuff first? It's really getting to me.'

He took her through the drawing room, lined with paintings of whiskery old gents who'd been lawyers and adventurers, soldiers and diplomats but now mouldered in the vaults of St Mary and All Angels on the far side of Garth Woods.

From the hallway beyond, McCall led her up a staircase fashioned from chestnut and wide enough to take a horse. The wallpaper was 1920s Chinoiserie - pagodas and rare birds amid cherry blossom. Here and there, the dimly silvered paper was slightly foxed through where paintings had once hung.

'I'd forgotten how spooky this old place is.'

McCall didn't answer but carried on down a landing of oak planks polished smooth by the efforts of maids long gone and the daily passage of those they'd served. They stopped at the last door.

'I work in here,' McCall said. 'It's quiet and out of the way.'

It was hardly more than a servant's chamber with an iron bedstead, a kitchen chair and an old pine table, empty but for an electric typewriter and a wire tray heaped with papers and press cuttings. Lexie looked about her, smiling, slowly shaking her head.

'This little room reminds me of Staithe End, Mac... the cottage, Norfolk, remember?'

'How could I not?'

'Happy times... if only we'd known it. Such happy times.'

'For a while, I guess.'

'You were my Byron, my skinny boy, always so intense. You still look consumptive.'

'And the golden curls aren't what they were.'

'Life can be a bit of a bastard, can't it?'

Lexie looked at him almost sadly but with great fondness and held out her hands.

'Come on, Mac. We're both a little older... what we had is still ours, still precious.'

She pressed him to her and he sensed her breasts against the crib of his chest. They kissed in silence. If neither spoke, the spell could not be broken and they were young again and every dream might yet come true.

They lay on the bed. And as they did, so the afternoon sun caught a row of six brass bullet casings on the mantelpiece and cast their shadows across the wall till the moment passed.

Four

Lexie had flipped McCall's life into the air on that morning of incalculable chance in Cambridge all those years ago. Heads or tails, someone wins, someone loses.

Each waking hour since they first met, McCall thought of little else but finding her again. He'd loitered about the Arts Theatre that weekend. On the following Monday morning, he saw her coming down St Edward's Passage in her camel-coloured duffel coat. And she wasn't with Mr Gannex.

McCall would have her to himself, if only for a moment.

She immediately gave him that smile again – that leftward tilt of her slightly parted lips, the slight widening of those eyes which knew so much and promised more.

'Hello, what are you doing here?'

'I thought… well, I often come this way. My college, not far from here.'

'Aren't you terribly cold?'

'No, not really.'

'You look it. Want a coffee or are you going to a lecture?'

'Coffee, yes. I'd like that.'

She winked broadly at the elderly stage door keeper, part concierge, part spy, peering from behind the fug of Woodbine smoke clouding his sentry box.

'Friend of yours, is he, Miss?'

'My brother. Just want to show him around.'

''Course you do, dear.'

It all smelt of sawn timber and fresh paint. Stage hands up ladders were finishing off flats of scenery. Here was a parallel reality which that night's audience would pay to enter before disappearing back into lives from which there was no escape.

A song called My Girl played on a transistor. McCall thought it an omen but that was an illusion, too. He followed her through an unswept corridor and down a set of concrete steps to a storage area lit by a bare electric bulb. Somewhere on the stage above, a nasally hysterical Kenneth Williams was in a final run-through with the other actors.

'It's our big night, tonight. A premiere.'

'What's it about?'

'These two thieves who rob a bank then hide their loot in a dead woman's coffin.'

'Sounds outrageous.'

'Joe Orton's written it so half the punters are bound to be offended and demand their money back but a bit of scandal is always good for the box office.'

She filled a kettle from a tap above a dirty sink, put it on a gas ring then found two cups and a bottle of Camp coffee in a cupboard.

'So, are you going to tell me your name, funny man?'

'Me? I'm McCall.'

'McCall? Is that it?'

'Well, it's Francis but usually it's just *Mac*.'

'Saturday was great, wasn't it? Meeting up like that.'

'Yes… it was lovely.'

'I hoped we'd bump into you again.'

'Did you? Honestly?'

'Yes. Why wouldn't I?'

He dried, couldn't express what it was he so wanted to say. She smiled at his gaucheness. Everything was understood between them.

The kettle whistled. She poured their drinks and apologised for having no milk or sugar or anywhere to sit.

'You didn't ask, but I'm Lexie.'

'Sorry, that was rude. What's Lexie short for?'

'Alexandra.'

'And you said you're the dogsbody around here?'

''Fraid so but I start my first proper acting job next week.'

'Really? I bet you'll be brilliant.'

'It's hardly the West End, just touring round lots of schools putting on Shakespeare.'

'But you'll steal it. I just know you will.'

'Flatterer.'

'No, seriously you will and I shall come and watch every performance.'

She laughed but wasn't mocking him. Her eyes seemed to peer deep within him. McCall sensed she'd really like him to be there.

'What about your studies? You can't just walk away from them.'

'I almost have already.'

'But you told us you're only in your first year.'

'I am but it'll be my last. I know it.'

Lexie looked at him as if her mercurial mind has made a decision. She took his cup and put it on the floor by hers, drew him close, her fingers in his twisting gypsy curls. She kissed his lips - kissed him because this is what she wanted and time was short. Her lipstick tasted vaguely sweet and her perfume carried the scent of pleasures unknown.

Then her hands ran the contours of his gaunt, drum-tight body which craved only hers. Lexie backed him through a rail of Victorian dresses left over from some past production.

They lay in the musky, dusty darkness beyond and she unzipped him and took him for herself. There was an elemental remoteness about her, almost animal, disconnected from the then and there. McCall held to her, drawn by such a force of nature he'd never encountered before.

And when at last she was done, when she opened her eyes and was satisfied, then came that coded smile between initiates who now shared a secret. He hadn't language equal to the moment or to calm his trembling elation.

'Oh God, Lexie…'

'Oh God, what?'

'I've never… you know, I've never - '

But they heard footsteps approaching. Lexie quickly led him through another subterranean passage and into the light of a day for which he was born and could never forget.

'Listen, I have to see you again.'

'Sure, but I'm late for work now.'

'I know, but when can we meet?'

'There's a big party here tonight. Come to that.'

'Can I? But what about Mr Gannex?'

'Evan? He doesn't like parties.'

'But he's your fiancé, isn't he?'

'How wonderfully archaic that sounds.'

'Yes, but he is, isn't he? You're going to marry him.'

'Who knows? Who cares?'

'Me - *I* care. Please don't, Lexie.'

'Listen, you really have to go now or I'll be fired.'

'Don't do it, Lexie. Don't marry him. Please, I mean it.'

'Go on, funny man. See you tonight.'

So the cruel drama of their affair began. McCall was to be tortured by infatuation and jealousy, the ache of separation, of being alone while knowing she was with *him*. In that moment outside the Arts Theatre where all was make-believe and pretence, he could only shiver at what he feared and had yet to understand.

But slowly, very slowly, McCall would begin to learn the convenience of lies.

Five

Lexie folded herself into one of the wing back chairs either side of Garth's wide brick inglenook. The wind sent spatters of rain bouncing down the black void of the chimney to hiss against the burning logs. She wore a red check shirt with the top buttons missing so the soft white slopes of her breasts were just visible.

McCall had been persuaded in bed that there could be a story in the disappearance of Lexie's ten year old niece, Ruby. Lexie was never to be denied.

'She's an unusual child,' she said. 'Quite brilliant in one way but so, so vulnerable.'

A photograph taken at Manor Hill primary school in north London showed a querulous-looking child, small for her age with wild curly hair, a floral pinafore dress and sandals. Police had rung Lexie's apartment in Bristol to check if Ruby was there.

'I told them she's so unworldly that she barely understands the concept of money or buying tickets for a train or a coach,' Lexie said. 'She gets bullied a lot so escapes into her own fantasy world of fairy castles and unicorns.'

Other children said Ruby had been taken over by demons. She'd hit one and made his nose bleed and been excluded from school last term.

McCall poured Lexie a glass of Italian liqueur made from almonds and set it down on the hearth by her side, glowing gold in the firelight.

'So there's something wrong with Ruby... psychologically?'

'It's called Asperger's syndrome,' Lexie said. 'It means she can't read other people's feelings, hasn't got a clue about the effect of what she says or does has on anyone.'

'It must be a great strain living with her. How does your sister cope?'

'Badly, I'm afraid. But Etta's never lived in the real world, either.'

'How do you mean?'

'She's into tarot cards and mythology, paganism. All that alternative tosh.'

'So you two don't get on?'

'No, we grew apart but then I started feeling bad about her struggling to bring up Ruby on her own. I'm her only relative and I said she could move to be near me and work in this business I've got.'

'What's that?'

'We supply vintage clothes and props for the theatre and TV companies.'

'But she didn't want to?'

'No, she didn't want any charity, which was nonsense because she would've had to earn her wages and not sit dreaming all day... but that's always been her problem.'

'What about Ruby's father?'

'Him? A one-night stand, never to be seen again.'

'Hardly sounds like a happy home. Could Ruby just have run away or wandered off?'

'No, I really don't think so. She depends so much on her own routines which is why I know something's happened to her.'

'What are the police doing?'

'Talking to the neighbours, doing the usual searches of lock-ups and empty building and there's been some publicity in the local media.'

'But nothing's come of any of it?'

'No, and when I ring, they just say they've no new developments to report.'

'Then that must be the case. What does your husband think?'

'Evan? No idea. He and I were divorced ages ago.'

McCall knew this already but had reason to feign ignorance.

'Sorry to hear that,' he said. 'So what do you want me to do?'

'Don't think I haven't noticed your by-line in the press over the years, Mac... and all

those credits on serious TV programmes.'

'But how does that help?'

'Look, I know how the media works. Ruby isn't the kind of cuddly, blonde-haired kid missing from suburbia that the papers would go big on every day. She's a plain Jane from a grotty council estate with a weirdo mother so her disappearance isn't getting the sort of coverage we need to keep what's happened in the public mind.'

'So you want me to try and put a piece together... a feature, something like that?'

'That'd be terrific - and if someone prominent like you turns up asking questions, the police can't just put Ruby's case on the back burner.'

'Have they dragged the reservoir yet?'

Lexie winced at this question, grimly logical though it was. She shook her head then unfolded a large sheet of paper from her shoulder bag and handed it to McCall. It was a minutely detailed pencil drawing of a huge stone castle, almost photographically reproduced with turrets, castellations, arrow-slit windows, studded oak doors and all perfectly reflected in a tree-lined lake.

'What's this?'

'Another place the police have searched.'

'I thought Ruby lives in north London not in Scotland.'

'So she does. This is a fake castle they built years ago to disguise the pumping station on the reservoir just around the corner from where Ruby lives and that's where she always goes to act out her fantasies.'

'And the cops found nothing?'

'No, but there's something you need to know.... Ruby drew this picture.'

'A child of ten did this?'

'Yes, she did.'

'I don't believe you.'

'It's true. She might be the weirdest kid you'll ever meet but she's incredibly gifted.'

'I've never seen anything like it.'

'And she'll have done it from memory.'

'It's astonishing. This alone would walk her story into any of the colour supplements.'

'She only has to see something once, a building or a face, and she can go home and draw it.'

'What an amazing talent. Shouldn't she be at a special art school?'

'You'd think so, but I doubt it'd happen.'

'Why ever not?'

'Well, I'm sure Etta does her best but a pushy mum she isn't. Life hasn't been easy for her with Ruby so if she's occupied drawing and pretending she's a princess in a castle and has a pet unicorn, Etta gets a few hours peace but she can't see beyond that.'

A colour supplement article was already forming in McCall's head.

Six

Three days before McCall chanced upon Lexie filming her cough and spit of an appearance in "Inspector Morse", a press conference about Ruby's disappearance was held sixty miles away at Manor Hill police station.

Her mother made an emotional appeal for information. A twenty second clip aired on regional BBC news that night.

Lexie called in a favour from a props buyer in the drama department who wangled her a cassette of the uncut rushes from the film library. She'd brought it with her for McCall to see.

He now inserted it into his machine and they sat back to watch. From the look of dread in her eyes, Etta could have been facing a firing squad, not a thinly attended presser.

She walked uncertainly between a uniformed policewoman and a civilian press relations officer, almost as if she was in custody.

'Hey, that PR guy, that's Malky Hoare,' McCall said. 'I know him from Fleet Street days. Wicked old sod, couldn't even lie straight in bed.'

Hoare's amiable face seemed to overflow his tight blue collar. He was an alumnus of a minor fee-paying school which gave him a faux posh accent, a facility to recite lines of rote-learned poetry and a belief he was a wordsmith when under the influence.

Etta looked trapped. McCall immediately thought this suspiciously like policing as theatre, testing how a suspect performed under media lights and questions.

Hoare placed a photograph of Ruby on the desk in front of them and thanked the hacks for attending.

'OK gents, you've got my briefing. This is Mrs Etta Ross, the mother of the little girl who's been missing for three days now and she wants to make a personal appeal through you to get Ruby home where she belongs.'

Etta was attractive, not beautiful, small boned, late thirties and unlike her sister, had the fashion sense of an office temp - prim black skirt, white silky top, simple silver chain around her freckled neck.

The cameraman tightened from a wide three-shot to a single. Etta's reddened eyes had done more weeping than sleeping. Her hands shook as if the prepared statement was a warrant for her execution.

'My daughter is the world to me,' she said.

Her voice trembled but gave no hint of its origins.

'I... I just want her back... if you're watching this, Ruby, you're not in any trouble, darling, no one's angry with you, honest they're not.'

Whatever composure she had summoned up began to slip. The policewoman put an arm around her as Etta tried again.

'I... just want you to come home or tell someone in the street who you are and ask them to find a police officer and then they'll bring you home. I miss you so much, Ruby.

'The flat isn't the same without you... and if anyone out there knows where she is, please, please let her go.'

Then Etta pushed back her chair and ran out crying, hands over her face. The policewoman quickly followed. Hoare filled in by asking for questions. An uninterested local paper reporter wanted to know if Ruby had gone missing before.

'No, and this is why the police are so worried about her.'

'Could we be talking kidnap or murder?'

'We're not speculating on either at the moment. This remains a missing child inquiry and we're doing all we can to find her alive and well.'

'Is it true what the neighbours say, that this Ruby's a bit of an oddball?'

'Ruby has some behavioural, psychological problems,' Hoare said. 'She sometimes finds it difficult to interact with people.'

'So you're saying she's a nutter?'

At this, a man in a pale cotton jacket and jeans emerged from behind the camera and propelled the hack towards the door. The camera mic picked up his parting words.

'Listen, sonny. Ruby's a little kid in danger, so get on your bloody typewriter and help me find her.'

The screen went blank. McCall turned to Lexie.

'Good for him - whoever he is.'

'Believe it or not, he's the detective in charge,' Lexie said.

'You mean you've met him?'

'Yes, with Etta when Ruby first went missing. He's called Benwick.'

'But if he's running the case, why didn't he take the press conference?'

'No idea but when I talked to him, he wasn't like any policeman I've ever known, a real charmer like one of those American cops on television.'

McCall would ring Hoare to line up an off-the-record briefing. Lexie could call Etta to arrange for him to meet her, too. He needed more examples of Ruby's extraordinary drawings - and other photographs of her, too.

But if McCall felt himself morphing into a hack again, it wasn't only Ruby's face which hovered between him and redemption.

*

From her bedroom window, Etta Ross could make out the silhouette of the reservoir's dominating castle, top lit by a rising full moon. It was not cold but she shook. Someone was walking up and down on her grave.

Candles shone behind the rocks of purple amethyst on her dressing table. Amethysts are said to promote clarity of thought but aid the passing of souls to the next world, too.

Her mind was a turmoil of regret and remorse, made no easier by the detective who'd just left. His smile couldn't hide the menace behind his eyes. Those pictures he showed her... men who didn't know they were being photographed. She told him she'd not seen any of them before.

But she was lying. Mr Ginger was all too familiar.

Etta drew her heavy purple drapes to shut out the world beyond the window and to be alone in the place where only she had all the clues - and all the answers - for the truth was always in the tarot.

She sat before her reflection in the mirror and shuffled the pack. The first card she turned was the High Priestess. Such irony. Of all the 22 major arcana cards, Etta most identified with this one - the mysterious keeper of supernatural knowledge, sitting between pillars of light and dark, life and death. Only the High Priestess knew what was hidden behind the curtain - and how to keep it secret.

But any parallel with Etta ended there. Within the figure of the High Priestess was imprinted the legend of Persephone, abducted from a field of flowers and spirited into the underworld.

Persephone's mother searched the earth to rescue the daughter she loved. But not until the goddess of witchcraft finally guided her to look in the land of the dead did she find where she had been taken - and would have spent the rest of eternity.

Etta threw all the cards on the floor. She lay face down on the scarlet covers of her empty bed, alone and in great distress.

There was no magic which might undo what she herself had brought about, no tears could wash away her wickedness, no deity help her through what lay ahead.

Seven

Everything about Detective Inspector Larry Benwick intrigued Hoare and stirred his tabloid curiosity. He was more Miami Vice than Inspector Morse, not yet forty and with an assured but anonymous face and fair hair long overdue a cut. Benwick could have been anyone but a hardly regular cop.

Hoare asked around the press office about him. Someone thought he'd recently returned from an overseas posting then parachuted into Manor Hill for the Ruby Ross job.

He managed to get a better steer from an anti terrorist contact in specialist operations. They'd met for a gargle in The Albert on Victoria Street where Scotland Yard's officer class went range-finding on each other's weaknesses.

'So, you gouty old reprobate, still glad you quit poaching to become a gamekeeper?'

'*Force majeur,*' Hoare said. 'Fleet Street's a young man's game.'

'But you always lied about your age.'

'Till I dyed my hair grey and fell foul of the young Turks.'

'Well, at least you've gone respectable now.'

'Again, no choice. My ex and her lawyers need their pound of flesh.'

'And you've a cross to bear?'

'Too right. My bloody shoulder's full of splinters.'

They sat in a corner alcove, well into a bottle of Merlot. Hoare lit a cigarette from the butt of another. He'd washed up in a hack's last refuge - PR - but hadn't lost habits like trousering other people's receipts for his own exes.

His companion checked his watch. He was running a live operation to find - and if necessary, kill - a Provisional IRA active service unit intent on turning the London Stock Exchange into a car park. Hoare took the hint.

'Look, I'm doing the words on a missing kid case for a DI called Larry Benwick and I'm trying to find out a bit more about him.'

'Why would you want to do that?'

'Because he's a bit of a mystery. I'd like my card marked now I'm working with him.'

His source finished his drink then offered some parting words of advice.

'I've heard tell that some blokes in our game go off the books for years.'

'Really? Is that where Benwick's been - off the books?'

'Do yourself a favour, matey. In this job, it's often safest to hear nothing, see nothing and say a damn sight less. Do you get my meaning?'

So now he waited for Benwick in the communal yard behind the shabby, low rise block of council flats where Ruby lived. Hoare knew two questions niggled Benwick when he'd read into Ruby's case file – why didn't Etta ring 999 immediately she realised her daughter was missing and why was she reluctant to say what she herself was doing that Friday afternoon? He'd not believed her story about being in bed with a migraine and drowsy from painkillers.

Murder was usually a family affair so she was brought in. They'd sweat Etta in an interview room as a witness, under suspicion but not arrest.

While that was going on, Benwick wanted to conduct a second search of the flat but with his PR man present.

'Forensics tell me the kid's body isn't there,' he'd said. 'But it's coming time for you to be let in on a few secrets.'

*

Linden House was once a Utopian design for living to replace many acres of diseased Victorian slums. But the complex of maisonettes had itself now become a warehouse for the socially disadvantaged, those from many nations whose refugee tongues could be heard in dark stairwells running with the piss of drunks and dogs.

Here were watchful eyes, briefly glimpsed behind rainbow-hued veils before a door closed or a window shut. But they could tell of torture and of those they had loved who'd disappeared into the night, never to be seen again.

Some flats were boarded up - squats where heroin and crack cocaine were dealt to the walking dead who drifted by Hoare, barely making a shadow.

From this place and from such people, police needed help. A child cannot vanish without someone seeing, someone knowing.

Hoare had struggled to generate much media interest in Ruby. The papers were preoccupied with the Gulf War, Britain's military role in it and oil prices rising. If Benwick expected more coverage, he was on a loser - unless they found a corpse.

A silver Vauxhall Cavalier drew into the yard. Benwick emerged in his Florida cop outfit and nodded for Hoare to follow him to Etta's ground floor flat. He unlocked the door and they stepped straight into the kitchen.

'No offence, but let me give you the gypsy's warning,' Benwick said. 'If anything you're about to see gets leaked back to your old pals in Fleet Street before I'm ready, I shall be at the psychotic end of really hacked off. We understand each other, yes?'

Behind Benwick's smile, his unblinking eyes remained fixed on Hoare in the same impersonal manner of a gangland enforcer he'd interviewed in a previous life.

'Anyway, notice how clean it all is, Mr Hoare... no blood and guts for us to find.'

Every surface gleamed – the aluminium sink and drainer, a Formica-topped table, the black and white linoleum under their feet. The bathroom and toilet were the same, shining, relieved of all germs and contamination.

Ruby's bedroom was equally dirt-free. Coloured pens and crayons and an unused pad of A3 cartridge paper were neatly laid out on a small table by her pine-framed bed. On the wall above was an architecturally detailed pencil drawing of the castle-like Victorian pumping station at Manor Hill reservoir.

'God, this is amazing,' Hoare said. 'It's like a photograph.'

Hoare, three stone overweight, forehead damp and prickling in the humid air, loosened his tie and struggled out of his creased suit jacket.

'Do you think Mum could've given Ruby a slap so she's run away?'

'Maybe… if we're lucky.'

'Meaning what?'

The detective's eyes narrowed as if weighing the risk of sharing his suspicions further. He led Hoare to Etta's bedroom. It took a moment to adjust to the darkness. Benwick turned up the dimmer switch and a gantry of soft lights came on.

'Have a good squint… then tell me I'm wrong to be worried about Ruby.'

The room looked part brothel, part Satanist's den. The atmosphere was heavy with stale incense. It clung to the swags of purple velvet curtains and the richly painted burgundy walls covered with prints of waterfalls, forest sprites, winged horses. There were books on witchcraft, the Wicca religion, paganism, mythology. Lumps of sparkling crystal were arranged on an altar-like dressing table alongside a pack of tarot cards, a few black candles and carved images of symbolic Egyptian gods.

But above Etta's double bed - and dominating all else - was a huge print of a pentagram encircling a horned goat. Under this were the words *The thoughts attached to the real desire of the seeker will lead us to him and him to us.*

'I'm guessing Mum's not big in the Women's Institute?'

'And maybe Ruby's starting to look like a better story?'

'Too right it is. The Sunday red tops would kill to get in here.'

The detective wagged a cautioning finger. Benwick pulled open the drawer of the bedside cabinet and scattered a dozen or so condoms across the deep red coverlet on Etta's bed.

'People, Mr Hoare... who'd believe what goes on behind their closed doors?'

'Keeps us in work though, doesn't it?'

'Why the hell do we bother?'

'To pay the rent. But nothing's illegal here, is it? No law's being broken.'

Benwick answered with a shrug then opened the door of Etta's built-in wardrobe. Hanging inside was the tiny black skirt and frilly white top of a fake nurse's outfit. The DI then emptied a shoe box full of banknotes over the condoms on the bed.

'That's ten grand, give or take a fiver... not the pay of an angel of mercy, I think.'

'So Etta knew her ceiling professionally... but how does all this help find the kid?'

'It doesn't but maybe it gives us a reason why we can't.'

*

Benwick said he was late for a meeting so Hoare told him about the phone call he'd had from McCall and of the meet they'd arranged next day.

'You know him personally?'

'Good pal from way back. Freelance, obsessive, doesn't do drive-by journalism, only long gropes for the colour supplements and television. His family had connections, not short of a bob or two so he can pick and choose what he works on.'

'Bit of a dilettanté, then?'

'Wouldn't say that. He's broken some half decent stories in his time.'

'So why's he interested in Ruby? No-one else appears to be.'

'That could be the reason - a clear field. He'll want to talk to you, of course.'

'OK, I'll ask around about him,' Benwick said. 'I'll ring you later - and don't forget to keep the shutters down on what you've just seen, even to this guy, McCall.'

Hoare was left to walk the half mile to Manor Hill bus station, jacket over his arm in the clammy evening heat. He wasn't any nearer to figuring out Benwick. If he wanted publicity - not least from an upmarket hack like McCall - it didn't make sense to blank any mention of Etta's colourful private life. That was a spread in any paper.

Hookers began to appear along the street as Hoare passed by, conjured out of nothing and nowhere. They leaned their insolent derrieres against the front garden walls of once respectable Edwardian villas, smoking, waiting, painted faces alert for the next trick.

Far in the distance, London rumbled towards dusk as the sun sank behind the reservoir's fortress pumping station. Its alien silhouette towered into the sky like a medieval highland keep, dominating and threatening all who dwelt beneath.

Eight

McCall, unable to sleep and up before day break, drank tea and watched over Lexie. He still wasn't entirely sure about her motive in re-appearing in his life after so long. She'd always been self-obsessed and impulsive, driven by an almost feline instinct to do only that which made her content. If others benefited, fine. If they suffered, she might be upset - but not for long. Lexie could no more change these ways than the colour of her eyes. Against this, her concerns about Ruby seemed genuine enough.

Yet for all his uncertainty, to lie with Lexie last night had been to disregard the passage of time. She was as she had been in those first insane days - a lover one dreamed about, however changed they'd become, however destructive the memory of their attraction. McCall knew he would do her bidding for reasons far deeper than he would ever admit.

Lexie murmured something unintelligible and turned onto her left side. The blue bed sheet covering her nakedness slipped a little, exposing the creaminess of her belly till it darkened between her legs. Here was mystery just as it had always been.

He combed the rounded firmness of her behind with the tips of his extended fingers. She woke and smiled and desired only to yield again as the moon waned and the sun rose and nature reawakened without and within. And all which remained unspoken between them was as nothing.

*

McCall drove to Essex after breakfast. Hoare was at a college in Harlow, lecturing media students about police-press relations. But he was free for a late lunch.

'Malky, you old fraud - still not been rumbled?'

Hoare happily took this as a compliment. They found a wine bar and ordered a bottle of house red.

'OK, cards on the table, Mac, what's your real interest in Ruby Ross?'

'I told you on the phone. I want to write a warts-and-all piece on every aspect of a missing child investigation.'

'Hundreds of kids go missing. What made you choose Ruby's case?'

'Because I saw the mother and my old mate making a TV appeal to find her.'

Hoare didn't look entirely persuaded but trotted out the officially approved line on the Ruby investigation. He omitted the sexiest of angles - Etta being on the game and fascinated by the occult and how that might have a bearing on Ruby's disappearance. But McCall knew Hoare rather too well.

'I didn't ask for a press release, Malky. That's for those who've never done you any favours in the past.'

'I'm giving you the official picture. That's the truth.'

'No, the truth is that being a spin doctor doesn't suit you. You're still a hack at heart and you know a good story when you come across one.'

'How do you know Ruby Ross is a good story?'

'Because I've got friends in low places.'

'Yeah, maybe you have but you've not got my problems.'

'What do you mean?'

'OK, I'll level with you, Mac, but absolutely not for quoting. Agreed?'

'Sure, everything's off the record.'

'Right... so this case is being run by a detective inspector called Larry Benwick and on my life, he's the least likely cop I've ever come across in a long march through Fleet Street.'

'Why is that a problem?'

'You must promise to keep this to yourself but I've a source in the anti-terrorist squad and he's tipped me the nod that before this Ruby job came along, Benwick had been working under cover for years.'

'Was he, by God? So that's why you fronted the press conference and not him.'

'It's got to be, hasn't it?'

'What kind of under cover work was he doing?'

'I don't know but as sure as the good Lord made little apples, he's not adjusted to everyday police work yet. There's an anger in the guy, only just below the surface, like he doesn't give a damn about anyone or anything.'

'But why put a UC like him on a case you say doesn't amount to much?'

'Can't help you there but I wouldn't want to cross him, I seriously wouldn't.'

'So you're accepting there's a half decent story in Ruby's case?'

'You didn't hear this from me, but yes... and judging by the little I know, it's a belter.'

'Great, now we're getting somewhere. So tell me more.'

'Sorry Mac, no can do. I just daren't. I know I owe you big time - '

'Then do me this little service and we'll call it quits.'

'It's not that easy, old sport. I'm still on my uppers after the divorce.'

'But I'd keep your name out of everything.'

'That wouldn't save me,' he said. 'Benwick knows about our meet today and that we're pals. If I anything leaks, I'm out on my ear and with no way back this time.'

*

There had always been something of the monk about Lexie's ex-husband, Evan, something austere, not entirely joyless but a man driven by a certainty of purpose.

McCall parked outside his house, a large dormer bungalow behind a screen of   willows already shedding their yellow leaves. Evan would be in his study. It looked out across the river slipping between the sloping lawn of his rear garden and the water meadows beyond and in the distance, to the spires of Cambridge where he taught.

But Evan's connections weren't just academic. He had access down corridors where few others ever went.

'Mac, it's been too long. You should've rung and I could've organised supper for us.'

'Thanks, but I can't stay. I'm on my way home from Essex.'

McCall was under no obligation to tell Evan that Lexie had reappeared in his life, still less that he'd become her lover again. Yet it felt right that he should, however subconscious his need for approval.

'I hope you survive this time,' Evan said. 'I wouldn't want you hurt again.'

His voice held neither jealousy nor resentment, only the concern of a fellow casualty. McCall told him about Ruby and how Lexie feared she could have been murdered.

'What an intolerable strain for her to be under.'

'It is, which is why I've come to ask if you might help.'

'In what way, Mac?'

'By making a few discreet inquiries with your anonymous friends about a detective in London called Larry Benwick.'

'Why, what's he been up to?'

'All I know so far is that he's just been taken off long term under cover work to run the Ruby case. I find that interesting.'

'Couldn't he have just finished one assignment and been given another?'

'Possibly, but someone in a position to know told me to keep digging on this tale.'

Evan nodded but said nothing. McCall left it there. Evan was a source who could join the dots for himself.

They walked to the front door. McCall still saw no sign of any female presence in the house save for the sterile neatness imposed by a cleaner paid by the hour.

'Mac, before you go, I should tell you my news.'

'What's that?'

'I've bought Staithe End.'

'Say that again.'

'I've bought the cottage.'

McCall stared at him. After twenty-five years of knowing each other, this outwardly cautious, measured man could still amaze him.

'How on earth's this come about?'

'I saw it advertised and I didn't like the idea of a stranger mucking up our memories.'

'Lexie simply won't believe it. She'll be overjoyed.'

'Then you two should go across to Norfolk and keep the place aired for me. I'll give you a key.'

Nine

Malky Hoare lived in a shoe box of a service flat near King's Cross Station. Each evening, he looked down on the toms - brown girls, white girls, aimless, shameless girls in the wide, wet streets which were their market place. They'd caught trains from the north or coaches from the west, each believing they'd make it big, make it better.

None ever did. So now they click-clacked their way from one litter-blown corner to another or sheltered in doorways to be serviced with a French-kissed rock of crack cocaine from the pimps whose creatures they were.

For Hoare, all was noise, dirt and traffic. Buses, cabs, cars, users and dealers, fast food, human flesh, human weakness – this was life as it had become, coarse and transitory and weighed nightly against how it had been before.

Only in the confines of this expensively rented privacy was he obliged to confront all he had given up for the career he'd had. The mirror foretold an unhappy ending. This much he knew from his ex-wife - a nursing assistant. The pains in the heart he didn't have and the tiny yellow deposits of fat beneath his whisky-brown eyes were evidence of coronary disease. He should beware. His clock was winding down.

But old habits, like addiction itself, were hard to break. Sitting on his single bed, he wrote three A4 pages of notes for an old-style reporter's aide memoire of everything he'd learned about Ruby's case that day.

Hoare added these to the manilla folder in which he had already put copies of all the confidential internal briefings, pictures and material he'd snaffled from the Ruby investigation - and from her flat, too. It was a sacking offence but something about Larry Benwick - and the whole Ruby affair itself - puzzled him and brought out his need for insurance. How interesting that McCall was onto it, too.

It was almost midnight. He should be attempting to sleep while the city outside refused to try. But he heard footsteps coming up the stairs, scuffing and deliberate like a drunk's.

They got closer and turned along the bare wooden landing outside. Hoare felt a rush of guilt and slid his folder under the mattress. He waited for whoever was outside to pass along to the only other bed-sit on that corridor. But the footsteps stopped outside his door. Then a key was inserted into the lock.

Hoare gripped an empty wine bottle by the neck. He couldn't figure out how this could be happening but knew he was too unfit to fight some drugged-up burglar. He'd have only one chance to strike. He was already imagining the headline in tomorrow's Evening Standard.

Then the door was pushed open and Hoare only stopped himself braining the intruder when he recognised Benwick.

'What the hell are you doing breaking into my flat?'

'I didn't break in. I've got a key.'

'Where've you got that from?'

'I've got keys to lots of places.'

'Like hell you have. And you're pissed, too. Why didn't you go to an hotel?'

'We're colleagues, aren't we?'

'So what? You can't just steal into my place like this.'

'Do I detect some grumpiness, Mr Hoare?'

Hoare stared at his uninvited guest, angry but ashamed, too. Someone had blagged their way in to his private world and looked upon what was never intended to be seen.

'I'm sorry,' Benwick said. 'Life's a bit complicated at the minute.'

'So is mine so I'm right out of sympathy.'

'Sure you are… got any tooth mugs?'

The detective reached inside his leather jacket and pulled out a flat, quarter bottle of whisky. As he did, Hoare saw something heavy and darkly metallic, tucked by his left armpit.

'For Christ's sake! You're half cut and running round London with a gun.'

'No, that's just my new portable phone.'

'Don't treat me like a fool. You're carrying.'

'You're mistaken, old man.'

'If it's a phone, tell me the number.'

He gave him a tipsy grin and reeled it off. Hoare wrote it down, still shaking his head. Benwick opened a wall cupboard and found two glasses which he rinsed in the sink below then half filled each with Scotch.

'A toast,' he said. 'To a good long walk down Felony Lane together.'

Hoare, too sober for his own good, knew he was in for an unforgiving session. If he thought Benwick would let his guard slip and reveal some personal secrets, he was mistaken. But as the night wore on, he learned Etta Ross had answers for everything. She kept cash in the flat because she didn't trust banks and was saving up to pay the fees at a special school for Ruby. Any suggestion of prostitution offended her. The men - and some women - neighbours saw coming to her flat were punters paying for tarot card readings or sharing her harmless fascination with the occult.

'What about all those French letters she had?'

'She's a single mother, thirty-eight years old,' Benwick said.

'Doesn't want to get pregnant at her time of life.'

'And the tart's nursing outfit?'

'Left over from a fancy dress party two years back.'

'That means you're no nearer to proving anything against her.'

'Nope.'

'So what are you planning next?'

'We drag that reservoir.'

'So you *do* think Ruby's dead?'

'Look, if she'd only fallen in, she would've floated to the surface by now but if she'd
been weighted down - '

'God almighty. You can't think that of any mother.'

'That's what cops do, Mr Hoare... think bad of people. Talking of which, how did the meet with your reptile friend go?'

'McCall? Fine, but you'll need to size him up yourself.'

'I'll be doing that, don't worry.'

'OK, but a word to the wise - he'll not buy any old nonsense. He'll scratch away till he gets the story he wants.'

They finished the whisky. Benwick dozed in the flat's only easy chair. Hoare saw inside his open jacket. It definitely wasn't a phone in his pocket. But why would a cop need a gun on a no-mark job like this? No doubt McCall would ask the same question. Hoare barely slept. Ruby's disquieting little face swam in the darkness of his night. She seemed to be struggling for breath though the lungs of London rose and fell to the rhythm of the dawning day. Its clamour would soon begin again and all her cries for help be drowned out.

Ten

Nothing ever quite stays the same on a beach. Dunes move, sand shifts and cliffs fall into the sea. Yet Staithe End cottage had remained unaltered in all the years since Lexie and McCall last stayed there, a doll's house set under an artist's sky and remembered from days they thought gone forever. Now they walked the wind-blown beach they'd known so well, solitary figures under shelving grey clouds which might yet bring rain.

Within each was an unspoken desire to recover what time steals and seldom, if ever, returns. For them, words were not necessary. Memories were enough.

*

McCall is smoking on the empty upper deck of a bus butting its cautious way through a North Sea gale. They pass a derelict windmill, its sails gone, iron innards exposed within a domed wooden cap rotting in the salt sea air. A farmer on a blue tractor is ploughing a field. The soil glistens cold and damp as it peels before the blade and the tumbling white gulls which follow.

The bus reaches its turn-round stop by a granite war memorial in the coastal Lincolnshire village where Lexie and her troupe will stage their final show early that afternoon. They have performed at ten schools in two weeks. Eight young hopeful actors in a tin box of a Bedford van she has hired, filled with props and costumes till there is no space for a passenger.

So McCall has followed on, hitch-hiking across the farmlands of East Anglia to stay close to Lexie. Not all the strolling players approve of his dog-like devotion to their female lead. He has seen the contempt in the eyes of those who know and admire Evan, the man to whom she is betrothed yet is betraying.

But McCall is young and knows everything but guilt.

He hasn't eaten since breakfast. That was a slice of toast and an apple bought at a café in the market place at Wisbech. He's slept in the van every chill night except one when Lexie smuggled him into her bed while the flea-pit landlady immolated supper. But obsessive love has a price. He is starting a fever, feeling alternately hot then icy cold with pains in his back and limbs.

He fears college may already have written to Bea and Francis to say no tutor has seen him for three weeks. They will be worried, maybe angry. He should ring home but lacks the courage to disappoint them yet again.

McCall walks the last mile of a drovers' road to the Thomas Newton School where Lexie will transform herself into Lady Macbeth. He can make out a complex of squat modern buildings of steel and glass within a grove of leafless young trees.

The threatened sleet cuts across the bare thorn hedges from the open fields and stings his face. But it will be warm in the school canteen. They will give him something to eat then he will want only to sleep and not wake again unless Lexie is by his side.

*

Come, you spirits, That tend on mortal thoughts!

Unsex me here, And fill me from the crown to the toe top full,

For a moment, McCall isn't sure where he is. Then he remembers - lying on a heap of coconut matting in the wings of the school assembly hall. There's a tightness in his chest and his head throbs. He hears Lexie's voice from beyond the drapes.

Of direst cruelty; make thick my blood,

Stop up the access and passage to remorse –

Other members of the cast enter and exit between the tabs in their home-made costumes, mindful only of their lines and cues, not McCall's distress.

Nought's had, all's spent, Where our desire is got without content:

'Tis safer to be that which we destroy than by destruction dwell in doubtful joy.

McCall is barely conscious during the rest of the play. He misses the scene where Lady Macbeth sleepwalks into madness, tortured by nightmare visions of the evil she has done in pursuit of her own ends.

Only as the final curtain comes down and the audience applauds does McCall stir. A teacher sees him and calls a colleague who does first aid and has a bottle of aspirin.

Lexie takes charge. She unilaterally donates all the props and scenery to the school to make space for McCall to lie in the back of the van. They drive to King's Lynn station for the rest of the company to catch trains to London or Cambridge.

Within an hour, she and McCall are at the Ship Hotel, further up the Norfolk coast at Brancaster. She has telephoned ahead for a double room for one night as a married couple.

A doctor lives only a few streets away. Lexie persuades him to leave his supper to attend her sick husband. McCall's given tablets and advised to rest, to eat more and take plenty of sea air.

In the hotel lobby, Lexie sees an advert on the notice board for a fisherman's cottage to rent overlooking the beach. It's called Staithe End and the owner lives nearby. She pays him thirty five shillings for a week, starting next day.

McCall lies in bed, exhausted by her energy. She'd stored up all the adrenalin from fifteen performances and let it burst in a single night to bend everyone to her will.

They drive to Staithe End after breakfast. It's built of flints and russet red bricks and is near where they say Admiral Nelson learned to sail and Roman soldiers once guarded a harbour which is no more. It has small sash windows either side of a leaf-green door reached by a path of pebbles taken from the beach. Inside, the walls and low-beamed ceiling have been newly whitewashed. The quarry tiles by the open hearth are cracked where kindling has always been split with an axe.

'Wow, McCall... just look at it. Isn't this a dream?'

'A dream, absolutely... can't argue with that.'

'Don't you just love it? I could stay here for ever.'

McCall, still weak, sits down heavily on the sofa. Lexie unpacks their cases and takes them up to the bedroom. There is a lumpy mauve eiderdown across a brass bedstead and a chamber pot on the plank floor below because the earth closet is down at the far end of the back garden.

They go for a walk. A gathering north easterly lifts the surface sand and a fine skim of crystal grains begins to twist and turn of its own accord across the beach. Adrift in this magical, disorientating tide, each is aware of their fleeting presence within it and the need to commit the moment to memory.

Then the rain begins. They take armfuls of driftwood from the strand line and head back to the cottage. McCall sets light to the fuel they have found and Lexie heats a pan of tomato soup on the oil stove.

The rain turns to hail which cracks against the windows like grape shot. They pull the sofa closer to the fire. Lexie fetches the eiderdown to cover them and they lie together, orphaned by the storm.

'I don't want any of this to end.'

'Why should it, lovely man? It's only just started.'

'Yes, but nothing lasts, does it?'

'It does if you make it.'

'But will we?'

'Will we what?'

'Make it last.'

'All that matters is to live in the moment, McCall.'

But how can he? Someone else will always be between them - Banquo at McCall's feast. Yet if he mentions Evan's name, she puts her finger to his lips. McCall is fascinated yet scared by Evan. He doesn't know how Lexie met him or anything about his background or why she is cheating on the man she may yet marry - still less, why he lets her.

But McCall cannot risk letting her think she has to choose between them. That he would fear like death itself. The clock on the chimney breast above them marks each disappearing minute. *Now* will soon be *then* and he is afraid of the uncertain future.

*

They wake next morning to the pealing bells of St Mary the Virgin. McCall feels no better. He has a temperature and is breathing rapidly. Lexie leaves him in bed and goes out. McCall is sleeping fitfully when she returns. The weather has closed in and an ill tempered sea sucks against the dunes.

'I've been to ring someone, Mac.'

'That doctor, again?'

'No, someone else. He'll help us.'

She wipes his forehead with a damp flannel and goes back downstairs to wait. It is lunchtime when McCall hears a car pull up outside. Lexie opens the cottage door. He struggles out of bed and kneels by the low dormer. It is Evan. It could only be him. McCall sees them through the window, embracing like the lovers they are.

'Thanks for coming.'

'Missed you.'

'Me too.'

*

The sound of the sea rushing and shushing across the sands comes to McCall all through the early hours yet cannot lull him to where questions stop and confusion is laid to rest.

The rain clouds have drawn back. The night sky is aglow with uncountable stars and a quartered moon silvers the floor by the bedroom window. There is no wind to shake the windows and the last of the logs in the hearth below pop and crack like burning bones then fall to ash and are no more.

Lexie lies warm and naked by McCall's side. Her breathing comes and goes in little tides and her breasts rise and fall with the current. She looks as innocent and content as the child she was till a dozen years ago.

All is still and at peace in Staithe End. But McCall's preoccupied mind still refuses to grant his body the gift of sleep. And in the silence, he can hear Evan on the sofa downstairs, inhaling and exhaling as rhythmically as the woman who will become his bride.

Eleven

Evan gives the impression of being at odds with the vulgarity of the mid 1960s. His car is a grey, razor-edged Triumph Renown - the preferred saloon of bank managers and accountants. Yet it fits him, fits the Cambridge don that he is, goes with the sports jacket, the cavalry twill trousers and the hand-made shoes.

This is McCall's rival for Lexie... Lexie, this wilful, earthy girl who now runs bare-legged and laughing through the waves that spill across the shore as both her lovers look on.

'Quite wonderful, isn't she?'

McCall can only nod in agreement. He has yet to grasp the basics of this three cornered arrangement. Its language and conventions are uncomfortable and new.

'Always doing her keep-fit exercises, you know. Theatre work's pretty punishing.'

They leave Lexie, her feet slap, slap, slapping against the wet sand, her hair damp with spray and unfurling behind her in the wind. McCall follows Evan to the cottage, half a pace behind like a younger brother.

'We're going to have to look after you, aren't we? You're run down. Lexie's told me.'

'I caught some infection,' McCall says. 'Knocked me sideways.'

Evan boils their eggs on the paraffin stove, timed at exactly four minutes by his watch, then brews tea in a big brown pot. McCall fetches a bottle of milk from the larder and reaches down two cups from hooks on the painted dresser. They sit either side of a plain scrubbed table sharing the plate of bread which Evan buttered.

'Eat up, Mac. You're going to need all your strength in the days ahead.'

McCall does as he is told. What else can he say to this paradoxical man? It's been two days since Lexie summoned him. He came with pills and cough medicine and personally gave them to the boy bedding his fiancée at every opportunity.

Even in these liberated times, where is the polite conversation to cover that? And yet he seems entirely without malice, as if conceit and male affront are beneath him.

They wash and dry their plates and cutlery, standing side by side at the earthenware sink. If there is any tension in the little kitchen it is due to McCall's nervousness, his dread of being called to account for what he cannot help but few would excuse.

'Lexie's got to get the van back,' Evan says. 'The hire runs out tonight.'

McCall looks up, even more wrong-footed. He wants to be with her, not left with Evan. But his thoughts have been read.

'She'll drive back to Cambridge this afternoon and we'll follow on tomorrow.'

His tone is kindly enough but firm. McCall is in no position to argue. He resigns himself to face a trial he cannot escape.

Lunch is dressed crab and salad. They clear away and Lexie kisses them both, throws her bags in the van then drives off. Evan and McCall stand side by side and watch till the Bedford is out of sight.

'Come on, let's go for a toddle,' Evan says. 'We've much to talk about, you and me.'

*

The grey-green North Sea breaks across the glistening beach, rolling its scattered pebbles ever smoother, ever smaller. Gulls hang in the louring sky and rooks lift off from fields the waves wait to reclaim.

It seems to McCall that he and Evan are the last two people alive. They keep seaward of the debris left by the last tide. Evan's brogues leave deeper impressions than McCall's shoes for he is bigger and heavier. The wind picks up and bends through the spiky grasses stitched across the dunes.

Evan is in his Gannex coat and wears a squire's check cap to cover his thin fair hair. The hood of McCall's parka keeps blowing back so he walks bare-headed in acceptance of his noviciate role.

'You're in big trouble, disappearing like you did,' Evan says. 'Your tutor's a friend of mine. Seems there are two options. Either you find some acceptable personal reason for leaving the university or you will be sent down.'

'I was planning to quit anyway.'

'It's a shame because you're a clever young man, you write well and have insight but you lack discipline, won't apply yourself. That's your problem, isn't it? Too ready to peel off and do something more immediately interesting. Bit of a butterfly.'

Ships pass on the curve of the far horizon, names unseen, crews unknown. The anonymous life appeals to McCall, goes with his desire to travel but never arrive.

'I'm an historian, Mac. I research people who are no more and times for which there are only the sketchiest of records. Events and people and their motives back then were as endlessly complicated as they are now so it is unwise to jump to conclusions about anything or anyone too quickly.'

McCall knows this outdoor tutorial is no accident. Whatever Evan says today will have a purpose, coded or otherwise. But at its heart is the joust for a lady's hand. There can only be one winner. Those are the rules of the game.

'Most people are rarely what they seem... take you, for instance.'

'Me? Why?'

'Well, to anyone who doesn't know better, you're a bright undergraduate from a well off and well connected family with a big old house in Shropshire. But what's the real story about you?'

'That's not something I talk about.'

'Well, let me try. You're called Francis after the husband of the couple who adopted you, the Wrenns, because your father was his rear gunner when they flew bombers together in the war. Tragically, your parents were killed in a car crash when you were little. They were quite poor so the Wrenns raised you as their own in rather pleasing surroundings near

Ludlow. Mr Wrenn is now a diplomat in Moscow and has hopes for your success in Cambridge. Unfortunately, they're not going to be realised, are they?'

There is no hint of triumph or recrimination in Evan's words. McCall has never been confronted with the facts of his own life by an outsider before. What Evan said is a shock. He has seen behind the veil.

'How have you found all this out?'

'I know what to ask and of whom to ask it.'

'But why have you bothered?'

'Because you've crossed my path and I need to know about you so I can work out how best to deal with the situation that has arisen.'

McCall is now aware his infuriatingly conciliatory rival might appear to turn the other cheek but never unclenches his fists. Maybe Evan cannot conceive of life without Lexie, either. Odd as it seems, McCall does not dislike him – quite the opposite.

He feels Evan actually understands how raw he is inside. It is this compassion which makes him more of a man than one who would knock him to the ground.

But his inner steeliness disturbs McCall. His own desire for Lexie, the blood-hot, base infatuation to possess her, is no less but now seems shaded by his opponent's more calculating passion. For all this, McCall remains in the grip of a blind madness. It's already caused him to step off life as he has known it - and always thought it would be - and drop into the fearful unknown. And the malady has yet to run its course.

*

They make toast on a long brass fork by the fire then spread it with Norfolk honey for supper. There are two bottles of house red which Evan bought earlier at the Ship Hotel. The room is lit by candles and feels like a den where schoolboys might share secrets.

'You must understand, Mac… I do realise how difficult all this must be for you.'

'*Difficult?*'

'Yes, it cannot be easy for you… this... this situation, I mean.'

McCall can think of nothing to say so keeps quiet.

'Lexie and I have known each other many years. She is a singularly complex person for reasons which, if you'll forgive me for saying, you cannot understand at your age.'

'I understand that I love her. Isn't that enough?'

'Sadly, no. The fact is Mac, I shall marry Lexie and you will find someone else. That is what will happen.'

McCall empties his tea cup of wine in a single swig and refills it from the second bottle. He wants to be drunk. He has a sudden urge to shout and fight and draw blood from his enemy then steal his car and drive to Lexie. But where would she be? He doesn't even know where she lives, only that she lives with Evan. Everything comes back to Evan.

Tears of frustrated anger well up into McCall's eyes and he hurls his cup into the hearth. It is a pointless, juvenile gesture which he regrets immediately. Evan clears away the mess with a brush and pan and wipes the wine stain from the chimney breast with a damp cloth.

McCall sits with his head in his hands. Evan leans against the jamb of the kitchen door, arms folded.

'If you will let me, I'll help you. Nothing that's happened means we can't be friends.'

*

McCall's meeting with his tutor is brief. He leaves with a suitcase containing only a few clothes and the books he intends to keep. He looks haggard and distressed. Of Lexie, he knows nothing. Evan drove him back to Cambridge the previous day. The atmosphere was strained. McCall went to the Arts Theatre but they said Lexie wasn't there. No one knew where she was or when she might return.

It is coming mid-day. McCall is at Cambridge Station waiting for a train to London. He might tag along with a blues band he knows and put a soundtrack to a life that's come off the rails. He dreads having to tell Bea and Francis the worst possible news.

The station's buffet is crowded and steamy. He buys a cheese roll and a cup of tea then finds a window seat. Through the condensation, he watches one train depart then another. In his mind, the moment he actually steps inside a carriage will signify he accepts he is beaten. He will have lost everything – and for what? Lexie always belonged to Evan. McCall only borrowed her for a day here, a night there.

He thinks of a tutorial discussion about a letter from Jack Kerouac's friend, William S. Burroughs... *There is no intensity of love or feeling that does not involve the risk of crippling hurt. It is our duty to take this risk.* And what then, comrade?

Another London train is announced. McCall knows he must catch it. He makes for the door. Before he can open it, a girl in a duffel coat walks in... a girl with dancer's legs, hair the colour of sunshine and a smile which promises pleasures to come.

'I guessed you'd be here,' she says. 'I've got a car outside. Let's go back to the cottage.'

So they did for that was what Lexie wanted.

Twelve

Being a Scotland Yard press officer gave Malky Hoare a status he'd never had before, a feeling of managing serious events, not just peddling tabloid scandals from the margins as before. Some of his pre-divorce chutzpa was coming back - thanks to Benwick. He'd pinned a hero-gram on the PR department's notice board lauding Hoare's handling of the televised press conference when Etta Ross ran out in distress. Who wouldn't be thinking cosmetic dentistry?

Hoare was calling various news desks to alert them to a photo-opportunity in the Ruby investigation when McCall rang from a phone box in Norfolk.

'Glad you've touched base,' Hoare said. 'There's been a significant development. Benwick's having the reservoir dragged the day after tomorrow. You need to be down here early.'

'So he's given up hope of finding Ruby alive?'

'Got to face facts. If they're not found in the first twenty-four hours, it usually means the worst and the kid's been gone for well over a week now.'

'How's the mother?'

'In a hell of a state, apparently.'

'I'll need to talk to her... and Benwick. Let's meet before any other hacks pitch up.'

'What about a coffee, seven-thirty on the day? There's a greasy spoon in Woodberry Street just by the reservoir. Café Leila, it's called.'

'OK, you're on. One last question - is the mother a suspect in any of this?'

'Christ, Mac. You know I can't say anything about that - even if I knew.'

*

McCall decided against telling Lexie about the reservoir being dragged. If Etta finally answered one of her sister's many phone calls and mentioned it, he'd still advise against Lexie being there. A body recovered from water can be a gruesome sight.

They'd time for a walk along the dunes before leaving for Garth Hall. Lexie needed to collect her car then attend to business in Bristol. McCall would head for London.

'Evan's a lovely old sweetheart, isn't he, Mac?'

'For buying the cottage?'

'It's like we've got a time machine to travel back to where everything was happy.'

Lexie squeezed McCall's hand a little more tightly.

'Are you ever going to tell me what you were doing in Oxford that day I saw you?'

'There's not much to say, not really... just dealing with something from the past.'

'Go on, I'm listening.'

'Some African stuff... something catching up with me.'

'Don't talk in riddles. What happened in Africa?'

He withdrew his hand from hers and hunched forward slightly as if to make himself a smaller target. Lexie stopped and made him face her.

'Come on, Mac. Tell me. It's obviously bothering you.'

McCall looked away, looked anywhere but into her eyes. It began to drizzle. The sky sank into the sea over Lexie's shoulder.

'Some people got killed... some villagers there.'

'Killed?'

'Yes... murdered. Six of them.'

'You weren't there, were you... on a story?'

'That's what I do, isn't it?'

'God, Mac. That's awful but how's this connected to Oxford?'

'Through a shrink there. He was recommended to me.'

'Ah, so that's it. What happened was bad enough to trouble you, psychologically?'

'I'd seen worse... but I was younger then. Life was still a game.'

'Was the shrink able to help you?'

'Not a lot, no... right out of magic wands that day, apparently.'

*

Neither spoke much on their drive back across England. McCall regretted opening up to her on the beach. Admitting to mental stress felt like confessing to a weakness. But it also exposed him to questions he wasn't prepared to answer - not to her, anyway. He needed to divert her attention.

'So, come on, I've given you a confidence so you tell me why you've really pitched up in my life again.'

'Because Ruby is missing.'

'No other reason, then? Just because me being a hack might help you?'

'Well, that and I've thought about you lots over the years. Felt guilty, I suppose.'

'But *we* were a long time ago.'

'True but you were special.'

'But not special enough for you not to marry Evan.'

'You know, Mac... if you think about it, you should be thankful I didn't marry you.'

'*Thankful*?'

'Yes, grateful even.'

'How do you work that out?'

'Simply because I would have destroyed you and your career back then.'

'In what way?'

'My unfaithful streak was a mile wide. Can you imagine what I'd have got up to while you were away on stories for weeks on end? You could never have trusted me. You'd never have been happy.'

'So you were doing me a favour, dumping me?'

'I know you were hurt and I'm truly sorry but I knew only Evan could put up with me in the long run. I couldn't have given you loyalty, not then. Evan represented the security I needed.'

'So it wasn't love between you and Evan - just a matter of convenience?'

'I always worked on the basis that if I had two men who cared for me and one went, I'd still have the other.'

'Do you regret anything?'

'Well, I've never had kids with anyone. But as my mother always said, if you've none to make you laugh, you've none to make you cry.'

Thirteen

Hoare waited at Café Leila, booted and suited and ready for the world. Benwick might play the Florida cop but Hoare was old Fleet Street, dressed to meet duke or dustman and cause offence to neither.

He'd breakfasted on steak and eggs with two cups of coffee, black, well sugared then the first cigarette of the day. This was always the best. It cleared his head for plots and schemes. Benwick had only wanted a photo call for the frogmen's search of the reservoir. But Hoare knew a theatrical agent who could lay on a Ruby look-alike for a reconstruction of her last known movements.

'We'll get terrific press pictures and better TV coverage.'

'Great idea,' Benwick said. 'Glad I thought of it.'

Hoare saw McCall crossing the street towards Café Leila in a blue cotton jacket and stone-coloured Chinos. McCall always looked nervy and drawn but that morning, seemed even more so. Hoare bought him a coffee and asked for a receipt.

'OK, I've talked to The Sunday Telegraph,' McCall said.

'They want twelve-hundred words and pictures on Ruby.'

'That's a whole page.'

'Yes, I sold the idea hard but I must have the mother exclusive, Malky. The piece won't work otherwise.'

'I'll talk to Benwick. It should bring a smile to his face but don't bet the farm on it.'

'So what else can you give me for old time's sake?'

'Listen, Mac. You can't keep leaning on me like this. I'll give you Benwick's mobile number and his confidential direct line then that's it. Debt paid.'

Hoare left to meet Benwick for a final briefing with the frogmen who would search the reservoir. Despite their friendship, McCall didn't trust Hoare enough to tell him about Ruby's brilliant artworks, still less that he was her aunt's lover.

He stayed in the cafe to write up his notes about what he'd already observed of Ruby's habitat - its litter, the dog shit, kebab smells, noise, traffic, the roaming neighbourhood kids whose unthinking cruelty she sought escape in a private fantasia of castles and princesses. Such a child with such an imagination - and so rare a talent - could hardly be of this world and might already be in the next. That was the tragedy unfolding here which was why her story was so compelling.

'You are from the newspapers, yes... about Ruby?'

McCall looked up. A woman stood over him, late middle age, white apron, darting eyes and scraped-back hair reddened by henna.

'Yes, I'm writing about Ruby. Did you know her?'

'I am Leila. This is my place. Ruby come and have food here almost every day.'

She sat down beside him. Her long, geranium-coloured nails dug into the flesh of her palms as she told him about an unlikely friendship.

'I never send Ruby away. Not me. Always hungry, no playmates. Her mother, not good woman, don't deserve Ruby.'

'Why wasn't she a good woman?'

'Men come to her, all times. Many men. Sorry but it's truth. If only Ruby visit *me* that

day... but no... and now all this.'

'Sounds like you were very fond of her.'

'Yes... such a strange child, like no other... so clever but no one knew.'

'In what way was she clever?'

'Listen, you come. You come with me.'

McCall followed her upstairs to living quarters furnished like the inside of a gypsy caravan – prints of snowy mountains, vases of artificial flowers, two plaster dogs either side of a gas fire. She unhooked a framed pencil portrait from the wall.

'See this? This is me.'

It was Leila all right – hooded eyes, laugh-lined and knowing, slightly Semitic nose and an alluring, full lipped smile, generous and kind.

'Ruby did this of me.'

'What, she sat you down and drew you?'

'No, from memory she does this. She just come in one day and give it me. Believe me, if Ruby die, some of me die, too.'

*

Viewed from the reservoir's edge, the very stillness of such a huge volume of water appeared threatening. Hoare figured it would take him at least twenty, twenty-five minutes just to walk the cinder path around it.

He lit another cigarette and sent the match fizzing into the reeds. The rain was holding off but a bank of cloud started massing behind the battlements of the pumping station. Benwick approached shaving his chin with a battery razor.

'Another night on the tiles?'

'I wish,' Benwick said. 'Big day, today. You all set?'

'The kid actress and her mum should be here shortly.'

'And the reptiles?'

'Couple of TV crews lined up, the local papers are all sending and I've just had a word with that freelance guy I told you about.'

'McCall... yeah, interesting bloke.'

'You've checked up on him?'

'Always best to be prepared.'

'You need to watch him. Like I said, he won't be fobbed off with any old fanny.'

'So I gather.'

'He'll want a long talk with Etta. You happy with that?'

'So long as you sit in.'

'What about giving him an inside track on Etta's private life? That'd spin the story very big.'

'We'll see. Meanwhile, you do all that front of house guff with the TV people.'

'OK, but won't they be wondering why you're not doing it?'

'Not too sure I care a damn what they wonder.'

They headed to the pumping station car park to meet the divers. A slight wind began to disturb the perfect reflection of the castle on the far bank. Benwick paused, hands in the pockets of his jeans, staring across the reservoir.

'She's out there, Mr Hoare... poor little sod... somewhere, out there.'

Fourteen

McCall watched the rubber-suited frogmen bob about like seals, sleek and glossy as they worked their systematic way from the main sluice towards the trees Ruby was known to climb. He got shots of them diving into the watery gloom only to emerge to give the thumbs-down.

He'd also covered the child actress being filmed for television in a copy of the green polka dot dress Ruby had on when she vanished. Police had the look-alike walk from Linden House to the parade of take-away shops and convenience stores on Woodberry Street, hoping to jog the memory of anyone who might have seen Ruby.

Women watched the performance from doorways or hanging out of windows to catch a glimpse of what might be on the TV news that evening. But the plastic Venetian blinds at Café Leila remained down. The sight of this play-acting little ghost caused the owner to shake with dread.

McCall told Lexie he'd ring later to say if he discovered anything new. For now, he couldn't help smiling, seeing Hoare comb back his silver hair as a TV camera crew set up to interview him. Weekly paper reporters stood behind the tripod and scribbled down his every word. If only they knew.

'We need people to think back hard,' Hoare said. 'Do they remember seeing Ruby that afternoon? If so, what was she doing? Where was she going, was she with anyone? It
is vital we find out every last detail.'

The young TV researcher asked Hoare why the reservoir was being searched.

'We have to explore every possibility. We know this was Ruby's playground, a place where she felt safe and free but she could've had an accident.'

'So something could've happened to her here?'

'We have to fear the worst but hope for the best.'

Hoare knew a snappy sound-bite when it came to him.

McCall kept the intriguing DI Benwick in sight. There was much to talk to him about. But that could wait. More urgent was McCall's need to have a face to face with Etta. He took Hoare to one side after he'd done his TV interview.

'Malky, old mate - where's Mum?'

'Bear with me. I think she must have slipped out of the flat for a minute.'

'So she's been at home all this time? I could've talked to her there.'

'Someone's looking for her right now. We'll find her then she's all yours. Honest.'

*

The first gusts of rain hit the reservoir like fistfuls of gravel. It did not trouble the frogmen but drove all the other hacks and photographers except McCall back to their offices. He saw Benwick and Hoare in a huddle as if something was not going to plan. McCall went to shake hands with Benwick.

'Sorry to barge in. I'm Francis McCall.'

'Yes, I know.'

'OK, well, time's getting on and I need to talk to Ruby's mother for my feature piece.'

'So do we.'

'How do you mean?'

'She's gone walk-about.'

'What, she's missing?'

'Uniform are looking for her. We'll find her.'

They were interrupted by two identical ivy green Rovers pulling into the pumping station car park. The drivers got out and put up brollies for their passengers - four men and a woman - who hurried through the downpour to the security manager's office.

'That'll be our pizzas,' Benwick said.

'Or your oysters and champagne.'

Benwick turned to McCall and asked what he meant.

'The tall guy, you must recognise him - Guy Inglis, rising star of the Tories. Even his enemies have him down as a future prime minister.'

'How do you know him, Mac?' Hoare said.

'I interviewed him on a defence story a while back.'

'So what the hell's he doing here?' Benwick said.

Then one of the chauffeurs came out and beckoned Benwick inside the building. Waiting for him was a parliamentary sub committee inquiring into operational police costs. They'd chosen the Ruby investigation for an unannounced inspection.

*

Rain clouds gave way to blue skies and sunshine which drew tiny wisps of vapour from the warm earth and beaten down weeds at the reservoir edge. Hoare suggested taking the MPs to the pumping station roof to get an overview of the search as Benwick briefed them on the case so far.

McCall saw Inglis looking at him, as if trying to remember why he knew his face. The female MP was all bosom and bluster. The creases in her fleshy pink neck looked damp. She struggled up the last narrow steps to the top with her briefcase and clipboard then leant heavily against the parapet.

'You say this little girl... this Ruby... she's handicapped in some way?'

'Asperger's syndrome,' Benwick said. 'It means she's quite naïve and unworldly and any child who's that vulnerable – '

'Yes, yes. I've heard of it. But tell me, what are the daily financial implications during a case like this – overtime, transport costs, specialist teams, that sort of thing.'

'I'm sure these things are important but my priority is finding a missing child.'

'Of course it is but to what extent do you consider costs during an investigation?'

'That's for the accountants. I repeat, my sole interest is in finding Ruby.'

'So you would bring in this diving team for instance without a second thought?'

'How else would you suggest I find out what's at the bottom of a reservoir?'

'No need to be defensive. I am trying to understand your decision-making processes.'

Before Benwick's contempt became any more obvious, Inglis intervened with a chairman's emollient tact.

'I'm sure the inspector realises we know he's got a job to do,' he said. 'But by the same token, our duty is to improve our police systems in the future. We have to make sure the public purse is wisely used at all times.'

These were not people who knew anything of Benwick's world - or McCall's. They were versed in double entry bookkeeping, profit, loss. Theirs was the language and logic of management, drier than dandruff and about as inspiring.

The MPs started to head back to their limos when Benwick's eye caught something in the middle of the reservoir. He shouted to the frogmen, pointing to what he'd seen. The parliamentary delegation leaned over the battlements.

'God almighty,' Inglis said. 'That's not her, is it?'

McCall got focus and saw a pale, distorted shape through his viewfinder. It was like a starfish slowly floating towards the surface. Benwick was already clattering down five flights of metal stairs followed by Hoare and the unfit MPs trying to keep up.

Two of the divers began paddling a rubber dingy to the centre deeps. McCall fired off shot after shot. The body was recovered then rowed to where Benwick helped to lay it gently on a bank of marshy grass.

She'd not a mark on her, only a smear of mud here and there. It made no sense for her not to wake, to rub her eyes and rise up.

Instead, she gleamed in the sunshine like a flawless marble statue retrieved from a civilisation lost beneath the waves. A circle of onlookers gathered. No one moved, no one spoke. Nothing disturbed this almost photographic composition - still life with figures.

McCall put his camera away. This was less out of respect than the guilty realisation he could almost be back in the bush, taking pictures he could never use to satisfy a compulsion to stare into the face of unnatural death.

This much he knew as he gazed on the naked body.... not that of little Ruby Ross but of her mother, Etta.

Fifteen

Men make plans, God laughs - Jewish proverb.

Etta's apparent suicide altered everything. It robbed Benwick of a prime suspect. The course of Lexie's life would change forever if Ruby turned up alive as she would have to care for her. And McCall's piece about a missing child's rare talent now needed a radical re-think.

But his story might yet be blown away by the tabloids if Etta's fascination with sex and Satanism leaked out. The manner of her death fed suspicion, not sympathy. Lexie was acutely aware of this as she tried to take in the enormity of what her sister had done - and all its implications.

'Why in the name of all that's holy would any mother kill herself while the police are still searching for her missing child?'

McCall hadn't an answer, not when they were surrounded by the paraphernalia of the occult - and possibly prostitution, too. This had to be the story Hoare had hinted at. The old muck-raker must have wished he still worked for a Fleet Street red top.

Lexie had caught the last train from Bristol after McCall rang and told her to get to London quickly and bring her spare key to Etta's flat. He didn't tell her the full story till they met at Paddington Station. There were tears then but of anger, not grief.

'Selfish, wicked, stupid bitch,' she said. 'Never a thought for anyone else. Self, self, self - that's always been Etta's way.

What's her poor kid to do now? How's she going to understand what her mother's done? I should've stayed with her when Ruby disappeared but she didn't want me to, told me she needed to be on her own. I understand why, now. What's she been hiding, McCall? What the hell's been going on in her life?'

They drove to Etta's flat and got some answers in her bedroom. Disbelief and alarm broke across Lexie's face.

'I've never been in here before,' she said. 'What was she getting into?'

'Lots of people are interested in all this fortune telling stuff.'

'Come on, I read tarot cards for fun but this magic's much blacker, believe me.'

'None of what's happened is your fault. Your sister was an adult.'

'On paper, maybe. No wonder Ruby didn't have a chance.'

'She wouldn't have understood any of this, even if she'd seen it.'

'This is all going to come out at the inquest, isn't it?'

'Depends on how relevant the cops think it is to her death.'

'If this gets into the papers and Ruby's still missing, they're bound to think Etta was involved in some way.'

'Let's cross that bridge if we come to it.'

They saw the condoms in Etta's bedside cabinet - and the nurse's uniform and a shoe box stuffed with bank notes. It all served to prove what Lexie feared most.

'So this is how she ended up... my baby sister... on the game.'

McCall bought a Chinese take-away in the parade of shops along Woodberry Street. They sat in Etta's uncommonly clean kitchen, careful not to let any of the king prawns or fried rice spill from their plastic forks. Lexie became very quiet. Her fatigue seemed freighted with shame and guilt. She needed the refuge of sleep and left McCall rummaging through a small document box he'd found in Etta's wardrobe. It was ebony inlaid with mother-of-pearl and held utility bills, cheap costume jewellery, Etta's passport and a tenancy agreement.

But it was an invitation card with gold lettering within a border of church bells and confetti which brought back all the hurt McCall had felt when he'd received his.

*

It is Bea who answers the door when Evan arrives at Garth Hall on the off-chance.

'Mrs Wrenn, I'm so sorry for not ringing beforehand,' he says. 'But I've been giving a talk at Shrewsbury School and on the spur of the moment, I thought I'd drive on down here to see Mac - if he's at home, that is.'

'Are you a friend of his?'

'Yes, I'm Evan Dunne... from Cambridge.'

'I see,' says Bea. 'Cambridge.'

'It's all right, I know what's happened. How is Mac at the moment?'

'A worry to us all, to be truthful. He's not the same boy who went up.'

'I'm sorry to hear that. Maybe there's something I can do to help.'

'He's probably in the woods. He spends a lot of his time down there now.'

McCall had gone to Francis's retreat, a corrugated iron dacha painted red oxide and half hidden amid the ash and cherry trees by a stream called the Pigs' Brook.

'Take the path through the woods,' Bea says. 'If you hear a record playing, just follow the music because that's where he should be.'

But all is quiet save for the bleating of sheep in a distant field. The door of the empty dacha is open. A newspaper on the arm of a scuffed leather armchair reports the hunt for an escaped train robber called Ronnie Biggs.

Evan finds McCall sitting on a bench staring into the stream.

'Mac? Hello... are you all right?'

McCall turns and stares at him.

'What are you doing here? Are you on your own?'

'Lexie isn't with me, if that's what you mean.'

Evan sits beside him. He's not sure what to say. This isn't the McCall he remembers. His spirit has gone, he looks hollowed out as if on the point of a breakdown.

'Look, you can't hide away like this for ever. You've got talent, you can write. You're young. There are things happening in this world that make you angry, that offend your sense of right and wrong. Don't waste the gifts you've been given. There are other routes to go in life.'

'Where's all this leading, Evan?'

'Wherever you want it to.... but I've a suggestion.'

'And what's that?'

'Someone I know has read those pieces you wrote for Varsity. He thinks they show considerable promise and he'd like to meet you.'

*

Bea is delighted when Evan agrees to stay the night. She's taken to him and is clearly charmed. Without Lexie around, McCall sees a different Evan - no longer the cuckold but a raffishly entertaining guest from high table, clever, well-read and attentive to an alluring and flirtatious hostess. Bea conducts him through the warren of fading apartments in Garth Hall with its antiques and portraits and legends of love and misfortune. Then it's supper of rabbit and pigeon pie, served in the drawing room scented by wood smoke and candles and where ghosts from the days of the first Elizabeth might still appear to flit amid the shadows.

'So, Mr Dunne... what are we to do with young Mac?'

'Well, that's for him to decide but I think he's ideally suited for journalism.'

It is as if McCall isn't there, allowed only to observe from the sidelines.

'Journalism? Wouldn't that be a rather tawdry business to follow?'

'Possibly but he's just the sort of subversive chap that editors like. Always wanting to show our masters for the fools and knaves they are.'

'Do you see that as the purpose of newspapers?'

'What else, Mrs Wrenn? Is it better to be led by a drunk like George Brown or a crook like Harold Wilson? How would we common folk know about either until a reporter such as Mac might become, ferrets out their secrets?'

Soon, the long case clock chimes ten from the hall. Bea leaves them sitting in the wing backs either side of the inglenook.

'Mrs Wrenn's a marvellous tease, isn't she?'

'Yes, everyone falls in love with Bea eventually.'

McCall shows Evan to a spare bedroom and they say goodnight almost formally. Later, in the dark and where he has slept since childhood - and where Lexie lay with him only days before - McCall finds it impossible not to dwell on the nature of his duplicity and why Evan is showing him such concern.

It makes life more complicated. He cannot get a fix on Evan's motives. They defy all male instincts, however base those generally are. But the effect on McCall is for him to think even less of himself, to believe he is wretchedly dishonourable.

*

By coincidence, Francis arrives back from Moscow next morning. He's driven up from London and parks the Alvis in the stable yard. Bea takes his suitcase and is kissed on both cheeks. She introduces him to Evan. They have coffee together then Francis suggests they walk down to his dacha. He doesn't change his travelling suit, bird's eye in grey worsted made for him by Bodenhams of Ludlow.

The dacha is his place of safety where he can hear the wind move through the trees and the stream bubble over its pebbles. And thus for a while, the perils of his world become as nought.

McCall thinks he detected an ease between Francis and Evan, a familiarity almost. It contrasts with McCall's own feeling of Francis being cool towards him since the great disappointment of Cambridge. But what else did he expect?

He watches from an upstairs window as they head across the orchard lawn then pass through the wicket gate into Garth woods. Again, McCall feels excluded, as if the grown-ups are deciding important matters about him behind his back. Within an hour they return. Evan has to drive home to Cambridge. McCall sees him to his car.

'So are you interested in what I mentioned earlier?'

'What was that?'

'Meeting the fellow who likes your writing. Mr Wrenn thinks you should.'

'I suppose so. Who is he?'

'He's called Roly Vickers, an Oxford man but we shouldn't hold that against him.'

'What does he do?'

'He publishes books on international affairs. Has great contacts who'll help you.'

'To become a journalist?'

'That's what you want, isn't it?'

'Do I have much say in the matter?'

'We all have free will, Mac. It just depends how we choose to use it.'

Evan starts his car and winds down the window.

'There's a pub called the Ye Olde Mitre in Holborn,' Evan says. 'It's down an alleyway - Ely Place, I think. Vickers has lunch there most days.'

'How will I know him?'

'You don't have to. He knows what you look like.'

With this, Evan hands him an envelope and drives away. On the card inside are words printed in gold which McCall never wanted to read.

Mr Evan Dunne and Miss Alexandra Nadin cordially invite you to their wedding at noon on Saturday the 7th of August 1965 in the Cambridge Register Office to be followed by drinks in the RAF bar of The Eagle in Bene't Street.

So she is going ahead with it. She will marry Evan as Evan always said she would. McCall's pleading had only won him a consolation prize - a pint in a pub with a man who might get him a job.

'Marriage is only a piece of paper, Mac,' Lexie had said. 'Nothing more.'

'It's not *nothing*. You'll be legally together and for always.'

'You're a hoot – and so old fashioned.'

Lexie insists such things don't matter. McCall cannot agree. For him to attend Lexie's wedding, to walk the streets of Cambridge again and pass those ancient halls where he'd neither the wit nor wisdom to stay the course, would be to compound his sense of failure. Yet not to see her on such a day cedes all victory to Evan, albeit theirs was never a struggle between equals.

So he'll go, tough it out at the ceremony, find a brave face for the reception. He will kiss the bride and shake the groom's hand. If he gets maudlin drunk then that is what happens at weddings when all that's on show is the happiness of others.

*

In the week before the wedding, McCall meets Roly Vickers in the snug of the Mitre, a darkly panelled medieval pub at the end of a narrow alley in the diamond quarter. Vickers is ex-army, prematurely grey hair slicked with brilliantine. He's no Colonel Blimp. Far from it. He claims Labour Party membership though is troubled by the influence wielded by communists who're covertly infiltrating its branches.

'But I'm more interested in your politics,' Vickers says. 'I gather you're a pretty liberal-minded sort of young man.'

'Left of centre, I suppose. Nothing too radical.'

'Given your upbringing, I'd expect very trenchant and independent analysis of the world and the many threats we face in this country.'

McCall reads this remark as an oblique but knowing reference to his adoptive father's very anti-Soviet views. He threw Vickers a curve ball.

'Are you one of Francis's associates, then?'

'We know of each other, yes.'

'Through intelligence work?'

'I'm a publisher, Mac. But I know where my loyalties lie. What about you? Do you think our western values are worth defending?'

'I thought I was here to talk about my Varsity articles and about getting a job.'

'We are, Mac... we are,' Vickers said. 'And I think Evan's right. You've a journalist's eye for detail and you know your own mind. Good qualities, I'd say.'

One of his Fleet Street contacts has agreed to give McCall a three-month trial.

'It's on the Daily Mail so you'll have to prove yourself,' he says. 'It'll be tougher than Cambridge so harden up and learn fast. But stick with it and I'll make sure you go on to bigger things before long.'

McCall doesn't ask himself why a man like Roly Vickers should favour him in this way, still less what he'll want in return. But his parting words offer a clue.

'Information is a commodity, Mac. You'll want it, I want it. That's the trade we're in.'

*

There's an odd assortment of guests at The Eagle – academics being modestly jolly amongst themselves, Lexie's theatre friends acting loud, socially awkward relatives in big hats and ill-advised outfits keeping to the fringes as befits their insecurities.

Against all McCall's preconceptions, Evan's father is not a learned professor but a   farm labourer. He and his Toby jug of a wife live in a tied cottage in the Fens. Neither can see beyond their pride to begin to understand the genetic quirk which produced so brilliant an offspring.

McCall is stalked by conscience. He's sure the eyes of others are constantly upon him. They must know he is Lexie's lover and disapprove of his shameless presence. If only she wouldn't leave her hand on his arm for so long, adjust his tie, smile so fondly into his face. But it's her way of compensating for the heartbreak she cannot stop herself from causing.

Evan observes them from the winner's enclosure. He could be a solicitor or a doctor in his muted olive green suit. Lexie is dressed more spiritedly - for the anarchic times if not the occasion - in a naval officer's jacket from Carnaby Street and a collarless mauve shirt with bell-bottom jeans. Lexie has a public image to create and maintain which explains why a photographer from the Cambridge Evening News is there.

Evan comes over and steers McCall to a discreet corner table. Above them on a ceiling smoked yellow by nicotine, is warrior graffiti from the last war – the names of British and American air crew scrawled in pencil or burned with cigarette lighters during nights of drunken revelry between bombing raids and dog fights from which some returned but many did not.

'I'm glad you've seen Roly Vickers, Mac. You'll have a focus to your life now.'

'Yeah, I suppose so,' McCall said. 'Tell me, is Roly a spook?'

'Not officially. He's what the real spooks call an *alongsider,* someone they trust, a propagandist publisher who specialises in books about the iniquities of communism and the need for the West to win the ideological war against it.'

'So he's a Cold War warrior, then?'

'Yes, but don't underestimate his ability to help you in journalism. Roly is privy to many secrets, knows lots of people. You'll have a direct line to him.'

'But why me? The Mail might sling me out after three weeks, let alone three months.'

'Roly thinks ahead, that's why. You're an asset for the long war, Mac. But play your cards with care.'

'How do you mean?'

'Nobody is indispensable in that world. Their rules are just that - theirs.'

McCall sees Lexie across in the other bar, glass of wine in one hand, cigarette in the other, half listening to her new mother-in-law while trying to lip-read a lover's conversation with her husband. He feels ever more awkward. Part of him wishes he'd never come. Evan returns to Lexie and embraces her. It is time for McCall to slip away, to make a discreet exit before the newlyweds make theirs.

Sixteen

Hoare insisted on taking McCall for a drink in the Manor Hill Arms after the undertakers carried Etta's body to their blacked-out van. He'd been tasked by Benwick to find out McCall's angle now the wrong body had been found.

'The boss was dead certain it'd be Ruby down there,' Hoare said. 'The job's hit a bloody big wall now Etta's taken a dip.'

'So he still thinks she's key to all this?'

'That's why he kept ramping up the pressure on her. Sooner or later, she'd crack.'

'She cracked, all right... now you'll never know if she was holding something back.'

'That's the bind we're in. No one thinks we'll find Ruby alive now.'

'As bleak as that?'

'Looks like it. Anyway, how does what's just happened play in the piece you're planning to write?'

'It's no longer the feature idea I put up. It'll need completely re-thinking.'

'I bet it'll become a knocking piece - cops drop a clanger and all that.'

'That's what you'd write, is it?'

'Come on, I only ever did tabloid stuff. My career was a mile wide but an inch deep but you just dig and dig, you bugger.'

'Only when something doesn't add up... like in this Ruby business.'

'Don't try tempting me again, Mac. I've signed the Official Secrets Act.'

'More fool you. Anyway, I still need my sit down with Benwick.'

'I'll get back to you on that. He's not in the best of moods. Want another drink?'

'No, I've got to be going.'

'Yeah, I suppose I'd better be off, too. We still haven't traced Etta's sister to tell her the bad news.'

'Lexie, you mean?'

'How do you know her name?'

'We've been friends for years. I'll be talking to her later.'

'You've never mentioned that, you sly old sod. What else do you know?'

'Not as much as I'm going to find out, matey... with or without your help.'

*

A pathologist ruled Etta's death was suicide. Only reservoir water was found in her lungs. She'd been drinking heavily but showed no evidence of sexual assault, defence wounds or illegal drugs.

Benwick left the mortuary ill at ease, the stench of dead flesh in his nostrils, in his hair, on his clothes. Etta had been sliced, diced and sawn up then stitched back together again. A mortician's powder puff and lipstick would create the final illusion of a sleeping beauty. There seemed little point. Etta was soon destined to be a heap of ashes.

This thought, callous as it might be, wasn't the issue. Could it have been her guilt - or his pressure - which had driven Etta to wade into the water and leave the child it was his responsibility to find without a mother? He needed to believe Etta's death was down to her guilty knowledge and the life she'd led.

Her fingerprints were on the empty bottle of vodka the search team found under the tree where Ruby played her games of make-believe. And the jeans, blouse, bra and pants dumped in a heap alongside were Etta's, too.

Benwick should've thrown a scare into her when he'd had the chance. A night in a cell might have induced her to open up about precisely who - and what - he believed she was involved with.

The reconstruction of Ruby's last known movements hadn't brought in much worthwhile intelligence, either. And that tricky loner, McCall, was already snuffling in the undergrowth. He had trouble written all over him.

Yet Benwick knew not to let a bigger picture be obscured by anyone or anything. He'd have to make his move soon. Time was short. Just because something cannot be seen does not mean it isn't there.

*

Hoare sat on a green leather pew in the Central Lobby of the House of Commons, gazed upon by the four patron saints of the British Isles in their mosaic panels on the walls above. The footfalls of clerks and ushers intruded on a babble of innumerable conversations echoing over the tiled floor and into the groins of a vaulted ceiling.

He was early for his appointment but hadn't time to hurry back through security for a calming smoke. What could Guy Inglis possibly want of him? When he'd phoned, he mentioned only a matter of "mutual interest".

'We'll be off the record. But best not mention it to anyone else, agreed?'

Everything was politics at Inglis's level. Some game was afoot. It hadn't been easy for Hoare not to let on to Benwick when he'd pitched up the previous night for another drunken session of palliative care with crisps and peanuts.

'This Ruby job's all going to rat shit,' Benwick said. 'You can't tell me Etta wasn't as guilty as hell or else why did she go for a midnight swim?'

'You seem under a lot of stress, if you don't mind me saying. Have you thought about going sick for a while?'

'You're joking - in the middle of all this?'

'Take some leave then, come back and look at it all afresh.'

'Can't do that, either.'

'Well if you don't, I'd say you're going to become somewhat vaginated.'

'Does that mean fucked?'

'It did at my school.'

Hoare checked his watch yet again. An unsmiling, matronly woman approached him under the glow of the Lobby's huge chandelier, a clipboard protecting an ample bust. She nodded for him to follow her down a corridor where outsiders were rarely allowed.

He saw the tension in the faces of those scurrying by, intent on the business of government even in recess. There was danger in the air and war on the TV monitors. The skies over Kuwait were on fire as the invading forces of Iraq put their enemies to the sword and threatened to ransom the world's supply of oil.

*

'Glad you could make it,' Inglis said. 'Tea? Coffee? There's water if you'd prefer.'

'Water's fine.'

'Sparkling or still?'

'Doesn't matter. From the tap would do.'

Inglis nodded to his hovering aide. She poured black coffee for him, unscrewed a bottle of something gassy from the Alps for Hoare then retreated through a door in the panelled wall.

Inglis's office looked over the striped canvas awnings of the Commons terrace and across the slow moving muddy waters of the Thames. His desk was the size of a snooker table, empty except for two black telephones and his red box for Cabinet papers. They sat either side of a coffee table by the window. All was hushed, like the library of a gentlemen's club.

Hoare sipped his water, crossed his legs and waited for Inglis to open the batting.

'I'll not waste your time. I'm looking to beef up my press team with a safe pair of hands. Might you be interested?'

Hoare immediately recalled the advice given to young hacks on first meeting a Member of Parliament... *always ask yourself, why is this bastard smiling at me?*

'That's most flattering,' Hoare said. 'Are you talking about a secondment from the police or something more permanent?'

'I'd much prefer the latter but I can promise you interesting times either way, bang in the centre of power.'

'Sounds quite a challenge.'

'It is but I want a no-nonsense PR with a Fleet Street background who knows how to handle the media. I was most impressed by your performance on television after that awful business at the reservoir.'

'All in a day's work.'

'How's that investigation going?'

'Not much progress, I'm afraid.'

'Why so?'

'Well, the mother was the main route into whatever has happened to the little girl. With her dead, there's no other prime suspect on the horizon.'

'You mean there's no forensic evidence, no DNA?'

'Nothing has shown up in their flat that links to anyone on police files and neither do her telephone records.'

'Being at the reservoir that day, I feel somewhat close to this case,' Inglis said. 'I'd rather like to be kept abreast of any developments... very much on the quiet, of course.'

'I'm sure something could be done.'

'Good. Now, let's go for lunch.'

Inglis's aide had booked a table at Rules in Maiden Lane. A black cab took them from the Commons and through the leaderless tribes of tourists in Covent Garden.

Hoare put him in his late forties, still unmarried, six feet tall, heavily built, probably played rugby or cricket in younger days. He could pass as a lawyer now - midnight blue Dege & Skinner suit, pressed white shirt, plain red tie in shot silk.

Hoare's researches of the public record revealed Inglis got a first in mathematics at Keble College, Oxford and was active in Conservative student politics. He'd become an accountant-cum-banker in the City before the party gifted him a seat in the midlands.

They knew Guy Inglis at Rules. He got bows and scrapes as a way was cleared for them to a corner table. Inglis ordered Mersea oysters and roasted squab pigeon. Hoare went for rack of Suffolk lamb and opted for the Chateau Mouton-Rothschild when Inglis asked him to select their wine.

'Good choice,' he said. 'Did you know that Bing Crosby and John Wayne would dine here when they were in London?'

'No, I didn't.'

Inglis unfolded his linen napkin then leaned forward and lowered his voice.

'I suppose you must've heard these whispers about Mrs Thatcher.'

Hoare shook his head. He felt like some favoured Lobby correspondent being given a confidential briefing.

'There are those who want a challenge mounted against her leadership.'

'But she's been your most successful Prime Minister in years.'

'She's drawn the unions' teeth and now it's time for a change.'

'So there's a putsch being plotted, is there?'

'Look, Lobby rules so keep this to yourself. My seat in the Cabinet is secure but if Thatcher is challenged, who knows which of us will end up in Downing Street?'

'Does that mean you could be in the running to be the next PM?'

Inglis gave him a modest smile. His eyes were almost as black as his hair but the grey skin around his jowls was starting to sag like a waxwork left in the sun.

'The horse-trading will go on behind closed doors first but don't rule anything out.'

Hoare then became aware of an unsmiling, aggressive-looking man trying to listen to their conversation from a couple of tables away. He was about fifty with gingery hair and a port wine birth mark spreading across his neck.

'Don't look round but we're being ear-wigged.'

'I'm afraid that comes with appearing on TV,' Inglis said. 'Complete strangers think they know one personally and just stare.'

He raised a finger and their waiter brought a second bottle of the Mouton-Rothschild. Inglis then changed the subject.

'Your colleague at the reservoir... that police inspector. Interesting chap, I hear.'

'DI Benwick? Yes, you won't get many like him coming out of Bramshill.'

'A bit unconventional, is he?'

'And how - hasn't been through the blander like so many others.'

'Someone told me he might have worked overseas for a time.'

'That's possible but I don't even know if he's married or where he lives. All I can say is he's utterly committed to finding that missing child.'

'Fingers crossed for him, then. The other thing I wanted to ask... there was a journalist knocking about that day. I thought I knew his face.'

'That'd be Francis McCall, does features for the colour supplements and researches television programmes.'

'Ah, yes. I remember. I wouldn't have thought this type of story was up his street.'

'Neither would I but it turns out he knows the sister of the dead woman.'

'Does he, by jove. I wonder how that will affect what he writes.'

'McCall's in no-one's pocket. He'll just go where the evidence leads.'

They parted after coffee and shook hands in the street.

'Have a think about things,' Inglis said. 'Then let's meet again. What's your club?'

'I don't belong to one.'

'Really? I could propose you for mine, if you wished.'

Hoare thanked him for lunch then disappeared into the crowds pushing towards The Strand. But as soon as he could, he slipped into a shop doorway and looked back towards Rules. For reasons which eluded him, Hoare was intrigued to know what Inglis would do next. And there he was - talking to the birth mark man who'd watched them across the restaurant.

A cab pulled up and they were driven off together. Hoare went back to Rules and found the waiter who had served him and Inglis.

'I forgot to tip you,' he said. 'So rude. Forgive me.'

He slipped a ten pound note in the waiter's apron pocket. Then he asked him for the name of whoever had paid the bill at the table where the ginger-haired man had sat. The waiter winked and checked the credit card receipts in the till.

'It was a Mr Gillespie, Raymond Gillespie.'

'What's his company called?'

'It's a trade union, actually – the Association of Federated Trades.'

'Is he a regular at Rules?'

'No, not that regular but I've seen him here before.'

'On his own, like today?'

'No, with the gentleman at your table.'

So an ambitious Conservative MP had contact with a trade union official. It was no big deal yet something about what he'd just witnessed didn't quite add up.

Seventeen

Lexie could only applaud the duty clergyman's acting skills at Etta's funeral. With barely a script and no rehearsal, his performance suggested genuine warmth for the stranger in the box.

Etta's three mourners heard she was the best of mothers, the most dutiful of sisters and that her tragic passing would cause sorrow to friend and neighbour alike. Lexie, McCall and Hoare could tell a different story. Each had seen inside the paragon's bedroom.

Lexie rejected the religious music offered by the vicar and chose a tape of The Lark Ascending instead. For her, this was the ultimate evocation of lost innocence.

As children, Lexie and Etta never understood why their mother wept whenever this was came on the wireless.

A button was pressed and the coffin moved forward. The first virtuosic notes of a violin rose ever higher between the bare brick walls of the crematorium as the lark sang Etta out of this world and all its temporal ills.

*

The birth of Etta had coincided with the Queen's coronation. Streets nearby were hung with Union Jacks and patriotic red, white and blue bunting. People bought televisions on hire-purchase and invited neighbours in to watch the young Princess Elizabeth take the throne of England and all its dominions.

But Lexie sensed something interesting happening at home, too. A district nurse arrived on a bicycle. Mum was still in bed which was unusual. She began screaming and Lexie thought murder was being done. Then the nurse came down looking for clean towels and caught her listening at the stair door.

'Away off and play or you'll get what's for when your Dad comes home.'

That much she knew only too well.

*

Lexie tightened her grip on McCall's arm. Another family waiting to mourn parted on the steps outside and let them through. In the memorial garden opposite, McCall thought he glimpsed a man with something like a camera around his neck. But the sun was in his eyes and he was too preoccupied to think any more of it.

The shadow of the crematorium chimney lay across the car park and a reflection of its hazy gasses shimmered on the asphalt beneath their feet.

'I need a steadier,' Lexie said. 'There's a pub across the road.'

Inside, wet-eyed women sat drinking spirits, self conscious men stood apart, pint pots in their fists, ill-fitting suits on their backs. McCall bought Lexie a brandy and asked to hear more about Etta.

'I still haven't got a clear picture of her.'

'Bit of a lost soul, really... lacked direction, hadn't much self-confidence.'

'Why would that be, do you think?'

'Our upbringing, I suppose. Everything goes back to childhood, doesn't it?'

'Wasn't your home life very happy, then?'

'No, not really... not looking back.'

'Would you rather not talk about it?'

Lexie thought for a moment and asked for another brandy. Then she lit a cigarette as if to delay her answer a little longer.

'Families,' she said. 'No one knows what goes on inside them... not truly, they don't.'

'That sounds pretty heartfelt.'

'Etta had it worse than me... wasn't as strong-willed as me.'

'Had what worse than you, Lexie?'

'Dad... Dad and his cuddling. That's what he called it. *Cuddling*.'

'You mean - '

'At that age, you don't know what's right or wrong or what's normal, do you?'

'Couldn't you tell your mother?'

'She knew, I'm sure she did but she was as afraid of him as we were so she chose to see nothing, didn't she?'

McCall would've carried on gently probing but Malky Hoare joined them. He'd collected Etta's ashes from the crematorium office as a favour to Lexie. It was his day off but even if Benwick hadn't ordered him to attend the funeral, he would've done so. He wanted to keep track of a story which had far from run its course. Lexie went to the loo so McCall had a chance to quiz Hoare.

'The possibility of Etta being mixed up in Ruby's disappearance, all that black magic crap and her being on the game, is any of this likely to come out at the inquest?'

'I wouldn't think so. There's no hard evidence against her, just suspicion.'

For Lexie, her sister's suicide was hard enough to take. Any official hint, however oblique, that Ruby's disappearance involved a background of sex and Satanism and the tabloids would start their own witch hunt.

Etta's death had affected Lexie more deeply than she would admit. She was showing a quiet vulnerability which McCall had never noticed before. It engendered an urge to protect her from more harm.

Lexie came back and said they should leave to miss the afternoon traffic. They had a long drive ahead, out of London and to life as it had once been.

*

Lexie and Etta were raised in Upton, a gossipy little town by a bend in the Severn, adrift between the whale-backed hills of Malvern to the west and Bredon Hill in the east. It was set on a marshy plain of brooks and ponds and pollarded willows where cows stood steaming in the early morning mists. Here were idyllic half-timbered cottages, bluebell woods and the bridal blossoms of orchards marking the coming of every spring.

They parked and walked for a while. The softly coloured counties around them were theatrically spot-lit here and there whenever the clouds blustered apart and let snatches of sunshine slip through.

'What did your Dad do for a living, Lexie?'

'He was a station porter... only became a big man when he got home.'

'This abuse you suffered, it must have had a bad effect on you and Etta.'

'It scarred our childhood, that's for sure. Psychologically, long term, who knows?'

'Did that have a bearing on you both moving to London?'

'Yes, just as soon as we could get away but then Etta fell pregnant by the first no-hope loser she climbed into bed with.'

'How did your parents handle that?'

'Dad disowned her. Can you credit that? Such hypocrisy. I just couldn't believe it.'

A wind was getting up. Larches on a hillside beyond began swaying before the storm to come. These forces of nature had inspired Edward Elgar to wonder once if the trees were singing his music or if he'd just composed theirs. McCall and Lexie ran back through a headland of spiky bracken to the Morgan.

The sky darkened and rain drum-rolled on the car's canvas hood. But the downpour stopped as quickly as it started, leaving the faintest of rainbows above all that Lexie was loathe to remember.

'Right, drive me to the river,' she said. 'If I don't do it this minute, I never will.'

*

McCall left Lexie clambering down the far bank of the Severn with the box containing her sister's ashes. She was still in her black trouser suit and coat from the funeral and wanted these last minutes to herself. The river slid by in silence, broad and powerful on its way from the mountains to the sea and spinning with the fallen leaves of autumn.

A church once stood close by but only its pepper pot of a bell tower remained. McCall sat on a bench beneath it. Soldiers of the English civil war marched by this place three centuries before, leaving their bones and blood in fields thereabouts.

As here, so in Africa. McCall's mobile rang and returned him to the present. It was Evan.

'Whatever it is you're up to, Mac, watch your step.'

'Why? What's going on?'

'You've just pinged on someone's radar. That's all I know. Can't say any more.'

McCall was puzzled. Why would anyone be remotely concerned with what he was doing? Namibia was months back, his very own private Gehenna. No-one knew he'd spiked his own story out there, still less why. His only press work since was researching Ruby's disappearance. Yet Evan must know something McCall didn't or he'd not trouble to make contact.

He looked up, unaware Lexie was standing close by. She asked who had phoned him.

'Just a contact with a tip-off. Nothing important.'

Eighteen

For McCall, the following morning was as surreal as it was cathartic. Lexie phoned her business partner from Garth before breakfast and was reminded of an unbreakable appointment in Bristol that afternoon. She tossed a travel bag into her Volvo, touched cheeks with McCall and drove off.

Hester observed this hurried adieu from the kitchen window.

'Looks like your friend's got a lot on her mind.'

'She's still in shock about her sister.'

'No, I don't suppose she'll get over that quickly,' Hester said.

'Lexie meant a lot to you once, didn't she?'

'She still does.'

'But she hurt you real bad... years back, I mean.'

'It's that obvious, is it?'

'When we're young, we never realise how fragile we all are, how easily we break.'

He nodded in agreement but didn't want to go where this was heading.

'But you've made your peace with her... promise me, Mac.'

'I'm getting there.'

'Good. Remember what the Chinese say... *he who does not forgive digs two graves.*'

McCall made for Garth Woods as others had done before. This was where they retreated in times of reflection and worse. In this - as in much else - he would forever walk in the shadow of a man he'd loved and still mourned.

He paused by Francis Wrenn's rusting tin dacha but hadn't heart enough to go inside. It had been cleared of the two leather armchairs in which they'd so often sat and talked, all the Whitehall papers he should never have kept - and his beloved gramophone.

Those irrecoverable days of childhood were played out to the sound track of Francis's records of tenors and sopranos and medieval plain song, drifting from the dacha and through the timeless woods to all the secret places only a boy could know.

Such voices hung in McCall's mind still, carrying on the air with the wash of water over pebbles and the sighing of wind through leaves. *Cleanse me from my sins for I acknowledge my faults... deliver me from blood-guiltiness, O God.*

But where was the deity who could absolve McCall of his?

Sitting alone on the bench by the Pigs' Brook - and without the diverting presence of Lexie - that same sense of self-doubt which unnerved him after Africa, threatened again. It was a fear of failure, of his judgement being unequal to the implications of all he now faced - as a hack and as a man. No one could gauge the eventual fallout from Etta's suicide or Ruby's disappearance, still less her possible murder.

The oddly coded warning from Evan only added to the sum of McCall's uncertainties. He heard twigs being trampled in the dried-up undergrowth behind him. It was Hester who knew exactly where he would be - and why.

'Come on, Mac. Staring into the stream won't solve anything.'

'It's OK... I'm just thinking about things.'

'Yeah, sure you are. Now listen, I want to take you some place.'

'No, I'd rather not. Today's not good.'

'That's where you're wrong, mister. You're gonna to snap out of it and come on a picnic with me.'

*

An hour later, they were hiking across a moor, high in the Shropshire hills. Far in the distance were the blueish peaks of Snowdonia and to the south, the Black Mountains, faintly drawn in the warm, hazy air. Wales rolled out west, all pale fields and dark, mystical forests.

Only Lexie's skylarks could be heard, lost in the heavens where her sister had already gone forth.

'What are you planning, Hester?'

'Something magical, you'll see.'

A grassy track led ever upwards, stamped by the iron shoes of horses and close-cropped by black-faced sheep. On either side were gorse bushes, alive with linnets and speckled gold with flowers smelling of coconut.

Ahead was a clearing and within it, the partial remains of a once great circle of standing stones. Stonehenge it wasn't but men had gathered here a thousand years before the time of Christ to mark the seasons, administer justice or offer sacrifices to their cruel and arbitrary gods.

'This is where I come to meditate, Mac... to get rid of all the modern noise we have in our heads till we can't hear the spiritual truth around us. Peaceful, isn't it?'

'Yes, I suppose it is.'

'I sense something timeless and symbolically charged here. Didn't Masefield describe landscapes like this as being *thronged by souls unseen*?'

'I'm afraid I don't know but then, my inner hippie doesn't get out much any more.'

Hester smiled and put down her rucksack.

'I know you've always thought I'm a batty old crank so I guess bringing you here just confirms that you've given home to a damn fool tree-hugger, doesn't it?'

'Of course not but people's opinions and beliefs usually reflect the lives they've led.'

'But there are other ways of interpreting our world, Mac - ancient ways which we've forgotten to remember.'

'Because science and the enlightenment changed how we think, surely?'

'Well, if you cared to look, you might begin to understand the significance of these stones and hills which were venerated by people we grandly think of as primitive.'

'Maybe, but their superstitions gave way to rational thought.'

'So it's *rational* to keep inventing better ways of killing people, is it? To profit from the earth while destroying it and making greed and selfishness respectable?'

She could easily have broken one of her new life's guiding principles - never to get angry. But Hester turned away, took a pure white table cloth from her rucksack and laid it on the grass by the tallest stone.

It stood six feet high, smoothed and blackened by animals rubbing against it for millennia. Someone had left a spray of pink carnations at the base as if this were a grave.

Hester brought out a batch of her coarse Celtic oatcakes which they ate with garden raspberries and cream. McCall asked why she'd brought him there.

'There's a word in Arabic, *sarba*. It means a journey leading to a kind of spiritual renewal and I believe this is an ancient site of healing which might help you.'

'Dear Hester... it's kind of you to be concerned about me but a ring of stones isn't going to sort out what's in my head.'

'No? Well, neither is denying that you're a prisoner of your past and always will be until you let go of whatever it is you blame yourself for.'

Not for the first time, McCall wished she would change the subject. He unwrapped the silver foil around a small lump of dope in his jacket pocket and began to roll a joint. Hester wasn't alone in having alternative leanings.

She opened a bottle of her rose hip wine and poured two glasses.

'Did you know you can draw dead straight lines between pagan places like this and lots of other sacred sites like really old churches and wells, all across the country?'

'Ley lines, you mean?'

'That's right. I know you'll mock but there are waves of energy along ley lines and in these stones. I can always feel it... gives me like a strange tingling in my hands.'

'See if this makes it better.'

He passed her the joint and refilled their glasses. Hester's wine was never allowed to age so was all the more potent for that. McCall stretched out on his back, feet towards the centre of the circle where who knew what sort of rituals had once taken place.

They finished the joint and a rare inner contentment came over him, an altered state of consciousness brought about by chemicals, hooch and weariness. He became aware of Hester kneeling behind him.

She began to gently describe circles on his temples with the tips of her fingers. He didn't object for her touch was as tender and innocent as he imagined a mother's might be.

Her hands moved over his forehead and closed over the pods of his eyes. When she spoke, her voice was calm and seemed to come from the clouds.

'Listen to me, Mac... I want you to let it go... start to release yourself from whatever happened in Africa.'

He didn't reply but felt no urge to get up and walk away.

'I know it won't be easy but just try... just for me.'

McCall still didn't respond but remained motionless under the shadow of the stone.

'Tell me what's in your head... tell me what's brought you so low.'

'Guilt, if you must know... guilt and blood.'

'Right, OK... but let's go back to the beginning. To Africa, but where exactly?'

'Namibia... in a kraal out in the bush... little settlement of huts.'

'What were you doing there?'

'Talking to these women whose men had been murdered for helping the insurgents.'

'Weren't they taking a risk talking to you?'

'A priest took me there and asked them to.'

'Who had murdered their husbands?'

'A counter terrorist unit called Koevoet, run by the South Africans. I was researching a story about their crimes.'

'So you're with these women... what happens next?'

'The priest leaves on his motorbike and I've got an hour with a woman who speaks some English but after a few minutes, she's becomes afraid.'

'Why? What made her afraid?'

'One of the others sees a plume of dust rising in the distance and shouts a warning.'

'What was it?'

'They call them Casspirs, troop carriers like huge iron pigs. Koevoet use them so they know the crowbar men are coming.'

'*Crowbar men*?'

'Koevoet means crowbar in Afrikaans.'

'What did you do?'

'The women hid me down this new latrine they'd dug.'

'That can't have been a nice experience.'

'No, but I can see what's going on by lifting a sort of lid contraption.'

'So the soldiers, what did they do?'

'They line everyone up at gun point and start screaming *Wit man! Wit man!*'

'Meaning what?'

'White guy, white guy... me.'

'But how did they know you'd be there?'

'Informers, double agents. Not easy for outsiders to hide in a bush war... spies everywhere. You're always worth something to someone.'

'But the soldiers didn't catch you?'

'No, and when they can't find me, they get angry, all psyched-up.'

'That must have been terrifying.'

'Then something moves or spooks one of them and they panic and just open up.'

'They shot these people, you mean?'

'Yes... that's what they did.'

'But they were women - '

' - five of them and a little boy.'

'And you saw all this happen?'

'Like watching an old newsreel... Nazis shooting people they didn't consider human.'

'That's so wicked, Mac... so wicked.'

'The earth where they were... it's reddish anyway but this, you wouldn't believe... then the silence takes over... not even the goats are bleating. It's like it's a film set and someone should shout *cut* but no-one does.'

'Mac, this cannot have been your fault.'

'You don't think so? Do you know what I did next?'

McCall rose to his feet almost in anger.

'I take photographs, that's what. Can you believe that, Hester? I stand over the dead and the dying, those poor holy innocents who'd been dumb enough to help me and I take pictures of them... and it's the kid I can't get out of my mind... his chest opened up from right to left... this vivid pink furrow ploughed through his brown skin getting ever deeper till the bullet exits and rips into his left arm and leaves it hanging by a few tendons. But that's not the worst of it, Hester... he's still alive and he's looking at me, looking into whatever passes for my soul and his eyes don't leave mine. What had I become? Was my ego worth any of this?'

'Death and wars go together, Mac.'

'No, these people wouldn't have died if I'd not been there. I was the target, not them.'

'You were only doing your job.'

'So my job was to get people killed for a bigger and better story, was it?'

He looked away as if unable to face her anymore and leaned his head hard against the standing stone as if it might heal.

But the eyes of a dying child had seen him for the pimp he had become. What was the point or purpose of his journalism now? Whatever wrong-doing McCall uncovered, nothing ever changed. The greedy got fatter, the corrupt still inherited the earth and the weak were cut down as they always had been.

'Mac, you have to carry on reporting the appalling things which happen in our world or there will be no change. You have to make a pact with your conscience.'

'How the hell can I? I can't raise the dead.'

'But those bullet cases on the mantelpiece in your room - '

'What about them?'

' - they came from this village, didn't they? Why keep them?'

But McCall wouldn't - or couldn't - reply.

Nineteen

The streets around Paddington were blown with noxious traffic fumes and greasy blasts of hot air from fast food joints. McCall paid his cab then hurried through a noisy surge of late night diners to meet Lexie off the last train from Bristol.

She came down the platform in jeans, a vintage black velvet jacket and carrying a repro Gladstone bag. His first instinct was to wave but he held back for reasons he didn't care to admit.

He wanted to watch her unseen, even if it felt like stalking. Time changes everything and everyone. In the end, it's all about trust... or the lack of it.

She'd only been away thirty-six hours - but in Bristol, that hinterland of her existence of which he knew nothing. Yet Lexie hadn't questioned McCall about his last two decades. Maybe his missing years presented less of a problem.

As she got closer, he thought her face drawn and grey under the artificial lights of the concourse. Delayed shock could mean she was still sleeping badly. But he detected something else, too - some pre-occupation outside of loss.

Lexie always said they had the empathy of twins. He stepped in front of her and apologised for being late.

'Doesn't matter. Let's get to Etta's flat. I've had a phone call from the council.'

*

Lexie spent yet another fitful night in Etta's disturbing bedroom so McCall left her sleeping. He showered and dressed then went into the street so she wouldn't hear him ring Hoare. To write anything on Ruby, McCall still needed a sit down with Benwick.

'You're out of luck, chum,' Hoare said. 'He went on leave last Friday.'

'Dammit. So what progress on Ruby?'

'The search goes on but you know the odds against a happy ending, don't you?'

McCall went back into the flat and poured Lexie a glass of mango juice from a carton in the 'fridge. She raised herself up on her elbows, barely awake and unsure if the black magic weirdness around her was real or imagined. Then she slumped back.

'Dear God, it's not a dream after all.'

'No, we're stuck with it.'

'But not for much longer.'

A housing officer had rung Lexie in Bristol, gently asking when Etta's flat might be vacated. He'd a long list of homeless families to deal with.

For Lexie, the apartment held memories she wished she didn't have. Etta's possessions held little value, sentimental or otherwise.

Most of her furniture could be given to a housing charity and the flat emptied by the end of the week.

Lexie now padded to the bathroom, pale and naked. On another day or in another place, McCall would have gone to her and laid her down somewhere soft, somewhere warm. But in that unsettling room where so crude a living had been earned, love would only ever feel like lust. He went to straighten the bed covers instead.

There was a bloodstain where Lexie had slept, vivid red and perfectly round like the mark of a plague sore. He covered it over with the duvet but said nothing. Lexie came back towelling herself, long hair dripping down her back and onto the carpet.

'I don't suppose there's anything to eat in the kitchen.'

'There's a café down the street and the woman who runs it was friendly with Ruby.'

'How do you know this?'

'She told me. I had a coffee in there on the day Etta was found.'

Lexie finished dressing and said there was something she had to do before they went for breakfast. She took hold of the satanic goat poster and tore it from top to bottom. McCall saw the satisfaction in her eyes, ripping the offending image into ever smaller pieces.

They would have left then but on the wall where the poster had been were three tarot cards, taped side by side.

'That's weird,' Lexie said. 'What are these doing here?'

The cards showed the devil, the hanged man and the sun.

'They're just cards. What of it?'

'Nothing you'd understand, I suppose.'

'Your sister was into things nobody understands.'

'I told you, I read the tarot and these cards arranged like this, well it's sort of strange.'

The devil had great bat-like wings, twisted horns and menaced a man and woman chained to the rock where he crouched.

The second card showed a yellow-haired man hanging upside down from the tree of life by his right foot while the third depicted the smiling face of the sun beaming over a child on a white horse.

'This is just a bit of fun at the fair, Lexie, nothing more.'

'To you, maybe. I wonder when Etta put them here… and why.'

McCall knew he had to be patient. Lexie was all about theatrics, creating dramas for personal effect. But she was also grieving and trying to rationalise Etta's suicide.

'Tarot cards have meanings if you've the knowledge to read them.'

'What are these supposed to be saying, then?'

'There's a message here... a message about why she was going to kill herself.'

McCall couldn't hide his disbelief.

'Look, you're upset but you mustn't try to explain the inexplicable.'

She ignored him and drew her fingers across the surface of each card, knowing the last hands to hold them were her sister's.

'See this, McCall? The devil could show how Etta felt she was being manipulated, tied down against her will and even enslaved by forces stronger than her to control.'

'Really?'

'And the hanged man is a card of sacrifice. It might represent her ending a struggle, putting self-interest aside and being a martyr for a higher cause and the sun and the child could suggest the truth being realised, of Etta finding sense amid the chaos and somehow releasing Ruby.'

'Releasing Ruby from what?'

'From whatever she and Etta had been caught up in but was beyond Etta to stop.'

'Lexie, love - you could interpret these pictures to mean anything you wanted in any situation, prove black was white… anything.'

'If you were unscrupulous, yes. But why did Etta hide them under a poster like this?'

'I've no idea and I know it's very painful but I can't see any of this helping you to come to terms with her death any more than why she killed herself.'

*

They ate scrambled eggs on toast at Café Leila. Leila fussed over McCall and smiled sadly when she heard Lexie was Ruby's aunt.

'My heart, it break for you,' Leila said. 'I send prayers for Ruby all nights.'

Lexie wanted to take a first – and last – look at where Etta died and Ruby played. To McCall, each new day revealed a softening in Lexie's tough exterior. She linked his arm as she had after the funeral.

They crossed to the footpath round the reservoir and its faux castle disguising the pumping station within. There was no wind to disturb the trees. All was settled and still. Neither of them spoke.

A plane banked on its long descent to Heathrow and in the far distance, an emergency siren rose above the dull drone of traffic. Lexie crouched at the water's edge and broke the placid surface with the tips of her fingers.

It was as if she was back on the banks of the Severn once more, communing with all she had lost. McCall kept his distance as he had then, yet still watching over her. But in the quiet of the moment came the barely audible voice of a child.

Six little mice sat down to spin, Pussy passed by and she peeped in.

What are you doing, my little men? Weaving coats for gentlemen.

McCall turned to look into the scrub of laurels and thorn bushes by the boundary fence behind him. There was no one to be seen.

'Did you hear that... like a kid reciting a nursery rhyme?'

'I did, yes. There must be a playground around here.'

Shall I come in and cut off your threads?

Still the child's words came to them, faintly as if from far away and long ago. Lexie got to her feet and took McCall's hand. She was more puzzled than afraid but there was something spectral and disembodied about the tinny little voice. They stood together, completely alone – alone on the sloping bank of grass and weeds where Etta had been laid, shadowed beneath a great overhanging chestnut tree.

No, no, Mistress Pussy, you'd bite off our heads.

It was Lexie who looked up first, looked heavenwards and caught a glimpse of her - a scrap of a girl astride a branch in the canopy of leaves high above them, singing songs to herself as she always had.

Twenty

Hoare had just left his flat when McCall rang his mobile to tell him about Ruby's bizarre reappearance in the place from where she'd most likely vanished.

'Sitting in a tree?' Hoare said. 'Even we couldn't make this up, Mac.'

'No, but like much else in this affair, it doesn't make sense.'

'I've been trying to tell you all along, it's a hell of a tale. The papers will love it.'

'Ah, slight problem there. Can you hold off releasing anything for a few days?'

'Am I hearing you right - a hack wants a press officer to sit on a bloody good story?'

'Ruby's in a bit of a state. God knows what's been happening to her so the last thing we want is the poor kid getting hounded by the pack.'

'Look, I'm on a day off and Benwick's away so I'll tell his stand-in what's happened then he'll contact you and maybe something can be sorted out.'

*

Rush hour traffic inched its way through the streets around King's Cross Station. Part of Gray's Inn Road had also been coned off for re-surfacing. It was quicker for Hoare to walk to his meet than go by cab.

He couldn't stop thinking about Ruby. Had she really been abducted or did this strange kid just run away and go feral for a couple of weeks? And where did her conjuring trick leave Benwick's suspicions about the mother?

All Hoare's instincts told him McCall wanted to scent-mark Ruby's story before any rival got a bead on her. As exclusives went, it'd be a smasher - provided the poor little stray could tell her own story. Still, the cops had trained interviewers who'd wheedle it out of her.

But if it ever came to court, how could any prosecution rely on testimony from a child as away-with-the-fairies as Ruby Ross?

Benwick's mobile was turned off and he'd not left a holiday number. By coincidence, Hoare had received a postcard from him that morning - a view of a sandstone church on a hill in a place called Blackrod. He'd not signed it but Hoare recognised the handwriting if not the cryptic message. *All shall be well, and all shall be well and all manner of things shall be well.*

The closer Hoare got to Benwick, the further away he seemed. But his secretive habits could have a simple explanation. Many a married cop he'd known played the field. No job provided better cover for supping and tupping till all hours.

Gulling wives - or husbands - was a breeze for detectives capable of standing in court, hand on bible, swearing to tell the truth... or a version of it cooked up in the canteen earlier. Hacks weren't even at the races when it came to fibbing.

*

Alone in an ornate booth within the Victorian glory of the Princess Louise, Hoare was half-way through a bottle of Mouton Cadet and the Daily Telegraph crossword.

The first drinkers of the day were coming in from another bright, Bloomsbury morning - academics from London University or the British Museum, men of suit and substance just needing a little help to face the world. He felt their equal these days.

Life as a grubby crime reporter had been like those parasitic birds in TV nature programmes, pecking for grubs off the hides of a big, bad tempered animal. Not anymore. He'd gone up in the jungle.

Hoare mused on this waiting for his one-time colleague, Teddy Lamb. He'd been the wiliest industrial correspondent of his generation - in bed with every side but screwed by none.

This made him beholden to nobody so he knew more than just where the dirty sheets went to be laundered.

Teddy arrived looking every inch a pinstriped city gent with a pink carnation in his buttonhole to match the Financial Times he carried to complete the illusion. They exchanged friendly insults and fell into happy reminiscences about their foot-in-the-door days, their buy-ups and stitch-ups and sins committed when too young to care if they'd left all their bridges in flames.

'It's tragic how Fleet Street's gone to the dogs.'

'There's no fun any more,' Hoare said. 'It's those bloody bean counters.'

'Shakespeare wouldn't write about killing lawyers these days, it'd be accountants.'

Hoare bought another bottle and chose to forget what had brought about the early exits of all the other members of their formation drinking team.

'To bigger and better exclusives,' Hoare said. 'And may all your exes be passed.'

Teddy allowed himself a sly smile.

'Always a delight to stagger down memory lane with you old chap, but what is it you're really after?'

'A little favour, Teddy. That's what.'

'Not going to land me in the arse-kicking cupboard, is it?'

'On my life, no. I'm just needing to check if you've still got your little black book of indiscretions.'

'Might have. Why?'

'Excellent. Let me top you up.'

*

An idea blew into Lexie's tired head like the spore of a poisonous plant and took root in a sunless corner. If life plotted out as it did on "Inspector Morse", Ruby wouldn't have been found alive.

Lexie might then have played the distraught aunt of a murdered child whose mother had just committed suicide. It would've been a tough role yet one she'd subconsciously rehearsed every day since Ruby went missing.

But reality rarely came with a script. It had no need of stars, only an endless supply of walk-on victims of circumstance, trying to cope as best they could.

After only half a day acting as a stand-in mother, Lexie was stressed to the point of exhaustion. It was gone ten before Ruby finally screamed herself to sleep - and not in her bed, either.

She'd made a nest of blankets and pillows beneath the kitchen table and burrowed into it. Such was the end of the oddest of days.

Ruby's resurrection was as unlikely as it was life-changing. Lexie's plans – maybe McCall's, too – were in disarray from the moment they heard her faintly robotic voice high up in that tree.

Lexie had called Ruby's name, quietly so she wouldn't be startled. She seemed not to hear. McCall began climbing towards her. Ruby stopped singing. The nearer he came, the more she made fearful whimpering noises like a cornered animal.

Lexie was scared she might fall and wanted to ring the fire brigade to bring a ladder. But McCall said a mob of men in uniform would frighten her even more. He had a better idea.

He ran to fetch Leila. She abandoned her customers without a thought. Immediately she saw Ruby, Leila dropped to her knees and made the sign of the cross for here was a miracle beyond understanding.

'Little one, come. I beg you.'

Nobody dared move or speak.

'Come, little one. Come to me, come down to Leila.'

Ruby began waving, as if saying farewell to someone or something in the castle-like pumping station on the far side of the black water. Then she swung a bare leg over the branch and let herself down the main trunk with the sureness of a cat – and with all its wariness, too.

'You gave us fright,' Leila said. 'But all OK now, my darling.'

Ruby stood at the base of the tree, hair uncombed, hands clasped together over her torn polka dot dress and staring down at her dirty white trainers as if waiting for punishment.

Lexie smiled and instinctively moved towards her but Ruby turned away and went instead to Leila's open arms.

'You safe, you home now, little one.'

Leila took charge. She gathered up Ruby like an infant and carried her from the reservoir, whispering that everything would be all right, nothing was wrong.

Ruby held tight to Leila so no one could see her face. Upstairs in Leila's private quarters, Lexie couldn't be sure if Ruby remembered who she was. They'd only ever met occasionally.

McCall stood apart, committing the drama of the moment to his reporter's memory. Where had Ruby spent this past fortnight? How could so naïve a child survive alone on the unforgiving streets of London? He didn't believe it possible. Someone had taken her and she must have escaped. Locked within this seemingly unreachable, dysfunctional girl was an extraordinary story, made all the more so by her precocious talent as an artist.

Leila brought in a glass of milk and a plate of biscuits then sat on the settee with a protective arm around Ruby's bony shoulders.

'You hungry, sweetheart? You want more food... proper food?'

She nodded and Leila went back into her kitchenette to make beans on toast. Ruby deliberately turned away from the room and hid her face in a cushion.

Lexie prayed no one could read her mind. There was sympathy in her heart but nothing truly maternal, nothing connected by blood. It had always been hard to like Ruby. She was a remote, rude and disobedient child with little understanding of how her behaviour affected anyone else.

Etta once said Ruby's abnormal tempers could spark off for no real reason like her pencils being moved from how she'd left them. Lexie knew she now faced an impossible choice - give Ruby a home or put her in one. It felt like she'd woken up in a car crash and was trapped in the wreckage.

McCall's mobile rang and disturbed her thoughts. The police were sending a female inspector and a doctor to carry out initial checks on Ruby. He and Lexie headed back to Etta's flat, struggling to keep hold of Ruby, playing the banshee and rolling around on the pavement.

'No! No! No! Won't do! Won't do!'

'Sweetie, come on,' Lexie said. 'Please, we must get you home and cleaned up.'

'No! Wrong way! Wrong way!'

McCall crouched down.

'It's OK, Ruby. It's OK. You show us the right way…come on. You show us.'

Her eyes were the palest cornflower blue he'd ever seen with all but the faintest trace of colour rinsed out. Ruby immediately looked away from him, as if she wanted no one to see inside her mind. Then she ran back to the café, stood on one foot, turned round twice and started walking on her own towards Linden House.

She took care not to step on a crack or any litter. McCall and Lexie followed a few paces behind.

'She's an obsessive, compulsive,' McCall said.

'What's that?'

'Imposes rigid routines on herself. She can't help it. It's the way she is.'

'And just when I thought it couldn't get any worse.'

'No, it's manageable.'

'Still going to be a nightmare though, isn't it?'

'Nothing like the nightmare Ruby might've just been through.'

'Do you think she'll tell us where she's been, what's happened to her?'

'Maybe, but it won't be easy to get it out of her. She could've buried it.'

'And how am I going to tell her about her mother?'

'Let's get some advice from the police and the doctor on that.'

'Doesn't matter what they say, it'll still be my responsibility. But I've never had to do anything this difficult in my life.'

Twenty One

The faint scent of flowers puzzled Hoare on entering his bedsit. Even his fags and booze-impaired faculties picked up an alien waft of the countryside within the staleness of the room where he crashed most nights. It wasn't important.

Of flowers, Hoare knew little - not those growing in gardens or arranged in bouquets to placate a wife. He could recognise the sickly reek of privet but what came through the dank of his flat was more like a fragrance remembered from a meadow - wild but subtle, hard to define.

Wherever it had originated - the other bedsit on his landing or those on the two floors below - he'd more tangible matters to attend to.

It'd been a more than satisfactory day. Teddy Lamb coughed up a few secrets to give him a line on the trade union eavesdropper at Rules. He'd also made up his mind to quit the police for Inglis's much higher profile PR job in politics. With this new life in prospect, he'd seen a Greek tailor in Soho to be measured for a three-piece suit in charcoal grey. He would look the knees of a bee during TV appearances yet to come.

Despite his lunch time jolly with Teddy, Hoare's low alcohol warning light was flashing. He poured a Scotch, lit the last cigarette from his third pack of twenty that day and began drafting a letter of resignation in readiness for Inglis firming up his offer.

Next, he wrote a detailed note of all the compromising trade union naughtiness Teddy let slip in his cups. As insurance policies went, it was cheap at the price. Hoare then switched on his portable television and lay fully clothed on the unmade bed to watch the early evening news.

But he nodded off and woke an hour later, crumpled and hungry. It was time for another all-day breakfast at the greasy spoon round the corner where his face was becoming known.

Before he went, he needed to hide the gold dust he'd winkled out of Teddy. It could go with all the paperwork and photographs he'd already liberated from the Ruby Ross investigation. This was in a large folder slipped into the narrow space between his wardrobe drawer and the floor beneath.

As he took hold of the file, it felt different - thinner, lighter. Then he saw why. All the Ruby material was missing. But the bedsit door hadn't been forced. His one window remained bolted from the inside. The intruder must have had a key. If this was Benwick's idea of a funny, it wasn't Hoare's.

But the wider implications of this little robbery sank in. Someone, whoever it was, now knew he'd been stealing confidential police documents.

People were sacked or even jailed for that. Nick the Greek might yet be stitching hubristic arrows on Hoare's new suit. He told himself not to panic.

Another Scotch would help but his mobile rang. A woman, well-spoken and sure of herself, asked if he was Malky Hoare, the police press officer.

'I might be. Who is this?'

'No-one important.'

'So why are you ringing me?'

'Just checking you're at home, that's all.'

'Who the hell are you?'

'Sorry, Mr Hoare. I've got to go. Good bye.'

He knew then he'd been rumbled. The apartment took on a cell-like feel. He moved the shirts drying on hangers above the sink and stuck his head under the tap. The cold water ran over his face and onto the unwashed plates in the bowl below. It wasn't flowers he'd smelt. It was perfume.

But the sound of heavy footsteps coming up the bare wooden stairs to his landing quickly drove this irrelevance from his mind.

*

However mildly she was coaxed by the police inspector, Ruby refused to answer any questions about who'd taken her or what'd happened afterwards. But she did allow herself to be examined by the doctor.

'There's no physical sign of sexual assault,' she said. 'We should hope she undergoes what's called dissociative amnesia, in other words, she blanks out what happened.'

Ruby was bathed and dressed in clean clothes. It was felt best to leave her drawing in her bedroom and despite everything, humming one of her made-up songs. She needed time to adjust - a luxury Lexie no longer had.

'What are we going to do, McCall? Just tell me.'

'Well, you can't stay here but wherever Ruby's going to live, a move to somewhere new isn't going to be easy, not for her or anyone else.'

'I'd take her to Bristol but my flat isn't big enough and I've got the business to run and I still get offered parts and I can't afford to turn them down.'

'So you'd be for putting her into a council home, then?'

'Don't say it like that, it sounds as if I don't care.'

'And do you?'

'You know full well I do but my whole life is being turned upside down.'

'What about Ruby's life? Hasn't that been turned upside down?'

'Of course it has but I've never had the responsibility of a child before, let alone one with all Ruby's problems.'

'Like the doctor just said, she needs calm and stability to give her any chance of coping with everything that's gone on.'

'Don't we all?'

'Yes, and that's why we need to get help.'

'But where from, sweetie? I can hardly sleep from worrying about it.'

'I was thinking that maybe we should ask Hester.'

'Your charlady?'

'Housekeeper, Lexie. You mustn't underestimate her.'

'I'm not but she doesn't look like she's moved on since Woodstock.'

'Maybe not, but for all Hester's kooky ideas, she's a woman of real humanity.'

'So you're saying Ruby might move up to Garth and live there?'

'She'd be with family and friends in a stable environment so I wouldn't see the welfare authorities objecting.'

It took a moment before a look of relief began to cross Lexie's face. And through the door of Ruby's bedroom came her endlessly repeated dirge... *and all will be well and all will be well and all will be well, well, well.*

*

Hoare was taken from his flat by two men with unreadable faces who could have doubled as funeral mutes. It wasn't a police car waiting outside for them but a black London taxi. Special Branch used them on surveillance jobs - but how come he warranted one?

His captors sat on the fold-down seats opposite so he couldn't see the driver. They pulled out into heavy traffic. All his demands to know who was taking him where were ignored. He felt breathless, unable to see outside the tinted windows and seized by claustrophobic stress.

Within ten minutes, they'd turned left down a ramp between two tall buildings. A metal portcullis rolled up to admit them to an empty underground car park.

The mutes led him through the semi-darkness to a metal gate in a far wall. They locked it behind them and descended a concrete stairwell.

*

The battery on McCall's mobile was dead. He left Lexie and Ruby and went to look for a working phone box. He dialled Hoare's bedsit to tell him they were decamping to the Welsh borders. But there was no reply or to his mobile. McCall tried his direct line at the Yard and heard the click of his call being diverted automatically. A man said Hoare wasn't there and asked who was calling.

'Just a friend. We're working on something together.'

'And what might that be, Sir?'

'Doesn't matter. I'll catch up with him later.'

McCall then rang Hester to tell her about Ruby - her talent as an artist, the suicide of her mother, of going missing then being found in the very place where she pretended to be a princess with a pet unicorn.

'It's all down to this condition she's got, Asperger's syndrome.'

'I knew a boy in the States with it. They can be extraordinarily talented kids.'

'Trouble is she doesn't like change but we need to leave the flat tomorrow.'

'And then what?'

'Well, if she doesn't throw a massive wobbly, we'll bring her up to live at Garth.'

'OK, I've understood everything,' Hester said. 'I've an idea how I help. Give me an address and I'll be with you around breakfast time.'

*

Lexie wasn't the jittery type. But Etta's occult junk made her nervy, despite being boxed up ready for the weekly rubbish collection. Even the exaggerated shadows of people passing the frosted glass of the door to the communal yard scared her that night. She wished McCall hadn't gone out.

It was still hard to believe he'd stay to help her care for Ruby. Most men would jump ship if a kid as difficult as her became part of the arrangement.

Lexie was too on edge to sleep. She needed a drink. There was ice and tonic in the fridge and the remains of a bottle of gin in the living room. She poured a decent measure and went to play one of Etta's videos to take her mind off the uncertain future.

On the shelf above the TV was something of Lexie's past - a VHS of Blow-Up, the ultimate time capsule of style and paranoid intrigue from London in the swinging sixties. Its packaging was scuffed as if Etta had watched it a lot though whether with sisterly pride or jealousy, Lexie couldn't know.

But Blow-Up was the first movie in which she'd appeared, if only briefly. That didn't matter. There she would be - forever young, dancing at a Yardbirds gig as the film's beautiful, boyish lead, David Hemmings, ran off with bits of a guitar Jeff Beck smashed against an amp. Such days did she remember.

McCall had idolised Jeff Beck once. He would've loved to have been on that shoot. But they'd split up by then and he'd taken it badly. She could still remember a line from one of his tortured letters... *when all of life turns into winter, heroin is a fur coat and a kiss on the darkest of nights.* She felt guilty at that. But she was meant to. Then Evan sorted him out. Evan sorted out everyone eventually.

Lexie took a sip of her gin and tonic. As she did, something within the ice cube which shouldn't have been there, caught her eye. It looked for all the world like a tiny frozen tear drop. She put the cube on the palm of her hand. Her skin felt on fire. The ice turned to water and slowly gave up its secret – a tight little twist of cling film.

She peeled it open with care. Inside was the narrowest curl of paper, barely an inch long. On it was written the name *Mr Ginger* in blue Biro.

She'd heard of this New Age fad - sealing the name of some feared or hated person in an ice cube to freeze out whatever threat they posed. But she'd never seen it done. This was Etta's doing without a doubt.

But who was Mr Ginger... and why had she been afraid of him? Was this another clue from beyond the grave about Etta's puzzling life and disturbing death? Lexie believed the tarot cards under the bedroom poster had been just that.

Yet if she told McCall about the ice cube find, he might think Lexie had written the name herself to create a drama. If not that, he'd just sneer and say it was only more proof of Etta's foolish ways.

Mr Ginger was best kept wrapped up for now.

Twenty Two

'Sit down, Hoare.'

'Why have I been brought here?'

'Because you're in a damned big hole.'

'Would that be the one you've just thrown me in?'

'It's not us who've been stealing documents from a police investigation.'

'But what gives you the right to break into my flat?'

'I do the questions and you do the answers. We find it works best like that.'

It would've been a gross misjudgement to think the interrogator's weary insouciance hid any lack of resolve. Hoare couldn't fail to note the hard, grey eyes of a man approaching a pension but who'd clearly given orders under all manner of fire.

'I still want to know who you are,' Hoare said.

'Let me see... I'm someone who could make or break you. Now, can we get on?'

Hoare's interrogator read from a file of typed notes. They sat either side of a desk in a windowless cinder block office lit by a neon tube humming above them.

'Says here you're overdrawn at your bank and behind with the maintenance and mortgage payments to your ex-wife.'

'Can't deny that but isn't debt the curse of the age?'

'Giving you every reason to make money on the side... like betraying the trust of the police who employ you and selling inside information to some rubbishy tabloid.'

'There's not a word of truth in what you've just said.'

'Wasn't truth whatever your newspaper decided at morning conference and all you had to do was go out and prove it, irrespective of whatever really was the truth?'

'Look, where's all this leading?'

'For you, probably to prison for perverting the course of justice and for theft.'

Three pictures were slid across the desk towards him - black and white ten by eights, shot with a long tom lens and showing Hoare leaving Etta's funeral with Lexie and McCall.

'Tell me more about the man you're with here.'

'Are you spying on him or me?'

'Being smart doesn't help you. Just answer my questions.'

'He's a journalist, Francis McCall - but I'd say you knew that already.'

'What sort of things have you told him that you shouldn't?'

'I've told him nothing which hadn't been authorised by DI Benwick.'

'Is that a fact? Well, let's listen to this.'

He pressed the *play* button on a small tape recorder.

Sitting in a tree? Even we couldn't make it up, Mac.

No, but as with much else in this affair, it doesn't make sense.

Like I've been trying to tell you all along, it's a hell of a tale. The papers will love it.

'This is scandalous,' Hoare said. 'You've been bugging my mobile phone.'

'And you've been leaking confidential police files to a journalist.'

'No, absolutely not.'

'McCall's the good pal you'd trust to pay you on the quiet for the story.'

'So when you snatch him off the streets, you can ask him.'

'We will and that's for sure. Now, tell me about Benwick.'

'Tell you what about him?'

'About his private life, where he spends time, girlfriends he's got. That sort of thing.'

'I know nothing about any of this.'

'You work closely together yet you know nothing about him out of office hours?'

'DI Benwick doesn't socialise or talk about himself.'

'So you haven't seen him drunk?'

Hoare shook his head. The interrogator switched on the tape again.

For Christ's sake! You're half cut and running round London with a gun.

No, that's just my new portable phone.

'So you bastards have put a spike mic in my flat, too?'

'You didn't report this drunken incident to your line manager. Why not?'

'Because I only thought I saw a weapon. I couldn't be sure.'

'All right, tell me where is Benwick at the moment.'

'He's on leave but he didn't confide his holiday plans to me.'

'And he's not been in touch with you in any way since you last saw him?'

'No, why should he?'

'If you don't know where he is, what about the child who disappeared?'

'Little Ruby Ross?'

'Yes, the girl... where has she been taken and who is she with?'

Hoare held the man's wintery gaze. Only then did he realise something was a mite more suspect than he'd first thought. If he was being questioned by a police officer, they already knew Ruby was being cared for by Lexie and McCall.

'I've no idea,' Hoare said. 'It's not something I'd be told about.'

'Really? I think you're a bloody liar. But we're through for the moment.'

'So I can go?'

'We'll drive you home shortly,' he said. 'But you're not out of the woods yet.'

'You've no damn right to treat me like this.'

'It's for a greater good, Hoare, for the benefit of our green and pleasant land.'

'You mean Benwick's some sort of risk to national security?'

'You can work it out for yourself. But if you want this nastiness to stop, resume your job and use every means to find out where Benwick is then tell me.'

'Aren't there official channels you could use rather than put my feet to the fire?'

'That's our business. Just you remember you've blundered into a drama bigger than your own. If you've any sense, you'll play ball because if you don't, you'll find the alternative will do your dicky heart no good at all.'

Twenty Three

Ruby always took refuge in the virtual reality of her imagination. Here, she could see what those without her gifts could not. Just occasionally, she allowed herself a part in the lives of others - never more so than when Hester drove into the service area behind Café Leila.

Her camper van looked like a gaudy fairground ride, painted with exploding stars, psychedelic swirls and a unicorn flying over the silver VW badge on the bonnet. Hester was no less exotic herself - untamed barley-twist hair, strings of beads, sweeping kaftan and slippers of gold. Ruby was captivated.

'Hi, honey,' Hester said. 'So you must be Ruby but they never told me you were such a pretty little girl.'

'You speak in a funny way.'

'I know I do but that's because I come from the other side of the world.'

'Do all the people there have old faces?'

'Only when they're very wise and have learnt magic powers.'

'My Mum could do magic but she's dead now.'

Hester tried not to be taken aback by the child's matter-of-fact voice or the unemotional eyes which hardly blinked. Nature didn't allow Ruby to be nuanced. Something was, or it was not. That was how she called it. In all her innocence, Ruby couldn't tell a lie - social or otherwise - still less, spot when she was being spun one.

Leila brought toast and coffee to their table. McCall poured and Lexie set about mending fences with Hester.

'I'm afraid I've been overwhelmed by some tragic events,' Lexie said. 'I'm really thankful for you helping me like this.'

'Please, it's fine. Only Ruby's important here.'

Ruby continued to stare at Hester, fascinated by the sparkling rings on her fingers, the silver triangles dangling from her ears. Hester unhooked the clasp of an emerald brooch and said it was for Ruby. She took it as a princess might a gift from a visiting dignitary and pinned it to her denim overalls.

'Now listen, honey,' Hester said. 'I've come to London because I need your help.'

'Well, you're silly because I don't go to school any more because I'm backward and naughty and I don't think right.'

'Whoever says that is so wrong,' Hester said. 'You know all about the unicorn who lives by the reservoir, don't you?'

'In the yellow castle. Yes, he's mine and not anyone else's.'

'I know, but he's ten years old now just like you and that's the age when all unicorns have to leave the castles where they were born and move to new ones.'

'No, he won't want to do that because he likes living near me.'

'But the castle that's been chosen for him is so much nicer.'

'Nicer than the yellow castle?'

'Sure is, sweetheart, and that's not all... you can live nearby when he goes.'

Lexie joined in at this point with feigned surprise and delight.

'Wouldn't that be lovely, Ruby? Can I come and live there as well, Hester?'

'Of course you can. We can all live together and then Ruby can visit her unicorn any time she wants.'

Leila smiled her approval of the plan.

'Go with them, special one,' she said. 'Go where you will be cared for.'

Ruby, ever literal and trusting, asked how the unicorn would know where the new castle was and how to get there.

'Because you and I will go across to him right now and we'll tell him.'

Ruby considered this for another moment before replying.

'You mustn't step on a crack on the way or you'll have to come back here and start all over again because those are the rules.'

Lexie and McCall stood at the café window watching them cross the road. Each of the adults felt uneasy about tricking Ruby but the alternative would have been worse.

'Looks like she's taken to Hester in her own way,' Lexie said. 'That's a first.'

'She's probably never met a grown-up who believes in unicorns before.'

'True enough, but please God she gets to trust her enough to say what's happened.'

*

McCall left the keys to Etta's flat with the Linden House caretaker after the last of her furniture was taken away by a housing charity. Hester was already heading towards the

Welsh borders with Lexie and Ruby. Packed in the back of the van were all Ruby's drawings, her pencils, art pads, bed, desk and clothes and the few family possessions Lexie wished to keep.

McCall was about to follow on in the Morgan when Roly Vickers rang his mobile.

'I've dropped on something that'll interest you,' he said. 'Can't talk on this but come to my office as soon as you can.'

It was best to sup with a long spoon when dealing with Vickers. He was McCall's best-placed contact for sourcing sensitive information. But he always wanted paying in favours. Most times, money would've been a less risky exchange.

McCall left his car in the yard behind Linden House and took a cab to Gray's Inn Road. Vickers, well into his seventies now, still ran his publishing business from rooms in an Edwardian mansion block in a street nearby.

His premises were as precise as the man - floor to ceiling shelves of books on politics and world affairs, a desk top of tooled green leather neatly arranged with telephone, diary, blotter and notepad. And close by, a fire-proof metal filing cabinet with a combination lock more commonly seen in a bank vault. Vickers had reason to take security seriously.

'You're trying to set up an interview with a detective, aren't you?'

'Could be.'

'There's no *could be* about it. His name's Benwick and he's a detective inspector.'

'OK, I'm researching a piece about a missing kid and he was in charge.'

'The Ruby Ross case, I know. Anyway, Benwick's supposed to be on leave, yes?'

'That's what I was told. Why?'

'Because he's not on his holidays.'

'Where is he, then?'

'That's the twist. He's folded his tent and cleared off.'

'Why - bedroom troubles, gambling debts?'

'Neither. Understand this - Benwick isn't your average plod. It seems he was carrying when he went AWOL - a Makarov, Russian job for close-quarter work.'

'He's armed? Christ. Has he had a breakdown or something?'

'I don't have a white coat but a bit of sleuthing on your part might pay dividends.'

'Where do you suggest I start?'

'Well, while you were running round bloody Africa to no good purpose, some people were getting bumped off closer to home.'

'Really? Tell me more.'

'A Canadian scientist called Gerald Bull, he'd be of most interest. Ambushed and shot in the head outside his flat in Brussels last March.'

'Why? What had he been up to?'

'Dig and ye shall find, my son.'

'But what's Benwick got to do with any of this?'

'That's what we'd all like to know, McCall.'

'I've only met him once, on this Ruby story. But like you say, not a bog standard cop.'

'And he disappears, armed and dangerous on the day after she turns up again. I'd say these are all interesting connections. Anyway, let me know what you find out.'

McCall knew it was pointless - bordering on insulting - to ask how Vickers knew any of this. But there would be a reason he was passing it on. There always was.

*

Hoare couldn't sleep after being delivered back to his flat by the men with no names. Who would ever let their guard down again knowing each sound and move they made was being monitored?

He needed time to think. He'd phone the office later and claim a migraine or worse. At first light, Hoare was dressed and walking the cold morning streets. The sun would soon burn through, birds start singing and all of London busy itself as if nothing out of the ordinary had happened. Yet his little world was falling apart just as he was getting back on his unsteady feet.

He ordered a full English breakfast at his favoured café and sat where he'd a clear view of the door. His first cigarette brought a little calm.

A crew of construction workers piled in from the building site opposite. They shouted orders for eggs, bacon and sausages and filled the place with noise and banter about their enviably uncomplicated lives. Hoare's problem was simple, too - his abductors had him on toast.

Try as he might, he couldn't figure what game was being played around him. He knew only that he could be taken out of it without warning. He wasn't even sure if he'd been caught up in a Special Branch operation or not.

If Benwick really was a security risk and this was a spook job, why weren't the funnies liaising with senior police to trace him? What was the point of complicating matters by blackmailing Hoare?

If he'd still been a hack on the road, he would think a damn good story was being covered up. Maybe that was the way to go - don't get mad, get even. Run the tale to earth then threaten to go public if the buggers put the squeeze on him again. He had the postcard from Benwick and his mobile number. That'd be a start to trace him, to find out what was really going on.

Then the doubts set it. What if the blackmailers called his bluff or leaked dirt on him to Private Eye or a diary column? He'd be rat-fucked to bankruptcy and never welcome in EC4 again.

By his third coffee and fourth cigarette, he knew the least risky option was what he was planning before the watchers swooped - bail out from the police and take Guy Inglis's offer of a PR job in Westminster. He'd then be jumping, not being pushed.

First, he had to get away to write the fullest note of all that'd happened the previous evening and everything he could remember from the vanished Ruby Ross files.

This time, he'd find a safer hiding place, maybe with a lawyer. McCall looked certain to get lifted soon. He considered warning him but thought better of it.

Hoare was under surveillance by men who could see through walls and had powers he hardly knew existed. Any move which confirmed their suspicious could compromise him even further.

Only number one was important now. McCall might come in useful later. This wasn't about a lack of trust or friendship. It was about fear.

Twenty Four

All Hester's repressed maternal instincts to protect and nurture welled within her as she looked down on Ruby from a bedroom window at Garth. The child stood in the middle of the front lawn like a cherub in a churchyard, gazing into the next world.

Hester had just answered the phone on the landing. It was McCall ringing from a call box to say he'd been delayed in London by something urgent. He sounded preoccupied.

It wasn't for Hester to be annoyed but she guessed Lexie might be. She'd wanted McCall there to help to unload the camper van and get Ruby settled in. In the event, he wasn't needed. Far from spinning into a temper about her new surroundings, Ruby became almost serene at her first sight of Garth Hall.

This didn't surprise Hester. For her, the ghosts of the old place were gathering this strange little girl to themselves, fitting her into the continuum of all their stories. It'd happened to Hester.

Impossible as it was to explain to the spiritually insensitive, she'd felt a presence, sensed an invitation to stay awhile, to rest and be content for Garth would still be there long after all who dwelled within had departed.

If this defied logic, so did the cat's bizarre reaction to Ruby. As she stepped from the van into the stable yard, Ludo - an anti social black tom once owned by Bea and Francis Wrenn

- purred round Ruby's bare legs and hadn't left her side since.

'How amazing,' Hester said. 'He usually makes himself scarce when visitors come.'

'My sister always said that Ruby had a closer affinity to animals than people.'

'Did Ruby have lots of pets, then?'

'Oh, no. Etta was allergic to animals.'

They watched Ruby and the cat walk the paths around Garth. Every ancient detail absorbed her - the great oak frame, bent with age, panels of narrow, hand-made bricks the colour of the Tudor rose and windows of imperfect medieval glass, glinting in the sun. Ruby recorded it all with a savant's concentration, as if she were a camera on a tracking shot.

For now, she stood unsmiling and motionless with the obedient Ludo sitting on the grass at her feet, looking up at Hester looking down on them.

Such an unwavering stare, such a mysterious child. Where had she hidden so that even the police couldn't find her? And to reappear *in a tree* - would the truth behind that ever come out?

Maybe she'd inherited her mother's gift for magic and illusion. How fortunate Ruby hadn't lived at the time of Salem.

Then Hester heard Lexie cry out from the next bedroom as if in pain. She turned from the window and went to see what was wrong.

*

The irony of Hoare's ex-wife living in a three-bed semi known as The Haven wasn't lost on McCall, waiting outside in his car. Hoare called it his sink hole because it swallowed almost every dime he ever earned.

It was close to the North Circular in an avenue indistinguishable from hundreds of others on this dreary edge of London - radiating corridors of identical brick boxes with bay windows, an apron of grass each, a cherry tree here, privet hedge there.

McCall was running late and wished the former Mrs Hoare would hurry home. Yet again, he was putting the professional before the personal. But any guilt about not being at Garth faded against the tantalising steer from Vickers - that Benwick had gone AWOL with a gun and might be linked to an assassination in Belgium. How - and if - this connected to Ruby remained to be seen. But it made a good story even better.

A friend at The Sunday Telegraph dug out a background piece on the murdered scientist, Gerald Bull, dated March 25 1990. Bull was obsessed with developing a super gun to launch a missile into space. The intelligence services of America and Israel hadn't bitten. But Iraq's maniac ruler, Saddam Hussein, had seen how he could dominate the Middle East with it. Bull's gun could lob a dirty nuclear or chemical bomb into Israel or any other regional enemy. So far, so nasty.

McCall now needed to pour enough hooch into Hoare till he coughed everything he knew about Benwick. But calls to his mobile, his flat and office, all went unanswered. Hoare's ex might know where he was. When she eventually walked towards the gate of The Haven in her auxiliary nurse's green uniform, she was weighed down with plastic bags of supermarket shopping.

She'd a night shift-worker's tired face and was cruelly aged. McCall had once sat at the Hoares' kitchen table, a net judge between her and him as they batted recriminations at each other over debts and burnt dinners and promises never kept. It could only ever be a contest without winners.

On the doorstep now, she took a couple of seconds to remember who McCall was.

'Malky's not here any more,' she said. 'We've been divorced almost year.'

'Yes, I'd heard, but can I come in for a minute?'

'The place is a mess.'

McCall said it didn't matter. He followed her into a barely used sitting room, musty and stacked with cardboard boxes containing the spoils of Malky's married life yet to be removed.

'He's not answering his phones,' McCall said. 'And we need to speak on something quite urgent.'

'He was here a couple of days ago. He's off work, not very well. Doesn't look like he's taking care of himself but he says he's starting a new job soon.'

'Really? Where at?'

'With some MP, doing his publicity at the next election.'

'That'll be interesting. Which MP, did he say?'

'He might have done but they're all the same to me.'

'True enough. So have you any idea where will I find Malky?'

'There's a caravan I rent from a farmer. Malky said he needed some peace and quiet because he's got to sort out something to do with this new job.'

'And where's your caravan?'

She wrote down an address near a village in the Oxfordshire countryside then said something which took him by surprise.

'It's handy for me because our daughter lives nearby, just across the field, in fact.'

McCall didn't let on but in all the years he'd known Hoare, no mention had ever been made of him having a child.

'How's she doing?' McCall said.

'As well as anyone with her condition. But she seems happy enough... well, happier than me, anyway. I get the train across there most weekends if I'm not on duty.'

'How old is she now?'

'Twenty-six next birthday.'

'It can't have been easy on you... or for Malky, I guess.'

'No, he took it hard, he couldn't accept her, you see. Every father wants a perfect baby daughter, don't they?'

'Does he visit, like you?'

'Not for years but then when he came this week, he asked me for a photograph of her.

I've never worked him out, you know... shouldn't have married him, I suppose.'

She had that same vacant look of a woman caught in those grainy wartime newsreels of the blitz, a face glimpsed amid the ruins, bewildered, powerless, unable to comprehend what was happening around her.

*

'Hester? It's Mac again. I'm sorry but it'll be a few more hours before I'm home.'

'You're not still in London, are you?'

'No, but I've got to stop off to see a guy who's really important to what I'm doing.'

'OK, but listen, Lexie isn't too well. I think she should see a doctor tomorrow.'

'Why? What's the trouble?'

'Female plumbing but try and get back before long.'

'Yeah, 'course. Is Ruby all right?'

'Sure, she seems fine, drawing away in her new bedroom.'

'Good. I've got to go now. There's a truck driver wanting to use the phone box.'

She went back to the bathroom. Lexie's sheets were soaking in the bath and needed transferring to the washing machine. Hester pulled the plug and watched the water drain away. It left a blood-red tide mark around the tub's white enamel sides.

Only after she'd made sure Lexie was still asleep did Hester wonder why McCall kept calling from phone boxes, not his mobile. Then Ruby distracted her with a pencil drawing of Garth.

It was stunning in its precision and execution. Hester smiled with warmth and admiration and told her she was brilliant and talented - words Ruby had rarely heard before.

*

McCall located Mrs Hoare's caravan early that evening. It had also known better days and was gradually turning a mottled, brownish-green beneath a line of sycamores on the far side of the owner's farmhouse.

Lights were coming on in cottages nearby and those on the low hills beyond. The damp scents of autumn hung in the air - decaying fruit, mist rising from the river, grey wood smoke layering out from the chimneys of sitting room fires, newly lit.

A large, elegant house of Cotswold stone backed onto the far side of the caravan field. It had been a vicarage but was now a private care home.

The caravan was in darkness. McCall swore to himself in frustration. Hoare could be anywhere. He might have hired a car or taken a taxi to a restaurant for supper. There was no point searching blind for him. He'd give it half an hour then leave a note.

McCall rolled a joint and stood, eyes closed, just listening to the night closing in. Rooks cawed back to their roost in a stand of trees and a tractor mauled along an unseen lane. Someone began playing nursery rhymes on a piano in the big house across the field. McCall thought of Hoare's daughter and the love he'd denied her. But why - and at what personal cost?

Still he didn't show. McCall walked to the caravan. The door wasn't locked. That seemed odd. It took a moment to adjust to the interior gloom and a clinging, left-over smell of fried food.

He put a match to the wick of a paraffin lamp on the table. By it was an empty bottle of Scotch, a large, spiral bound notebook and a Biro. McCall, no less a beggar or thief than any other hack, began reading. Sitting in the dim light, he was astounded by Hoare's revelations and how they confirmed the heads-up from Roly Vickers.

According to Hoare, DI Benwick was now being hunted as a threat to national security. The possible future prime minister, Guy Inglis - who'd witnessed the recovery of Etta's body - wanted a confidential back channel opened to the Ruby investigation. He'd even tempted Hoare with a PR job. But the spooks were blackmailing him over stolen police documents and they, too, wanted to know where Ruby was.

And tucked inside the notebook was the postcard Hoare said he'd received from Benwick. On the back was the most cryptic of quotes.

All shall be well, and all shall be well and all manner of things shall be well.

Hadn't Ruby sung something like this after McCall and Lexie got her back to the flat? There were so many coincidences. Hoare must have felt the same.

I can't say how but the case of the little girl can only be part of a bigger affair and therefore, she could still be in danger. Benwick has to know more or why else has he vanished and why are the spooks leaning on me for information about him?

Still Hoare didn't return. He'd have to leave him a message. Yet even as he wrote *Dear Malky*, the silence within the caravan was broken by the urgent ring tone of a mobile phone. McCall started out of his seat. It wasn't his.

It came from behind the curtained-off sleeping area. He found the phone on the floor and knelt to answer it. A man with a mature, cultured voice spoke without introducing himself.

'Listen, Hoare. You're not at your desk or in your flat but don't forget my warning the other night. You'd be well advised not to go on any travels before we talk again.'

McCall might have ad-libbed a reply had he not stood up at that moment. But he did and saw Malky Hoare, face down on the upper bunk and lying on what looked in the half light to be a black pillow and sheets.

He reeled back as he realised this was blood, pints of it, soaked into the bedding. It looked like a murder scene but wasn't. Hoare had succumbed to an alcoholic's dreadful fate. The blood vessels in his gullet must have exploded.

McCall suddenly had too much to take in to know what to do for the best. A complex situation had just become infinitely more so. He should ring the police or tell the farmer. But then he'd have to stay as a witness.

The revelations in Hoare's memo would inevitably become known. McCall didn't want that so he'd only one course of action. He ripped out all six pages of Hoare's notes and

pocketed the postcard, too. Then he blew out the lamp and
closed the caravan door behind him. No one must see him.

He stumbled through the shadows towards the Morgan and
could hear music - that piano again and the happy, discordant
singing of those who would always be children. McCall now
knew the face of one of them.

He'd just seen her picture, a photograph of a little girl in a
wheelchair clutched in her father's bloody hand at the end of
this, the most remorseful of days.

Twenty Five

Hester leaned back in her armchair by the Aga, slippers off, feet on a stool. The hall clock struck midnight and the soft echo of its chimes carried to the far corners of the silent house.

This was a favoured time, her chance to audit that day's words and deeds against her shamanistic code for living. It was not always easy to match her own ideals. But in Ruby, Hester knew her predestined purpose had been revealed.

She was to provide sanctuary for this singular child and protect her from other kids by home schooling. By doing this, Hester could also foster Ruby's artistic development. From the moment they met, a bond seemed to exist between them. Why else would Ruby have taken to her so readily and moved from all she had known with hardly a complaint? Their lives were ordained to intersect - Ruby orphaned by tragedy, Hester beginning to understand what all her days of haphazard wanderings about the earth had been for.

She thought back to her own beginnings in Shaniko, a huddle of wind-bleached shacks on the high plains of Oregon where her family grazed sheep to survive. She'd drifted south - to California and beyond, to communes and ashrams, jobs and lovers, most now beyond recall. All those meaningless, childless years, searching for something no god or cult could provide.

Then to the Welsh borders, drawn by that unknowable instinct to return, a memory of a song or a story passed down from those who'd left long ago, left their cottages to fall to ruin stone by stone beneath those green and shrouded hills.

But in this homecoming and in Ruby, Hester could at last see pattern and reason to her existence.

It was late and she was tired. She made her way up the back stairs to the bedroom Ruby had chosen to share with her. Ruby, so slight, so vulnerable, gave out an involuntary sigh as she entered. Ludo stirred, too. He looked up from Ruby's bed, his eyes saucer-wide and yellow in the momentary spit of light from the landing.

Hester leaned over and kissed Ruby's forehead as a mother might and was asleep herself soon after.

*

Lexie's wan face worried Hester at breakfast next day. McCall, unshaven and sleep deprived, was no oil painting, either. He'd arrived home in the early hours and spent the night in a guest room so Lexie wasn't disturbed. At least he was coming out of his depression by working.

Ruby sat across the kitchen table from them, eating toast and managing her trick of being physically close yet appearing to be somewhere else in her head. She always looked serious, as if about to ask a question though she rarely did. But it'd be a mistake to think Ruby wasn't absorbing all she saw and heard.

McCall knew this so suggested she give Ludo his breakfast outside after she finished her own. He'd no wish to frighten her with what he had to tell Lexie and Hester. As Ruby left for the yard, Lexie winced and put a hand to her groin as if in pain. McCall asked what was wrong.

'Just a bit of discomfort downstairs. I'll take something for it in a minute.'

'Lexie, you must see a doctor,' Hester said. 'You can't put this off any longer.'

'There's a morning surgery in Ludlow,' McCall said. 'I'll drive you there.'

Hester brought Lexie a glass of water and two pain killers. McCall waited till she'd taken them, anxious to have their attention for what he was going to say.

'You need to know that I've dug up more background on Ruby's case,' he said. 'I don't want to alarm you but what I'm finding out bothers me.'

'How do you mean, Mac?' Hester said.

'Well, for a start there are people making discreet inquiries about Ruby, like wanting to know where she is now.'

'You don't mean those monsters who took her in the first place?'

'No, what's strange is that these people are in positions of authority which makes what they're doing harder to understand.'

'But the police know that Ruby's safe with us. We've told them.'

'These people aren't the police, Hester.'

'I don't understand. Who are they?'

'I'm not entirely sure yet.'

'Then we've got to tell that detective on Ruby's case.'

'Benwick? That's the queerest thing. He's now gone missing himself and the same people who're asking questions about Ruby are looking for him.'

'Does all this mean Ruby's in some sort of new danger?'

'We need to make sure one of you is with her all the time,' McCall said. 'I've got to find Benwick because he's the guy with all the answers.'

Lexie listened without comment till then but now faced McCall, almost resentfully.

'I kept telling you Etta was warning us about something,' she said. 'But you wouldn't take any notice, wouldn't believe me but everything you've just said goes to prove it.'

'What I said was a few tarot cards stuck on a wall wasn't legal evidence of anything.'

'No? Well, what's this evidence of, then?'

She took a tiny screw of paper from her handbag with the words *Mr Ginger* written on it and told them how she'd found it in an ice cube from Etta's 'fridge.

'I've no idea why but she must have been really scared of this man,' Lexie said. 'No doubt it'll sound ridiculous and New Age to you, Mac, but Etta was trying to freeze this man out of her life in her own way, in a way she believed in.'

'So you're suggesting what?'

'That my sister killed herself because of whatever hold this man had over her.'

Nothing was said by McCall or Hester which might deride Lexie or her dead sister. Suicide was rarely a rational act any more than leaving a name in an ice cube. But a sense of unease and conflict settled in the room. Hester sought to defuse it by saying she'd taken Ruby to Ludlow Castle the previous day.

'I tried ever so gently to get her talking about whatever had happened to her while she was away.'

'And did she?' Lexie said.

'No, she still won't open up. The nearest she came to admitting anything was saying she couldn't see her unicorn so he must have run away and gone back home, too.'

'Was she upset about not seeing her unicorn?'

'No, not at all. And what's also interesting is that Ruby's stopped drawing castles now and all she's drawing is people's faces... just faces, all the time.'

*

Lexie walked across the surgery car park to where McCall was waiting in the Morgan. Her ashy-grey hair blew about in a wind bearing down from the summit of Cleehill to nudge scraps of litter along the shuts and narrows between Ludlow's medieval streets. If nothing else, it brought a hint of autumn colour to her pale cheeks.

'So what did the doctor say?'

'Wants me to see a gynaecologist.'

'Because of the bleeding?'

'Yes... says it's not good. He's saying I need an operation... sooner, not later.'

'But you've been having smear tests, haven't you?'

'Whenever I can, yes.'

'Don't say you've missed some. Is this why it's not been picked up before now?'

'You mustn't nag me, McCall... please. It'll all be all right.'

Lexie withdrew into herself on the drive back to Garth Hall. McCall wondered if the doctor had actually used the *C* word and she was in shock - or denial. How quickly, and without warning, can life seem frighteningly unreal.

McCall knew it from Namibia and other conflicts - that primitive fear of an unseen enemy, the possibility of dying. The mind closes down of its own accord to disassociate itself from the bullets above and the bodies below. It is as if it were happening far away and to someone else. Maybe this was how Lexie was feeling.

McCall couldn't ever fit Lexie - that most vibrantly alive of lovers - into any notion of mortality. Even when he looked at her now, he saw only the mesmerising girl with the dancer's legs and barley-coloured hair, in that cold, Cambridge street all those years ago.

Age and illness were but rumours then, places far beyond the horizon where they themselves would never tread. Yet the hours pass, seasons change and the tides carry us to the ends of our earth. And what was once so distant comes ever closer.

*

Supper was early and subdued - onion soup with bread Hester baked herself. Lexie asked McCall not to be offended but she wanted to sleep alone for the next few nights. He understood and they walked upstairs together. Each held to the other at the bedroom door. Lexie's body felt taut, as if everything was being held in, not least her tears. They kissed then McCall was left alone on the darkened landing.

But at the far end, silhouetted by a wall light behind her, Ruby stood motionless in her pyjamas, casting a long shadow on the polished oak boards between them. McCall went to her.

'Are you all right, Ruby?'

'I've brushed my teeth.'

'That's good. I'm going to brush mine in a minute.'

'Some of your teeth aren't straight.'

'That's true. They're not.'

'Hester's breath doesn't smell very nice sometimes.'

'That's why we all have to brush our teeth, isn't it?'

'I can hear people talking in this house.'

'You mean when you're in bed and we're all downstairs?'

'No, in the night. There are voices in the air, voices talking to me.'

'And what are they saying?'

'I don't understand them but it's voices, all right.'

'All old houses are like that, Ruby. The timbers creak in the wind and make little noises. It's nothing to be afraid of.'

'I know that, silly. But these are voices.'

He switched on the lights along the landing and took her into the bedroom. Hester had moved a Pembroke table by the window where Ruby could sit and draw. On it were her pencils and blocks of paper. He asked if he could look at her work.

'I don't care. It's night time.'

McCall still found it almost impossible to believe a child could recall such minutely observed details of a building or a face just from memory. Yet he saw her near perfect representations of Garth Hall - front and back elevations, complex roof, dentil mouldings. She'd also drawn Hester and Lexie and people met during trips out.

Ludo came purring in. He jumped on Ruby's bed and settled down by her feet. McCall mused on what enigmas they both were, how impossible it was to understand what was going on in either of their heads.

He would've gone back to the kitchen still thinking this had he not noticed the table drawer slightly open. Inside - and as if to be kept private - was a newly-started drawing book. Ruby was almost asleep so he flipped through this one, too.

And as he did, so he had to sit on her bed at the sight of what Ruby depicted - a boy and girl, neither older than her, each naked and pornographically revealed as if posing in some grotesque life class.

She couldn't possibly have seen such depravity before her disappearance. This picture was of childhood betrayed, innocence defiled. The inescapable conclusion was that Ruby must have been a witness to - and maybe even a victim of - events she described in the only way she knew how. But where had this happened and for whose perverted gratification?

And equally puzzling - how had Ruby escaped from those responsible for such wickedness?

He turned the final few pages. And there was someone he recognised immediately. It was Detective Inspector Benwick, intense eyes, long floppy hair, open-necked shirt. McCall stared at it for a full minute, increasingly confused. He wanted to wake Ruby and demand that she tell him where she'd seen Benwick - and what had he been doing when she did so.

He then looked at her last drawing - the only one where she'd added colour. It showed the hard, sneery face of a middle-aged man with cropped, gingery hair. But what stood out most was the fierce red birth mark she'd put on the left side of his neck.

Seeing this, McCall went across the landing to his writing room to re-read Hoare's memo. And there it was, a reference to the man with a wine stain birthmark who'd spied on Hoare and Inglis when they lunched at Rules.

Hoare's note explained how he'd identified him as Ray Gillespie, an official of the Association of Federated Trades based at its headquarters in Birmingham. He'd also combed out Teddy Lamb, the veteran Fleet Street industrial correspondent who'd swum the union world's unclean waters for years.

Teddy said Gillespie was a nasty piece of goods, a Scot and black arts merchant who collected embarrassing information on friend and foe alike because no one ever knew when it might come in useful. I asked if he meant for blackmail and Teddy said that's what it amounted to.

Gillespie is an old Trotskyite with a network of informers in the union who feed him information, either from fear or reasons of self-advancement. Nothing is off limits as far as Gillespie is concerned. Teddy says he runs the union's dirty tricks department under the guise of being a "communications officer."

As such, he wields power and influence for the leadership while they turn Nelson's blind eye to what's being done. I don't know why Inglis pretended not to know him to me but I saw them leave Rules together in the same cab.

So had Ruby drawn the face of *Mr Ginger*, the man who frightened her mother to death? McCall went down to the kitchen where Hester sat in the armchair by the Aga reading The Guardian.

He decided not to mention the pictures he'd just seen. She and Lexie were distressed enough already. He just said he'd someone to meet in Ludlow. He hadn't but the phone in The Feathers wouldn't have a listening ear on it as he guessed his probably would by now. An hour later, he was back.

'I'll be away tomorrow, Hester. You'll take care of Lexie, won't you?'

'Sure, I will. What'll you be doing?'

'Things you're better off not knowing.'

Twenty Six

McCall left the train at Birmingham, crossed New Street and stopped every so often to look in shop windows - but only to glance at whoever might be behind him. This wasn't paranoia. Paranoia was when you thought six people were following you but it was only four. He'd been on bumpy stories in the past and sensed that same undercurrent of threat now, no less because he was in Britain.

He was making for Digbeth, a one-time industrial district where most factories were now shut and workers queued for benefits in this, the fag-end of Mrs Thatcher's economic revolution.

Behind a back street pub called The Old Wharf was a railway viaduct where small-time outfits still managed to trade from under its blue brick arches. A man with oily hands fitted tyres to a truck and a joiner's workshop gave out the improbable scent of a pine forest from the baulks of Scandinavian timber being ripped to length on a circular saw.

The next arch was fronted with cement blocks, a thick metal door and looked like a secure storage facility. A painted sign read *Cyril Loader, Television Repairs*. McCall had need of services Cyril didn't advertise but for which a few anointed hacks - and other villains - paid him well.

He pressed an intercom to be buzzed in. Cyril had an air of dyspeptic misfortune. No one else's bowel was more irritable, their wife more like a robber's dog. McCall got half a nod as Cyril fiddled inside the guts of a broken TV on a workbench. He lit a cigarette from his soldering iron and without preamble, said he'd got some of what McCall had asked for.

'But I'm not very happy about this job, not one little bit.'

'Doesn't sound like you, Cyril. Is there a problem?'

'Yeah, there bloody well is because it's a police mobile you're after,' Cyril said. 'This all feels like it could come back and bite the bones of my arse.'

'So you're saying you can't get me a copy of the bill?'

Cyril wiped his long nose on a rag and said it'd be madness to even try.

'Straight forward this number ain't, my little ferret. But seeing as it's you, I've figured out a bit of a compromise... it'll cost you extra, though.'

'I'd never have guessed.'

'Take the piss all you want, McCall, but I'm running risks here, not a fucking charity.'

'Easy, Cyril. It'll be fine.'

'You'll be saying that when I'm banged up in Winson Green again, you sod.'

'Just tell me what you've got then we can do a deal.'

'Hmm... all right... well, my mate in the phone exchange was able to find out through his ways and means committee that this mobile was hardly ever used but it did call one particular land line quite a lot so that sort of stood out for him.'

'And where is this land line?'

'That dump up the M6, Manchester.'

'And I should be cheerful because - '

' - I've got you a copy of the customer's latest bill, name, address, the lot.'

'There's handsome, Cyril. Thanks - now what about the rest of my wish list?'

'Come back in a couple of hours,' he said. 'I'll have you a Sierra estate and I'll leave an untraceable mobile in the glove compartment. I've also got you a moody driving licence but listen you bastard, if you get collared, I hired that motor out in good faith. I'll admit nothing. You understand?'

*

It was still quite warm for autumn. Office workers in short sleeves gathered on the piazza by the Association of Federated Trades headquarters not far from New Street Station, eating sandwiches and drinking bottled water.

McCall found a bench opposite the AFT building - a steel and glass homage to the utilitarian brutalism of the sixties. He made sure the briefcase on his lap had the main entrance framed in the video camera concealed within it.

Black bag jobs like this fouled up more often than not, however much care was taken. All he could do was wait and blend in with all the other strangers in the sunshine. He wondered what secrets they kept, what lies they told. McCall had knocked about with Malky Hoare off and on for years, drunk and sober. Yet behind all his Fleet Street bonhomie was a daughter denied.

That wasn't a secret, it was a disgrace. McCall now thought far less of the man who'd believed otherwise.

He looked over at the AFT offices just as the revolving doors delivered his targets onto the piazza - Gillespie, the ginger-haired man with the strawberry birth mark from Ruby's drawing, and another individual built like a boxer.

McCall pretended to rummage in his briefcase to switch on the camera. He panned the case with them as they came towards him and walked through shot. Then he closed the lid and followed at a distance. Gillespie and his colleague headed towards the canal basin. All the waterside warehouses and old industrial structures alongside were being redeveloped as bars and restaurants for tourists.

They entered a trattoria and sat at an upstairs table overlooking a berth for gaudily painted narrow boats which would once have transported coal or produce. Now, they were crewed by families on holiday or those who'd sold up their semis for a life on the water.

McCall stood on the towpath with a stills camera, innocently firing off general views. But in between, he managed snatch shots of the AFT men laughing, wine glasses in hand. They were joined by a third male. McCall had enough images and should have quit while he was winning. But he went for one last close-up.

That was when he saw an angry-looking Gillespie pointing at him from the restaurant window. McCall got the picture then vanished.

*

Of all the rooms in Garth Hall, Hester preferred the kitchen. This was the warm, practical heart of the house where the rhythm of its daily routine was the preparation, cooking and communal eating of food.

It had a worn brick floor, beams and no modern units. Everything was stored in a housekeeper's cupboard, scuffed from years of use and abuse by cooks and scullery maids, or in a dark oak dresser with shelves bending under the weight of a blue and white dinner service.

Only in the late 1940s did an Aga replace the cast iron range which had served the house since the middle of Victoria's reign. At least eight people could sit to the kitchen table - sycamore, pale from scrubbing and with plain, tapering legs. Hester and Lexie sat across it now, drinking red wine, with the remains of their lamb stew yet to be cleared away.

Ruby was asleep and McCall preoccupied in his office. Lexie wanted to talk, needed some reassurance from another female before she went into hospital next day.

'I'm not certain Mac really appreciates what's happening to me.'

'That can't be right, Lexie. He cares a great deal but there's so much going on in all our lives right now that I don't think the poor guy knows which way to turn.'

'I've never been lucky for him, I've always brought him heartbreak.'

'Maybe once, long ago, but there's a great love between you. Anyone can see that.'

'I sometimes wonder if some part of me always knew I was going to get ill.'

'In what way do you mean?'

'Subconsciously, I suppose. I willed him to come back into my life because I knew I could depend on him but I also knew somewhere in my heart that it wouldn't last.'

'Why Lexie, why did you think that?'

'It's not because I'm going to run off with anyone else at my age but because I was never meant to make old bones.'

'I won't hear this, it's so negative. You've got to make yourself believe that you'll get through whatever the doctors decide is right to do for you.'

'I know but just say it turns out badly... what's McCall going to do then?'

'We have to deal with what *is* in this life, not what might be.'

'Maybe I should bail out now... do what I've always done and run away.'

'But you'd be forgetting Ruby, wouldn't you?'

'No... honestly, I'm not... but it's just that everything suddenly feels so weird, as if I'm living in someone else's life or they're living in what's left of mine.'

'Because you're in shock, Lexie. You've had one piece of bad news after another and now you've got to have a big operation. It's no wonder it's all affecting you.'

'That's about the God-awful size of it. Still, come on, let's finish this bottle because tomorrow... who the hell knows?'

*

It is a fear of dying which wills us to stay alive.

Lexie was about to be put to sleep by the medics who would cut the malignancy from her perfidious body. But she fought the anaesthetic, hated the idea of going under, of losing control.

That same childhood nightmare stole up to haunt her once more, slowly suffocating beneath the dentist's tight rubber mask when the gas went into her like a fog. But she slipped from this world again, an apparition in the depths of her own night. The past, the future - neither leaves the other in peace so it all bleeds into one. Then Lexie began to fall... fall to earth from wherein all her lovers rose up to kiss her one last time. Then they sank back as soon she must herself, calling in the darkness for her Daddy to stop what he was doing but hearing no word of reply.

Twenty Seven

Hester rang the hospital next morning. The sister on Lexie's ward said she'd come through the procedure well but wouldn't be properly conscious for some hours.

'She's undergone what is really emergency surgery,' she said. 'It'll take her a while to recover.'

Hester planned to drive over to Shrewsbury with Ruby to see her. She wanted McCall to go with them. But he looked preoccupied to the point of distraction.

'I can't, Hester. I can't even guarantee I'll be back tonight or even tomorrow.'

'Why? What's more important than being there for Lexie when she needs you?'

'Ruby, that's what,' McCall said. 'Whatever happens, don't let her out of your sight.'

'You're worrying me, Mac. There's still a threat to her, isn't there?'

'I'm not sure but we can't take the risk of thinking there isn't.'

He gave her his new mobile number but said she must only ever ring it from a pay phone, never from the landline at Garth Hall. Hester asked why - and why he'd left his own car in the garage.

'Because it's safer for me to be under the radar till I know what's really going on.'

'So where will you be?'

'Up north. I've got a fix on the missing detective.'

'You'll take care of yourself, won't you?'

*

Lexie was barely conscious when Hester and Ruby arrived in her ward. They didn't stay long and left flowers and fruit before driving the two miles into Shrewsbury. Ruby showed little or no understanding of her aunt's serious condition.

Hester parked by the river which slipped like a noose around the half timbered town. Ruby's eyes stayed fixed on all its ancient buildings, absorbing their form and line for later - but in silence. She rarely expressed an opinion. It was as if all her thoughts were written in invisible ink so no one else could read them.

Despite this - maybe because of it - Hester felt it important to open her mind to new places and experiences, to give her freedom but in conditions of safety. She also wanted Ruby to look loved and cared for, not like the urchin she'd first seen.

'Let's get you some nice new things, Ruby. What about a pretty dress and some shoes to go with it?'

Ruby seemed not to care for anything she was shown, except dungarees and T-shirts. After an exhausting hour, Hester gave way and bought her whatever she chose.

They set off along a narrow cobbled street for lunch in a café near a churchyard hemmed in by a row of crooked oak-framed houses. But Ruby kept looking behind them. The child's hand tighten its grip on hers. Something like fear crossed Ruby's face.

'What is it, my lovely? What's wrong?'

Ruby trembled slightly and pointed towards the people following them - window shoppers, an Asian woman with a baby, two pensioners linking arms, a man turning on his heel to go back the way he'd come.

'There's no one to be afraid of, Ruby. Come on, I bet you're hungry.'

'No, I want to draw in our room. I don't like it here.'

*

McCall had a theory that only guilty men bought houses in cul-de-sacs to make it difficult for hacks to secretly film them. A strange vehicle parked in one for any length of time quickly got rumbled and safe passage out was never guaranteed.

True to form, the house DI Benwick rang so often from his mobile was at the bottom of Boland Grove, a short U-shaped avenue of 1930s semis in the Fallowfield district of south Manchester. McCall parked at the top with a direct view down to number 9, the home of Adele and Gerard Green, according to his copy of their bill.

Long stake-outs could be tedious and concentration hard to maintain. The long term implications of Lexie's illness kept coming back to him. For her, the enemy was already inside the gate.

He forced himself to keep focus, to stay with Ruby's story. The Greens' bill showed that on the day Benwick vanished, someone from their house rang him once and a number in London three times. McCall rang this one himself. It was answered by a female and he asked if Mr Green was there.

'No, no one's here.'

'Is that his office number or a private house?'

'No, Mr Green is not here today. Sorry, bye.'

Her accent could have been east European, possibly Russian. This alone made McCall think back to the warning in Hoare's aide memoire.

If the spooks felt justified in tapping my phone and bugging my flat to find DI Benwick in the name of national security then McCall is involved enough be a target, too. He has background knowledge of what's happened and a connection to the missing girl through her auntie. I'm in enough trouble as it is or I'd tell him not to use his own phone any more and get eyes put in the back of his head.

McCall wondered if the watchers were already watching him watching Benwick's contacts - if they knew about them, that was. The documents Hoare lifted from Ruby's case file must have an incriminating significance beyond her disappearance. But how did the spooks know Hoare had copies? And why did they burgle his flat when they'd a right of access to them through normal police liaison channels?

Yet if McCall thought the situation sticky now, it would get worse. Hoare's body must have been discovered. The police were bound to interview his ex-wife and she was equally certain to mention McCall's visit. They would find his fingerprints - already on file from past misdemeanours - in the caravan.

He'd also removed evidentially relevant pages from the notebook in which Hoare had obviously been writing. The cops might yet ask where they were, why they'd been taken and why he'd failed to notify anyone about the body. He'd have no choice but to go no comment and risk the suspicion that would cause.

He looked up for a moment and saw an elderly woman with a walking stick, struggling with a bag of shopping as she entered Boland Grove. She leaned against a garden wall, as if exhausted. McCall went across to see if she needed help. It wasn't only Greeks who bore gifts. She'd strength enough to smile and nod. He took her bag and she took his arm.

A minute later, he was in her kitchen, two doors from where the Greens lived. The old lady slumped in an easy chair. He made her a cup of tea and fed her cat. It turned out she was widowed so had no one McCall could ring.

She thanked him for his kindness and wanted him to stay awhile for hers was a life with few friends. By the time he left, McCall knew the Greens were on a walking holiday, had no children, that Mr Green was something to do with computers but was currently overseas on a project for his firm.

Mrs Green called herself a legal executive and they drove a silvery-blue Rover car. Both were in their late thirties and had only lived at number 9 for six-months.

'Short dark hair, she has. Eton Crop we called it in my day,' the old lady said. 'Very private sort of soul, doesn't go out of her way to make conversation but then, your neighbours don't these days, do they?'

So what was the connection between this seemingly blameless, provincial couple and a runaway detective being sought as a threat to the State? Like Evan said, we never truly know anyone... least of all, those we're sure we do.

For the moment, that didn't matter. The only non-London number called from the Greens' phone in the days before Benwick went AWOL was 0204 68288. McCall had rung it the previous night. It was the Blackhorse Hotel in Blackrod, a former mining town in Lancashire and - even more encouragingly - the place pictured on the front of Benwick's cryptic postcard to Hoare.

Here was the joy of McCall's kind of hackery - digging about in the muck and litter at the side of the road then finally turning up a spraint left by the prey being pursued. McCall booked a room at the Blackhorse and now headed north.

*

For the life of her, Hester could not think who or what might have caused Ruby to be so frightened in Shrewsbury. But she was starting to recognise when it was wiser to retreat than fight. They drove back to Garth Hall. Ruby stared straight ahead during the entire journey. She refused any food and immediately went upstairs to draw some of the buildings her photographic mind had just registered.

Hester busied herself in the kitchen. The phone in the hall rang and she silently prayed it wasn't bad news about Lexie. She answered and a man with a regional accent she couldn't place, asked if McCall was there.

'No, not right now. Who is this?'

'Just a friend,' he said. 'I'm trying to find out where he is for a job I've got for him but he's not answering his mobile.'

'He could be anywhere. I'm only the housekeeper, he doesn't tell me his plans.'

'So you're all on your own in that rambling old place, are you?'

'Sometimes - so what?'

'Don't take offence but it's a bit creepy for a woman, isn't it?'

'Listen, I'm a bit busy for this.'

'All those creaks and bumps in the night. Must almost scare you to death.'

'Just tell me your name and I'll have him call you if he rings in.'

'No, don't worry. You've got other things on your mind... better go and make sure all the doors are bolted, hadn't you?'

Then the man put the phone down.

Twenty Eight

The name *Blackrod* derived from words meaning *bleak clearing* in the language of those from across the German Sea who invaded after the Roman legions left and the Dark Ages began.

In time, forests came to be replaced by farms. Stone cottages were built, women wove fine cloth and men lowered themselves into the earth to dig for coal. The town grew and had a railway to serve its brick works and factories.

But as McCall drove down the Roman road which was now Blackrod's main street, he saw scant evidence of the industries where those who'd once lived in the long, unlovely terraces he passed had worked.

He noticed a sign for *Ros Thorne Photography* in a parade of shops. He parked and looked into a window display of joyful wedding pictures and children's portraits. Ms Thorne was guillotining prints at her counter, a woman of forty summers surviving on the happiness of others.

McCall entered in his lawyerly blue suit, white shirt and dark tie and carrying a leather briefcase. He could be mistaken for anything other than what he was. There was rarely need to lie when people made assumptions of their own.

He smiled at Ms Thorne and said he'd a reel of film urgently needing to be developed and printed as blow-ups.

'Sorry, I couldn't get round to doing that for a couple days at the earliest.'

McCall kept the beguiling smile going through his fatigue and disappointment. He implied this was a delicate legal matter so he'd pay over the odds for any assistance.

'If it took you a couple of hours, I'd pay for four... in cash, if you wished.'

'There's nothing dodgy about these pictures, is there? I can't afford to get mixed up in anything dodgy, not round here.'

'You'll see them for yourself,' McCall said. 'And I don't doubt you'd quickly work out what sort of case this is.'

'Not a messy divorce, is it?'

'I wouldn't be allowed to comment, would I?'

*

It was still warm and the landlady of the Blackhorse opened the pub's front windows to catch whatever breeze might pass. The night sky was sour with sodium glare from all the street lighting between Blackrod and the distant Pennine Moors.

This had been a tiring day. McCall sat in the bar with a Scotch and much on his mind. But the news from the hospital was encouraging. Lexie was stable.

Hester might have rung him but didn't so he took it she and Ruby had no problems at Garth. He would home in on Benwick next morning, check the guest book and ask if anyone recognised the photograph he'd taken of him by the reservoir.

Ros Thorne arrived with a large manilla envelope as promised. She declined McCall's offer of a drink. She'd her wedding commission to finish. He went to his room and spread the snatched pictures of Gillespie on the bed.

It was the final shot of him sitting with the other union man and an unidentified male at the trattoria window that made McCall look twice. He stared hard at the blow-up but there was no doubt. Inexplicably, the third man was his very own *Deep Throat*, Roly Vickers.

*

A car's headlights cut through the trees along the pot-holed drive to Garth Hall then swept onto the front drive and threw shadows across the bedroom Hester shared with Ruby. Hester stood behind the curtains and looked down.

It was a police patrol car. This made her more anxious, not less. Two uniformed officers got out and walked round to the back of the house.

'You must stay in this room, Ruby,' Hester said. 'Tell me you understand.'

Ruby nodded and carried on drawing. Hester went across the landing to the bathroom and watched from there. A sergeant and a constable shone their torches into the stables. It was padlocked but they could see McCall's Morgan inside. This was what they were after. A few moments later, Hester heard the front door being knocked.

It took some deep breathing before she was calm enough to open it. The sergeant said they wanted to speak to Francis McCall.

'He's not here,' Hester said.

'But his car is.'

'Yes, but he's working away. Why do you want him?'

'It's the police in Oxfordshire who want him. There's been a suspicious death and they think Francis can help them with their inquiries.'

'How would he know anything about a suspicious death?'

'It isn't for us to say but the police down south want to interview him.'

'Well, if he rings me, I'll tell him.'

'Do you mind if we come in and have a look round?'

'Have you got a search warrant?'

'No, but we could get one if we need to.'

'You'd still be wasting your time. Mr McCall's in London for a few days.'

'How do we know he's not hiding inside?'

'You don't but he's not and I don't tell lies.'

'So who's moving that curtain up there?'

'That's my bedroom. It'll be the cat, he sleeps in there.'

'A cat... really? So what relation are you to Francis, Miss...?'

'Miss Lloyd and I'm not a relation, I'm his housekeeper.'

'And you're stuck out here, miles from anywhere in this big old house with just a cat for protection,' he said. 'Not of a nervous disposition, are you?'

'I was raised in the wilds of Oregon so there's not much that frightens me. Now, are we done here?'

'For the time being, yes. But we may well be back.'

Half an hour later, Hester drove to a phone box and rang McCall, not in a panic but unsettled by events beyond her control. She told him how frightened Ruby had been, thinking they were being followed in Shrewsbury.

'And now the police have just pitched up,' she said. 'They say there's been a suspicious death and you're involved. You have to tell me what's going on, Mac.'

'It'll be Hoare, the PR man. He's died but the cops will use his death as an excuse to find out where I am.'

'But why would they want to do that?'

'I don't know but like everything else, it'll be to do with Ruby's case. Is she with you now?'

'Hasn't left my side nor will she. Will you be back to visit Lexie tomorrow night?'

'I'll do my best but cover for me if I can't.'

Her coins ran out so she and Ruby drove home through the moonlit country lanes. On such a night, as soft and warm as a lover's first kiss, Hester ought to have been lying in a hammock on the orchard lawn, staring at the stars and questioning all those inner beliefs and thoughts which influenced her outer self.

It was said an unexamined life had no merit - and that wasn't in Hester's soul plan for this incarnation. But instead of visualising her universe, she was assailed by fears of kidnap, of menacing telephone calls and suspicious deaths.

All this worldly wickedness swirled around the motherless child at her side. Who could possibly want to harm her? For what reason or purpose? Every door and every window at Garth Hall would henceforth be locked against evil-doers. Ruby would be protected by Hester this time.

*

The landlady of the Blackhorse offered McCall a full English breakfast next day. But all his underlying worries caused him to feel nauseous enough without a fry-up.

'Just cereal and toast, please'.

'You look quite pale, Mr Sydenham,' she said. 'Not poorly, I hope.'

This was McCall's first outing using the moody name on Cyril Loader's even moodier driving licence.

'No, I'm fine honestly, just not too hungry.'

He was queasily aware of the pub's early morning smells - stale cigarette smoke, last night's spilt beer, disinfectant. The landlady brought his order then hovered out of hospitable curiosity.

'You from London, did you say?'

'Down that way, yes.'

'All that crime and rushing about there, not sure I could cope with it.'

McCall smiled and had reason to suggest she share his pot of tea.

'Might as well,' she said. 'I've no other guests in today.'

He poured for them both. They chatted about the pub trade and the weather before he reached in his briefcase for the close-up he'd taken of Benwick by the reservoir.

'Don't know if you can help me with this but do you recognise this man?'

She gave a canny half smile and asked if McCall was a private detective.

'Not quite but I'm anxious to trace him.'

'Yes, I know him. What's he done that you're after him?'

'It's complicated and rather personal but would you tell me how you know him?'

'Because he's stayed here a few times. In fact, he only left a couple of hours before you arrived.'

McCall cursed silently. He'd seen only one other name above his in the register - a Mr Terry Boland. There was no address but he should have spotted the clue in the surname, cribbed from the street where the Greens lived.

'So what brings our Mr Boland up this way so often?'

'He's a bird watcher, mad keen on it, apparently.'

'I didn't know that. Where does he go round here?'

'No idea but someone in the bar said they'd seen him a while back on the other side of Euxton, on a golf course up there.'

'You mean playing golf?'

'No, watching birds. Got all the right kit, he had. Camouflage outfit, binoculars, even a video camera.'

'So which golf course was this?'

'There's only one that way, Shaw Hill, it's called. Very posh, got this lovely old house they've turned into a country club.'

'I might head up there and see if he's still about. What sort of car is he driving now?'

'They're all the same to me, love. No idea.'

'Is the golf course easy to find?'

'It's right next to what we call the gunpowder factory round here.'

'Gunpowder factory?'

'Where they make the bombs and weapons and such like. It's all supposed to be top secret and we're not meant to know what goes on there... but we do.'

So this was where Benwick's trail was leading. McCall now had even more reasons to be cheerful.

*

Lexie believed herself to be in a field of tulips - vermillion, lilac, violet, apricot, black, white and every shade between. Their fleshy-bladed leaves brushed her bare legs as she passed. But where was this place?

She snapped a flower head off its stalk and put it to her lips to kiss. But within its satin chalice of petals was a heart burned black by passion, all but spent now. In front of her was a clearing and in this space, a million more deflowered tulips, tumbled into a great heap like an unmade bed.

Lexie lay on her back to luxuriate in the waxy silkiness of the blooms against her skin, sank ever deeper into all that rainbow beauty being crushed beneath her spread-eagled nakedness. Then she found her own velvety self as she first had when crossing the border from innocence to experience.

But that is not enough. She called into the silence for a lover and her voice echoed into the past. Who will smile gently now, genuflect before her and offer the sacrament she wants most? Whose back will she mark... McCall's or Evan's or one whose name and face she can no longer recall?

A man's hands cup her breasts. They move over her belly and further down so she reveals herself to him, arches to receive the pleasure he offers. And in that moment, she is entered yet doesn't feel what was expected.

She was being knifed open. Cut, sliced, ripped apart till her very essence was excised and removed. And the blood seeped from her wounds to discolour the flowers where she lay until all turned crimson and she and they were nothing but flames.

Lexie was no longer female. Her life was saved but lost. They had neutered her. An intensity of white light shone in her eyes so she saw only the wraith-like shapes of strangers floating by.

And she began to weep for the woman she believed she was could be no more.

Twenty Nine

A boy on a bike is rarely noticed. He is as unremarkable as a tree in a wood or a brick in a wall. Yet he sees much. The world and its ways are still a mystery to him. Each new sight and experience imprints itself on the blank page of his open mind – all the more if what he witnesses is so fearful he is too afraid or too confused to tell anyone else about it.

So it was with Ronnie Stansfield, eleven next birthday and good at mending things like his Dad had been. His Mum sometimes worked late shifts at the gunpowder factory. Then their house felt empty and sad so Ronnie stayed out till all hours on those nights.

On this calm autumn evening, he rode up the country lanes around Shaw Hill golf course. The rosaries of street lights were coming on in the valleys below and only the iron clunk of railway wagons being shunted in the underground chambers beyond the trees could be heard. This was where the munitions his Mum helped to assemble were prepared for dispatch.

Ronnie sneaked his bike through a hedge and rode the rough ground towards Hardfield Wood. His den was here, the place where he was the hero of his own stories and even smoked a cigarette. He'd filched it from a packet left on the mantelpiece by Mr Towner, the neighbour who came for meals now his wife had cleared off.

Smoking seemed manly to Ronnie but out in the open air, the real taste of tobacco made him giddy and sick. No more cigarettes went missing after that. Besides, Ronnie didn't dare risk his friendship with Mr Towner for Mr Towner was a loco driver and Ronnie was a train spotter.

And that night, Mr Towner was booked to drive a big Class 47 diesel on a job he'd said was very hush-hush.

'What's hush-hush about it?'

'Don't rightly know but it's going from your Mum's place and we've been told to keep our traps shut about it.'

Everyone thereabouts knew the gunpowder factory made bombs and bullets for the government. This was dangerous work with a special law against talking about it. Ronnie's Mum said anyone who did would be locked in prison and the keys thrown away.

'So is your train hush-hush because someone might blow it up?'

'No lad, that'll only happen if I chuck my fag ends in the wagons.'

'But spies are real, aren't they - like terrorists, like you see on the television?'

'True enough but this is just some special delivery, a special cargo.'

'What's special about it?'

'I shan't get to know that, will I? My job's just to drive the train to the docks.'

'So is it a special cargo because it's for a war?'

'Your Mum's factory only makes things for war,' Mr Towner said. 'War is what puts bread on the tables round here.'

*

Hardfield Wood was criss-crossed with animal tracks and hunted by owls and sparrow hawks. The ground beyond sloped down to the gunpowder works' perimeter fence and below that, the network of huge underground storage rooms Ronnie called the concrete caves. There were twenty of them beneath artificial hills covered in tons of earth to absorb any blast from an accidental explosion.

Each was honeycombed with brick-built chambers where TNT was kept with thousands of bombs and mines, grenades and ammo, all stacked in wooden crates.

But it was the factory's own private railway which really fascinated Ronnie. Every bunker had a siding running through a tunnel to an unseen platform where fork lift trucks loaded pallets of munitions into wagons.

These were shunted out to the factory's marshalling yard by a stout little Fowler 0-4-0 diesel and coupled up behind a big mainline engine for the likes of Mr Towner to drive to distant ports.

From there, whatever Ronnie's Mum and other women had so carefully produced could be shipped across the world to any country where people had to fight and others had to die.

But as Ronnie heard her say to Mr Towner, if folks round their way didn't make such things, the French would... or the Yanks, or the Russians or the Chinese. It was just a job of work and everyone needed to live, didn't they?

*

Ronnie left his bike in his den and ran across to the wire fence to watch the shunting. But something was happening he'd never seen before before - a man dressed like soldier, caught for a moment in the yellow light from a lamp above a tunnel. He had to be an army man because he was wearing a black beret and combat fatigues and had a short rifle cradled between his arms.

Ronnie felt an immediate tingle of excitement - but instinctive fear, too. He'd only ever seen soldiers in films or on television. Why would a real one be patrolling the concrete caves – and with a gun?

Then he saw a second soldier walking from another siding. Something unusual was going on, something hush-hush like Mr Towner said. The normal security men had dark blue uniforms and dogs but not guns.

Ronnie crawled further along through the grass and nettles to get a better view. His jeans and T-shirt were already torn so his Mum wouldn't mind. He watched the soldiers exchange a word then carry on patrolling.

Then the Fowler clanked into view from the nearest tunnel, pulling three red and grey munition wagons, each loaded and ready to be taken to Mr Towner's engine. The shunter waited for clearance to reverse from the siding and onto the line which looped around the whole site. Its engine was idling and drowned out the low rumble from the other tin-sided sheds nearby.

His Mum would be in one of them, standing at a conveyor belt rattling with brass cannon shells to be filled with explosives. Not far away, lines of thousand pound bombs, each bigger than a coffin, were being crated up alongside tons of machine gun ammunition.

Ronnie moved along around the perimeter fence towards the marshalling yard. He'd just passed three more concrete caves when he heard a yell.

Two people in dark overalls ran out of a tunnel and along the railway line, chased by two men who weren't in uniform and didn't have guns.

One of the runners looked round to see how close the pursuers were and seemed unaware of the diesel reversing with its wagons. Then the figure stumbled and was hit a glancing blow by the engine's buffer and spun to the ground, twitching and flailing as if having a fit.

The engine driver couldn't have seen anything because he didn't stop. One of the chasing men spoke into a walkie-talkie. Ronnie saw them lift the injured person by the arms and legs and carry them to the roadway that ran round the site.

No more than half a minute later, a car pulled up. The driver unlocked the boot and the fallen runner was put inside. The boot was shut, the men got in and drove away. Ronnie couldn't move for a few moments.

He had seen something happen – but what, exactly? The men were just shadows in the gathering gloom. There was nobody there now.

First the soldiers and their guns, now this. Ronnie felt himself trembling. Suddenly, he wasn't playing in Hardfield Wood any more. This wasn't a game. What if those men had seen him spying on them? What would they do next? And where was the other runner who'd escaped?

But Mr Towner's train was due off soon. He'd watch from the footbridge. But even then, this frightening night wasn't over. Behind the plume of oily smoke venting from Mr Towner's engine, Ronnie counted forty-two trucks, each with their sliding metal doors sealed shut. There would usually be no more than five or six.

That wasn't all. He saw more soldiers with rifles and packs. Two climbed into the rear cab of Mr Towner's engine and the rest headed down to the end of the train. And that was odd, too. Hooked up to it was an old bullion coach. Ronnie recognised it from his train spotting books. They'd carried gold bars before the army bought them to transport ammunition. The soldiers could only be there to protect whatever was locked in the wagons.

Ronnie checked his watch. It was almost nine thirty. Mr Towner must have called the control box at Preston from the phone in his cab because his train started edging forward in the darkness and whatever mission lay ahead. Ronnie waved and waved but couldn't be sure if Mr Towner had seen him or not.

It was best to go. He hurried back for his bike hidden in the wigwam of fallen branches which was his den. On other days, it could be a pirate ship or a fort besieged by warriors but on this night, it offered no shelter from his imaginings.

After what he'd just seen - or believed he had - the moonlight shifting through the trees made everything seem spooky and he was scared. As he took hold of his bike, something moved in the den.

It was a man. His face was smeared with green and brown make-up like soldiers put on in the jungle. He wore black overalls so Ronnie knew who it must be straight away. This was the other running man, the one who'd escaped.

'Don't be frightened, kid,' he said. 'I need you to help me.'

*

Another sixty miles and Shelley Lucas would be in the Lake District. She drew off the northbound carriageway of the M61 and into Anderton Services - a building she thought so hideous it could only be improved by an ounce of carefully placed Semtex. But the IRA had yet to do the decent thing so she'd forego breakfast that morning.

Taz was the more immediate concern. Her old terrier hadn't cocked a leg since leaving their overnight hotel en route from London. But beyond the car park was a public right of way down through a grass field to a brook at the bottom.

It was going to be another hot day. The back of Shelley's white cotton dress was already sticky with perspiration. She would change outfits before having lunch with a new author it was vital to impress. He was a PR dream - descended from slaves, gay and living in Wordsworth country. She simply had to sign him.

Taz was unleashed and romped off into the field. Like his mistress, he just about remembered being young. Shelley stood by a kissing gate on the bridge over the stream. On the other side were two railway lines and far the distance, a church and the town of Blackrod, according to her map.

But time was pressing. She bent to put Taz back on his lead. Then she noticed a running shoe in the nettles on the track side of the gate. It looked new. Shelley leaned over to see if the other was there.

And it was - and on the foot of a body lying on its side in a patch of withered brown lupins.

Thirty

Apart from Hester and Ruby carrying a picnic down to the stream, little else moved in the warmth of Garth Woods that morning. A bird might flit from the caves of shadow beneath the oaks and ash but that was all. The spirits of the magical trees themselves remained bound within their roots.

The air carried a charge of thunder from the slate blue clouds massing beyond the Shropshire hills. It might take another hour for the weather to break, for a wind from nowhere to stir the limp green leaves above where they sat and bring rain to make mud of the bare cracked earth.

'You pour our tea, Ruby, and I'll cut the cake.'

Hester was desperate to create a safe new childhood for Ruby out of the abnormalities of her life. She'd no template for how this could be done, only a feel for the way it might be achieved. But the disconnect between Ruby and those around her wasn't simply a consequence of her abduction which might heal in time.

This was how she was and likely to be. Ruby occupied a very private space in the world of others and could only interact with them in the way she was wired to do.

'We'll go to the hospital tonight, shall we? Call in and see how Lexie's getting on.'

Something of a frown crossed Ruby's quizzical face.

'No, that man will be there.'

'Which man, Ruby?'

'In the street, the ginger man. He was coming for me again.'

'I didn't see a ginger man.'

'Then you weren't looking properly. He was behind us and I'm not going back there.'

'You knew this man?'

'He put me in a bag.'

'He did *what*, Ruby?'

'It was dark and I was in a room with some beds and some children.'

Hester set down her cup, unsure how to react for the best. Prompting Ruby with questions might cause her to retreat into herself again. But the story of her ordeal was better out than in, however long or painful the process.

'This ginger man doesn't sound nice to know,' Hester said. 'Where did he take you?'

'I don't like this cake. I'm going back to draw now.'

*

McCall found Shaw Hill golf course and the grand, bow-fronted Georgian house which was its country club. He walked into reception with his briefcase, obeying the first rule of blagging for hacks - play whatever role that day's assignment demands.

'I believe a client of mine might be staying with you,' he said. 'Could you just check for me, please? His name's Terry Boland.'

The receptionist smiled, top lit by a chandelier, and scrolled down a list of guests on her computer screen.

'No... sorry, we've no Mr Boland with us,' she said. 'But there's a Mrs Boland. Could that be his wife?'

'Yes, that'll be her. I can go up, can I?'

'You could but there's a note here from the housekeeper. It says Mrs Boland didn't use her room last night and the bed wasn't slept in so there's no one there at the moment, I'm afraid.'

'That's OK. By the way, which of their cars did she come in?'

'There isn't a registration number shown here so I assume she arrived by taxi.'

McCall asked if he might take a stroll around the grounds while he waited for the Bolands. The receptionist gave him a location map and he set off towards the golf course.

He had to think. The existence of a Mrs Boland was new information. But then, an armed detective being sought by the spooks would need an accomplice. McCall had seen nothing about the hunt for Benwick in any of the papers. That suggested a news black-out which only happened in sensitive cases - or when lives were at stake.

One thing was for sure. Benwick wasn't risking his liberty for anything connected with nine irons or nightingales. The reason - whatever it was - had to lie in the sprawl of sheds and buildings on the other side of the golf course fence where the shunting of wagons loaded with the profits of war rarely stopped.

*

The body by the railway line wasn't much of a mystery, not according to the first assessment of the British Transport Police sergeant who'd been called out. Edgar Crowther was raised near Blackrod so knew where to go when they said a corpse had been found by Kittie's Crossing.

He remembered damming the brook there as a kid, putting pennies on the track to be flattened by steam trains hammering up to Scotland or south to London. Now, with a gold clock ticking in his head, the contorted remains of a stranger lay amid his boyhood memories, guarded by a constable barely out of school himself.

'What makes people do something like this, Sir?'

'I try not to guess anymore,' Crowther said. 'But this one could just be an accident.'

'How's it possible to tell?'

'Bad crush marks on the right side of his head, see? Hit a glancing blow from a train on the south-bound line then spun round a couple of yards onto the embankment here, probably dead before hitting the ground.'

'So don't suicides do it like this?'

'No, they mostly lie down or jump… horrible, that is… not pleasant at all.'

A photographer came to take pictures of the body, face down in the dead flowers. Crowther could then turn it over and begin a search of the clothing for any documents to establish identity. The overalls were new but hadn't any outer pockets. He knelt to unbutton them from the neck and put his hand inside to check for any there. But he withdrew it quickly.

'Christ, this isn't a bloke, it's a woman.'

'Boiler suit's a funny outfit for a woman to be wearing in this weather, isn't it, Sir?'

'Maybe she batted for the other side. Her haircut's like a short back and sides.'

Within an hour, she was zipped into a rubber bag and carried across the fields to Anderton Services where the undertaker's recovery van was parked. Crowther hadn't found a single piece of paper, credit card, purse or car keys on her to give him a clue as to who she was, where she lived or what she did for a living.

'Don't like loose ends,' he said. 'This time next week, I want this poor soul in her grave and me and the wife to be away in the motor home, job finished.'

But he knew in his water that many a door would have to be knocked before this case could be signed off.

*

McCall fired off a few long distance stills of the weapons factory's complex of low brick buildings and concrete bunkers then sat back against a tree and rolled a joint. He took the smoke deep into his lungs and exhaled slowly.

A skylark rose from the long grass in front of him, spiralling ever higher till it bequeathed its song to the earth and vanished. It made him think of Etta's funeral and of Lexie - and why he wasn't by her bedside.

He'd the excuse of chasing Ruby's story. Yet that's all it was - an excuse. There was something about the promise of happiness he'd never bought.

But if he hoped smoking weed would give him clarity of thought on this or his other concerns, he was wrong. The revelations in Hoare's memo remained as tantalisingly unexplained as when he'd first read them.

Why did Inglis - a potential future prime minister - want a secret channel to the Ruby investigation? What crime had Benwick committed to make the spooks blackmail Hoare into finding him for them? And how would an armed fugitive like Benwick react when fronted by a hack he'd no reason to trust?

There was only one way to find out. Benwick - and whoever his wife might be - might soon arrive back at the country club. McCall had to get back there and find a discreet corner to wait for the detective's return.

But as he got to his feet, he heard a sound in the woods behind him. It was no more than a shoe scuffing the dried undergrowth. He turned quickly and saw a boy, maybe ten or eleven, in a grubby T-shirt, ripped jeans and old fashioned red leather sandals. McCall smiled with relief.

'Hi, you gave me a bit of a shock,' he said. 'You looking for lost golf balls?'

'Sometimes I do, yes.'

'You must be a very handy guy to have around the place.'

He didn't answer. McCall zipped his camera back into his briefcase and prepared to leave. But the boy kept looking at him as if he had something to say.

'Are you called Mr Mac?'

McCall tried not to show any surprise when he asked how the boy knew his name.

'The man told me it.'

'A man at reception, you mean?'

'No, the one from the other night, the one who ran away.'

'Sorry, I don't understand. Who ran away?'

'This man who wants to talk to you, they were chasing him on the railway.'

'I still don't understand but where is he?'

'He's in my den and he's hurt his foot and he told me to tell him if any strangers were knocking about so I told him about you and he sent me to get you.'

McCall was suddenly conscious of his own heart beat, sure that he knew who he was about to meet. He followed the boy further into Hardfield Wood. It was cool and shady.

The den was a tent of fallen branches propped up either side of a low hanging a tree. The boy held back, uncertain of his role in this puzzling grown-up affair.

McCall peered at the man in the hide-out. Amid a litter of newspapers and fish and chip wrappings and no longer looking like the modish Miami cops he copied, lay Detective Inspector Laurie Benwick of the Metropolitan Police.

He was unshaven and unwashed, wore a black boiler suit and could just have emerged from a three-day bender. His right ankle rested beneath a pack of frozen peas the boy must have brought to relieve the swelling. Benwick raised himself on his elbows and managed a grim smile.

'Cometh the hour, cometh the investigative journalist,' he said. 'Pull up a log... there isn't much time.'

Thirty One

Benwick gave the boy a fiver and sent him off on his bike to buy chocolate. A wary silence hung between the two men. Neither could have foreseen so bizarre a meeting. A bout of mutual shadow-boxing began to exploit whatever advantages might be had.

'Are you wired up, McCall?'

'No. Are you armed?'

'Yes, but don't worry about it.'

'At least we know where we stand.'

'Or lie...'

McCall let this pass. He had a hundred questions but started with the most obvious.

'What the hell's happened to you?'

'Don't they say no plan ever survives first contact with the enemy?'

'I'm fascinated by what the plan was and who the enemy is.'

'I'm damn sure you are.'

'For instance, I'm still trying to work out what role a Mrs Boland plays in your life.'

'There is no such person.'

'Really? So you're not Terry Boland and your *wife* isn't staying at the country club?'

'No and no.'

'But you are in a bind, aren't you?'

'Are you volunteering to help me out of it?'

'You'll be needing a magic carpet for that.'

'Know anyone who's got one?'

'Oddly enough, yes. I've left it up in the car park with a change of clothes.'

'Is that a fact? So what would a person have to do to get air lifted out of here?'

'Do you really need me to answer that?'

'No, I guess not.'

'Why else would I bust a gut trying to trace you?'

'I'm impressed that you did. You'd make a half decent detective given time.'

'I doubt it. I'm crap at following orders... a bit like you.'

Benwick smiled then said talking to a journalist crossed a very risky line for him.

'Do you have a choice?' McCall said. 'If you'd anyone else to save you from the shit you're in, you wouldn't have needed to show out to me.'

'Still doesn't mean I can trust you.'

'That's a judgement call for you. I would've thought your immediate worry is the kid telling someone about the mystery man in the woods, then you really are screwed.'

Benwick knew the truth of this already. He took a moment to make up his mind.

'The Ruby case is much more complicated than you can imagine.'

'I think I'd already worked that out.'

'OK, but you need to understand what it's about.'

'So tell me.'

'Power... political and financial and the abuse of that power for great advantage.'

'Give me a little taster, something for me to think on in case I end up in jail for helping you.'

'I know who kidnapped Ruby and why they did so,' Benwick said. 'It was me who rescued her and left her by the reservoir the day you found her.'

'If that's true, it's a damn good story.'

'For you, yes, but for me, what's in my head will get me murdered if I'm caught.'

'You're spinning me a line, aren't you? You're not being serious?'

'Never more so but keep this in mind, McCall. If you help me, you'll be in no less danger and even if you only stand up part of this story, I guarantee you'll never see it published.'

*

It was becoming more difficult for Hester to invent new reasons why Ruby should stay where she could be seen. Polishing, washing, ironing and the preparation of food to freeze for winter, were all being neglected. So were any number of seasonal gardening tasks which marked the calendar of Hester's days.

She had to devote her waking hours to Ruby's safety. But Ruby wanted the freedom to explore the house and to invent another world for herself in Garth Woods. She kept hiding from Hester though she wasn't playing. She'd scream and shout and stamp the floor when found.

'I don't like you. Don't like it here.'

'But Ruby, sweetheart, Lexie's coming home soon and Mac as well, so we'll all be back to normal then.'

'You leave me alone. Don't like you.'

'I know it's hard but we have to stay close together.'

'*They* made me stay in a room. I didn't like it.'

'Who, Ruby? Who made you stay in a room?'

'The ginger man.'

'Where did he do this?'

'He locked the door, we had no windows.'

'You poor child. But that's all over now, you're safe here with me.'

'I want to go out. The unicorn said he's coming to see me.'

Ruby ran across the orchard lawn like a creature released into the wild. Hester put away her mop and left the kitchen floor awash with dirty water then followed discreetly.

Ruby was already on her rope swing in the crown of ash trees, going back and forth, back and forth. What secrets lay within that disturbed little head, what pictures were hidden behind her eyes?

A rising wind began to shake the woods. Hester shivered slightly. Autumn's hold on summer weakened with every leaf which fell.

The taller trees swayed and through this noise of nature came Ruby's spectral little song... *and all will be well and all will be well and all will be well, well, well.*

*

Death and tragedy have their own routines, some easier to fulfil than others. Edgar Crowther's holding report into the fatality at Kittie's Crossing was necessarily brief as he'd yet to establish a name for the dead woman.

The deceased was a healthy female aged between 35 and 38. There were no documents on the body to assist with identification. Her clothing consisted of an overall or boiler suit, black in colour, but with no maker's label attached. This had been removed as had the labels from the under garments she wore. Her shoes were size five and of a sports variety or trainer and made by Nike. As such, they are widely on sale throughout the United Kingdom and elsewhere.

Dental records of known missing persons are being checked. The estimated time of death is consistent with the deceased having been struck above the right temple by the goods train which passed through Kittie's Crossing, Blackrod at 22.18 and going south. The signal man at Blackrod Junction estimates its speed at less than 15 mph by then due to a delay following a signal check at Adlington.

The engine was subsequently examined and traces of human blood and tissue have been found on the buffer on the driver's side i.e. the right side looking at the engine head-on, and this has now been forensically shown to be from the deceased.

The driver, Mr Towner, was interviewed but has no recollection of hitting any object, human or animal, anywhere on his route that night. The guard travelled in the rear cab as he objected to Mr Towner smoking so was not in a position to see anything.

There is no artificial illumination at Kittie's Crossing and the engine headlight would only have provided forward visibility of a few yards. The buffer centre is some 3 feet 5 inches above the rail, suggesting that the deceased, who was 5 feet 6 inches in height, was in a falling position at the moment of impact.

All vehicles parked at the Anderton Service Station nearby have been accounted for. Unfortunately, the close circuit TV within the service station area was down due to a malfunction. The pathologist is of the opinion that death was caused by cerebral haemorrhage following a severe concussive blow. He found no evidence of alcohol or drugs in the body to impair the deceased's judgement or actions on the night.

Crowther re-read his report then photocopied it. It went in a ring binder with other relevant documents and photographs to hand on to his inspector.

He wished it'd been a more open and shut affair to end to his no-fuss career. Not knowing who she was - that niggled a bit.

*

McCall's first task for Benwick was a spot of house cleaning for a non-existent guest at the country club. Jane, the receptionist, was very understanding. He said he'd now heard from his client, Mr Boland. His wife hadn't returned the previous night because she'd been taken to hospital with suspected appendicitis. Could her belongings be collected and her bill settled? Benwick had given him cash to cover it.

McCall asked for a receipt, not for Benwick but his own paper trail. He'd no intention of not getting this story in print or on the screen. But it would need careful midwifery and every piece of supporting legal corroboration he could lay his hands on.

'I do hope Mrs Boland recovers soon,' Jane said. 'Appendicitis is horrible, especially at her age.'

McCall nodded in agreement but her remark threw him slightly. It suggested someone elderly but he'd assumed Benwick's accomplice to be under forty like the man himself.

Jane summoned a porter to unlock the room and help McCall to carry down any luggage. He wasn't needed. Mrs Boland travelled light with just one expensive-looking leather suitcase. McCall tipped the porter and said he could manage alone.

The wardrobe contained a long sandy-coloured top coat, a few frumpy skirts and matching silk tops with high necks and ruffles. These were an older woman's outfits, confirmed by the unstylish flat shoes beneath the bed and a walking stick leaning against the writing table.

She'd left her handbag on there, too. McCall rooted inside and found lipstick, a comb and a wallet with a hundred and fifty pounds in it but no credit cards. Her passport was there, too.

It revealed her as Emily Jane Boland, British citizen born in London in 1922. That would make her 68, borne out by her passport photograph showing a care-worn face with intense brown eyes beneath cropped grey hair.

McCall fetched her toilet bag from the bathroom. It felt bulkier than it ought. He took out what was expected - tooth brush, tooth paste, deodorant, nail varnish and the like. Folded in a plastic bag beneath was a wig - grey and short - and a partial set of front upper dentures. But they'd not be found in a glass of water on any regular bedside cabinet. This was a prosthetic worn over natural teeth to completely change the wearer's appearance.

Alongside this was Mrs Boland's third theatrical aid - a bottle of liquid latex used by make-up artists to fake wrinkles - and add years - to an actor's face.

Benwick was right. There was no such person as Mrs Boland. Whatever the passport said, the woman claiming to be its holder wasn't old or frail enough to need a walking stick. But who was she - and what had she been plotting with Benwick?

Whatever the answer, McCall pocketed her passport and various disguises as tangible evidence. But of what, he still couldn't begin to guess.

*

Ruby hid under Lexie's hospital bed during the evening visit two days after her operation. Hester and a nurse tried to persuade her out but she refused. She'd only agreed to come after Hester promised to take her to a safari park if she put aside her fear of the *ginger man* and got in the Volkswagen for the drive to Shrewsbury.

'Why's Mac not here?' Lexie said.

'He's away at the moment, doing something about the Ruby business but he's been out of touch for a day or so, now.'

'It was always going to be like this... me coming second to some story or other.'

Hester knew enough about McCall's single-minded ways not to plead his case.

'How are you feeling, Lexie?'

'Pretty groggy. They've given me stuff for the pain... but it's not that so much.'

'What is it, then?'

'I don't feel I'm *me*, any more, Hester... all that I was has been taken away.'

'You'll adjust in time, I'm sure. Just think what the alternative would've been.'

'I know you're right, but it's just, well... '

'It's natural to feel a bit down after an anaesthetic. Takes a few weeks to recover.'

'McCall's still a son-of-a-bitch, isn't he?'

'Maybe you feel that right now but he's a good guy, really.'

'I think he's punishing me for what happened between us years ago.'

'No, I don't agree. I guess he just feels it's important to chase down this Ruby lead.'

'Really? Well, it might look like it's for Ruby's benefit but it'll really be for McCall's,' Lexie said. 'Anyway, enough of him. Could you put a call into my business partner in Bristol and give her a message to come and see me? I've got to make some plans for the future.'

Ruby suddenly re-appeared between them and said she wanted to go.

'It smells nasty in here,' she said. 'Everyone's going to die and I don't like it.'

*

Benwick stripped off his boiler suit to put on one of McCall's spare shirts and a pair of jeans. As he did, McCall lifted the detective's backpack. It was lumpy and heavy.

'What's in here?'

'Things that cause damage,' Benwick said. 'Don't mess with them.'

He didn't need to. He could feel a handgun and several small cardboard boxes. Which side was this guy really on? McCall wondered if Ruby's story was worth the grief coming his way for aiding the escape of a cop who'd turned terrorist. He might yet be writing his exclusive from behind bars.

Benwick came towards the boy and hunkered down, smiling like an uncle.

'Time to move on, Ronnie,' he said. 'But we're like blood brothers now, you and me.'

Ronnie nodded, uncertain and embarrassed.

'So you'll not be telling anyone about our secret, will you?'

The boy swore he wouldn't and Benwick slipped him a twenty pound note.

'But if you break your promise, one of my soldiers will be round to your house... you understand what would happen, don't you?'

Ronnie nodded but looked terrified.

'OK, good man.'

Benwick then went into the woods to pee. The kid turned to McCall.

'He won't, will he? Not send a soldier after me?'

'I don't know what he'll do so you just better keep your mouth shut.'

'But I saw them, the soldiers.'

'What soldiers?'

'In the gunpowder factory, where it all happened.'

'Where what happened?'

'Where the shunting engine hit the other man, the one who couldn't run away.'

McCall heard Benwick limping back through the undergrowth towards them before Ronnie could explain any more.

He got the boy to whisper his home phone number then scribbled it down and said he'd ring him in a few days.

Benwick began gathering up all his litter so no sign of his stay in the den remained. It was nearly dark by then. All the golfers had returned to the clubhouse. Benwick straddled the boy's bike for McCall to push him along the edge of the trees to the car park. They shook hands with Ronnie and watched him pedal off into the night.

'What was all that about about your soldiers?'

'All in good time, McCall. We need to find a shop that sells pain killers.'

'Your ankle?'

'Yeah, good job my dance card's empty this evening.'

Thirty minutes later, they pulled up outside a late night convenience store. McCall left Benwick in the car checking a road atlas and went inside for the pills. Once he was alone, Benwick put the map aside and tuned in to Radio Lancashire for the local news headlines. The second item was of interest.

British Transport Police are still trying to identify the body of a woman in her thirties found by the railway line at Kittie's Crossing near Blackrod. They are appealing for witnesses or for anyone with information to come forward.

Benwick thought they'd be well advised not to hold their collective breath.

Thirty Two

It was getting late for anyone to knock at Garth Hall. Hester, tense enough already, looked down from her bedroom window. A man with a stiff, military bearing stood on the drive, hands behind his back, his face serious. He'd been brought to the house in a dark Range Rover by a driver who stayed in the vehicle. It all looked too official to ignore. Hester opened up but left the door on its chain.

'I'm sorry to trouble you at this time of night, Miss Lloyd, but this is most urgent.'

'How do you know my name? What's this about?'

'Our friend, McCall, I'm afraid.'

'What's happened to him?'

'Nothing yet but he's in some danger. Might I come in and explain?'

'You've not told me who you are.'

'Sorry, I'm Roly Vickers. I've known McCall for years.'

'He's never mentioned you.'

'Possibly not but I was also a friend of Francis Wrenn, the man who brought him up.'

'Maybe you were but you're still not coming in.'

Vickers hid his exasperation behind a strained smile.

'As you wish but I've come to tell you that the authorities believe McCall is with a man wanted in connection with an assassination in Belgium. This man is armed and very dangerous and it's in McCall's best interest that both of them are found.'

'What have you got to do with all this?'

'As I knew McCall and his people, it was thought you might help me locate him.'

'The police have already been here over a suspicious death some place down south now you're saying there's another in Belgium? For God's sake, he's a journalist, not some crazy killer.'

'But he often gets into scrapes and as scrapes go, this one could wreck his career.'

'I'm sorry but I can't help you.'

'Can't - or won't?'

'Take your pick, mister. You're getting nothing from me.'

'If that's your final word, be aware that you're doing McCall no favours,' Vickers said. 'By the way, I hope little Ruby is being well looked after in all this dreadful business. You wouldn't want the authorities to take her into care, would you?'

*

For the very first time in their friendly arrangement, Hester resented McCall. He'd no right to expect her to continue holding the fort on her own. His world wasn't hers. It threatened her, made her feel anxious in the very place where she'd finally found peace of mind.

'Ruby, sweetheart, I'm so sorry but we've got to go out.'

Ruby was in bed and almost asleep. Hester raised her into a sitting position and put a

coat over her pyjamas then slipped her trainers on.

'Don't want to,' Ruby said. 'Go away.'

Hester carried her downstairs and into the camper van.

'We'll only be gone a few minutes but I've got to make a phone call.'

She drove to the kiosk from where she'd rung McCall's new mobile before. Ruby screamed and kicked the dashboard. None of what was happening was the kid's fault. She needed calm and security but was getting neither. Hester locked her in the van and dialled McCall. When he answered, she told him about Roly Vickers putting pressure on her to reveal McCall's whereabouts.

'The little rat even suggested Ruby could be taken from us.'

'Look, I can't talk now. I'll be home as soon as I can but I don't know when.'

'I can't take much more of this, Mac, not all these threats and this talk of killings.'

'What killings?'

'Vickers says you're with a man who's wanted for assassinating someone. He says you're in danger and that's why they need to find you.'

'I can't explain his reasons now but what Vickers says isn't right.'

'I don't know what to believe any more. Only little Ruby matters in all this. Her and Lexie. I think you're forgetting what's important in your life, Mac.'

As Hester left the phone box, she was observed from a chauffeured Range Rover parked unseen in a field entrance. She'd done exactly what Vickers told his associates she would - called McCall's new mobile from a public phone.

She would've been warned by him that their line at Garth Hall wasn't secure.

So now their source at British Telecom could *de-pip* the number she'd rung and get it for them. With this, another contact in the mobile phone network would quickly triangulate McCall's location to within fifty yards. Wherever he was, the rogue detective wouldn't be far away.

*

McCall was finding it difficult to concentrate. Vickers leaning so hard on Hester - that bothered him. He'd wanted Benwick flushed into the open. When McCall hadn't played ball, Vickers turned nasty - not least in regard to Ruby. So who was he really running with?

More immediately, McCall had no idea where he and Benwick were driving. They'd travelled south from the golf club on minor roads. After about twenty miles, Benwick told him to turn into a thinly populated stretch of flat, wooded farmland. He seemed to know the area. They bumped along a dirt track towards a tangled hedge of alders and hawthorn.

Tucked behind were a corrugated iron implement shed and a small barn-like structure, almost overwhelmed by ivy.

'Pull into the shed,' Benwick said. 'Then kill the lights.'

'What is this place?'

'Just a little port in a storm.'

McCall parked then Benwick led the way into the barn. It had once been a kitchen and sleeping area for seasonal agricultural labourers. There was no electricity, just candles and a paraffin lamp.

But it had a cast iron range with charred wood in the grate from a recent fire. On the hob were a kettle and a brown tea pot and on the table, a plastic pannier of water, mugs, plates and cutlery.

'The Ritz it ain't,' he said. 'But we'll be OK roughing it here for a while.'

'What about whoever owns it, the farmer?'

'He knows me as a bird watcher, doesn't mind me using it.'

McCall couldn't immediately think of a reply. It was endearing, if puzzling, that a rogue detective who might yet turn out to be an assassin or a spy, should have so gentle a side to his character. But the terrorist, like the paedophile, is always a guy next door, the quiet one who goes unnoticed.

The barn had a single small window with a potato sack nailed over it as a rough curtain. Benwick pulled it aside and scanned the darkened landscape with a pair of military night vision binoculars from his backpack.

'You think we were followed?' McCall said.

'No, but I want to make sure.'

Benwick then began screwing up newspaper to start a fire with the sticks and split logs piled in the hearth. Some of the pages carried dispatches about Iraq's advance into Kuwait so were almost a month old. This must have been one of Benwick's long term bolt holes.

'It's going to be a long night,' he said. 'When this fire gets going, I'll boil some water for some tea and warm up a can of soup and there's bread, too, if the mice haven't got in the bread bin. Got to keep our strength up for the chase, haven't we?'

Benwick appeared almost euphoric, as if relishing playing a fox outwitting his pursuers. But McCall needed to know why they were being hunted.

'At some point, you're going to tell me what the hell is going on, aren't you?'

'Don't worry, you'll find out soon enough.'

*

Lexie, fading in and out of consciousness in the dimly lit ward, felt she was being digested in the belly of the beast. The essence of her very self had been torn out and devoured. Like the purblind victims around her, she would eventually pass through the system - but none as they had entered it. And not all would survive.

Yet on this night, she had to cling to the hope that she would, albeit life as she'd known it would be in remission. But she'd made a start on whatever future she had. Her business partner had driven over from Bristol. Agreements had been made, documents signed. There had to be something to plan for and Lexie knew now what it must be.

*

McCall and Benwick sat either side of the fire. The wind cut through the silver birch trees shivering beyond the barn and howled around the chimney. Neither man wanted to be the first to speak. Both knew the advantage silence gave against anyone seeking   information they'd rather not divulge. Yet this was different. Each had need of the other - and to give ground.

They'd eaten and were getting warm. Benwick poked at the logs. They cracked and sparked and threw ever bizarre shadows on a scene that was weird enough already. He reached into his rucksack for a half bottle of brandy and offered first swig to McCall.

'So, you want a bit of the back story to all this drama, do you?' Benwick said.

'I think I'm owed that much, don't you? A sort of payment in kind.'

Benwick took his pull of brandy as he considered his next words.

'Did you ever hear of a police investigation called Operation Kid Glove?'

'No, what was that about?'

'The sexual abuse of young children, not just by the usual grubby little perverts but a few seriously influential people.'

'Really? Like who?'

'Some politicians... high ranking household names, rarely off the TV some of them.'

'I don't remember reading about any of this in the papers.'

'No, you wouldn't.'

'Why not? They were committing crimes, weren't they?'

'The case never got to court, that's why.'

'You mean the evidence wasn't there?'

'No, there was plenty of that. The investigation was deliberately sabotaged.'

'In what way?'

'Some exhibits and statements went missing, witnesses changed their stories or just disappeared then as the arrests were being planned, guys in suits turned up at the nick early one morning and took away every incriminating file and every cop's notebook.'

'So it was covered-up?'

'Too bloody right it was. Someone, somewhere decided it wasn't in the national interest to pull down these pillars of society. That's what power and influence buys you, McCall. We're all equal under the law but some are more equal than others.'

'I get that but who were these MPs and why were they being protected?'

'Sorry, but you and I have a way to go before I'll give you chapter and verse.'

'I see... so you're just baiting the hook, then?'

'Only so that you'll understand there's a link between these untouchable politicians and little Ruby Ross.'

'For Christ's sake, you can't just leave a claim like that hanging in the air.'

'All I'm going to say for now is that if the cops on Operation Kid Glove hadn't had their balls cut off, those who put Ruby through her wicked ordeal would have still been locked up.'

Thirty Three

Benwick's words were edged with genuine anger, controlled but evident in his eyes. It seemed to McCall that the intensity of his feelings was rooted in something deeper than professional animus alone.

He was coming across as a man starting to make sense of himself to his priest for the night. If his past actions seemed incomprehensible, he might now offer context if only to keep McCall inside the tent while it suited.

Nothing of what he'd hinted at so far explained why he carried a gun or from what - or whom - he was running, still less his interest in a munitions factory. But this might come with patience.

'You'll have gathered I'm out in the cold,' Benwick said. 'But if I'm to tell you things I shouldn't, then you must be just as open with me.'

'What do you want to know?'

'How you found me... and this isn't just about my injured pride because you did, it's more about my neck.'

Benwick wasn't alone in having concerns about personal well-being. McCall didn't feel bad about holding back on the whole story.

'I saw the postcard you sent to Malky Hoare,' McCall said. 'This helped me to trace the hotel where you'd stayed in Blackrod then I asked around and dropped on someone who'd heard you went bird-watching near the weapons factory.'

'You're saying your first clue was Hoare showing you my postcard?'

'No, he didn't show it to me. I found it when I found his body.'

He stared at McCall even more intently as the implication of his words registered.

'Hoare's dead?'

McCall nodded.

'Christ, I thought the Lord above was supposed to look out for drunks and fools.'

'Well, Fleet Street's got plenty of both so even He would be hard pushed to keep up.'

'Was it natural causes?'

'It looked like it to me,' McCall said. 'Why wouldn't it be?'

Benwick fell quiet again but hardly with grief. It began to rain, steadily enough to seep through the barn's dislodged slates and drip on the floor by the window. He took another mouthful of brandy then came at McCall from left field.

'You've got a source, a man called Roly Vickers.'

'Have I?'

'Yes, a publisher, does books written by communist bloc defectors once they've been pressed dry of all useful information by the British and need a bit of extra money paid by the back door.'

McCall stayed as expressionless as he could but was alarmed that his contact with Vickers wasn't the secret he'd always taken it to be.

'How do you know him?'

'I swam in a small pond, McCall. Vickers might have always appeared to be your friend but he's a dangerous man to know.'

'Meaning what, exactly?'

'That he's an agent of influence for the spooks, does deniable favours for them when they'd rather not show their hand. Because of that, I don't think it was my postcard which steered you to me, I think it was Roly Vickers.'

This was Benwick displaying strength while probing for weakness.

'You must think what you want,' McCall said. 'But why would it concern you if he had given me a leg up?'

'I'll answer that once you prove your loyalty.'

'Why do I need to prove loyalty to you?'

'Because like it or not, we're in this mess together. We stand united or fall separately.'

'Does this mess involve you being mixed up in an assassination in Belgium back in March?'

'If that's what Roly Vickers told you then he was slipping you a *FUD*.'

'A what?'

'A FUD... the creation of fear, uncertainty and doubt among your enemies by the use of disinformation. It's this relationship you have with Vickers which bothers me.'

McCall waited. There were times when a denial as to a matter of fact or falsehood could be equally incriminating. This was one of them.

'I'm not sure how much I can trust you, McCall. You're quite amoral. You'd cut a deal with the devil himself if it got you the story you wanted.'

'Once upon a time, maybe.'

'Oh, really? That doesn't sound like the guy who once had nerve enough to run around some of the nasty countries where Vickers sent you on errands. Not exactly friendly to Her Majesty's Government, were they?'

'Good stories often happen in bad places.'

'Sure, but information is the currency traded by spy and journalist alike, isn't it?'

'What are you getting at?'

'You don't really need me to answer that. Still, I guess all the exclusive stories old Roly put your way in return made the risks worthwhile.'

McCall winced at the professionally damaging truth of this. Benwick could hold a gun to his head in more ways than one.

*

Lexie, weak and dosed with analgesics, couldn't be sure if the words going round her head were remembered from a script, a song or a book.

You've got to be lost before you can be found. Only now, capsized by disease and surgery and obliged to audit the ungrounded life she had lived, did she see their relevance to her.

She'd always presented an image of confident fulfilment. Yet lying in hospital on that sleepless night, Lexie was confronted not just by the fiction of such apparent self-belief but the vacuity of her life, of time wasted and mortality itself. She sensed a curtain coming down on all she had known and had been.

The slow, electronic tick of the ward clock came through the sighs and groans of other patients. In the bed by Lexie, the breath of an elderly woman guttered in and out from the rafters of bones which were her chest. The tired skin of her face sank into the many hollows of the skull within. And yet a lover might once have craved those lips, blue and bloodless now in this, the dimming of her day.

Who was she? What was her story? Something about her suggested a likeness to Lexie's mother - and to how she herself might yet become. Maybe they could exchange a word or a smile after breakfast for who will remember any of us in the end - and for what? We all walk the cobbles of the same coffin path, each weighed down along the way by different burdens.

Lexie was never sentimental but her emotions no longer seemed under control. Try as she might, she couldn't fend off the mood of remorse and regret welling within her.

Thirty Four

'All right, so you've got some black on me,' McCall said. 'But don't tell me you always played by the rules when you were an undercover cop.'

'Who says I was a UC... Roly Vickers?'

'Believe it or not, I do have other sources.'

Benwick stretched out his damaged leg towards the fire and took his time finishing the last of the brandy.

'OK, McCall... I'll tell you what's relevant to Ruby but don't push for any more.'

Benwick read linguistics at university then worked at the Foreign Office. Diplomacy was dull so he joined the police. He spoke Russian and some Arabic so was fast-tracked through the ranks.

'I'm walking to the tube one morning and - bang, I'm grabbed from behind, my eyes and mouth get taped over, hands bound and I'm shoved in the boot of a car, scared shitless that some terrorists had got me.'

'That can't have been pleasant.'

'No, but the car finally stops then I'm put into something like a metal coffin and left there. When it's finally opened and my eyes get uncovered, some guy's standing over me having a smoke and he says "...you'll do. Welcome to S.O.10."'

'To what?'

'Special Operations ten, the Met's undercover unit.'

'Quite some job interview.'

'Yes, but they needed to see how much stress I could take before I started gibbering.'

'Why did they choose you in the first place?'

'I guess I'd not been a cop long enough to look or sound like one.'

'Or were a plausible liar?'

'A useful attribute in both our trades, McCall.'

'Touché.'

'Anyway, I was given the identity of a boy who'd died young and I used his name to build a phoney legend with bank cards, rented flat, driver's licence, the lot.'

'So if any background checks were made, you'd look kosher?'

'Right, but I was really in a repertory company run by the cops.'

'Did you enjoy the work?'

'Loved it, living on nerves and adrenaline, being privy to secrets. All so addictive.'

'So how did this lead to you investigating Ruby's case as a regular detective?'

Benwick threw more logs on the fire and said it started by him being assigned a role as a lobbyist, cultivating new sources in Westminster.

'I hooked into this really strange guy fronting a freelance dirty tricks campaign for the benefit of the Labour Party,' he said. 'Always in the market for any dirty gossip about Tory MPs, boozing, extra marital affairs, stuff like that. Every

Tuesday, he'd hold court in a curry house in Soho and buy lunch for anyone who delivered the goods.'

'What did he do with this gossip?'

'If it came up to snuff, he'd plant embarrassing stories in the papers. He was a bit like Vickers in that way, a cut-out for those who wanted to keep in the shadows.'

Benwick registered this new snout as *Auric* because his information was '...as good as gold'. Auric told him about a young trade union official who arrived one lunchtime, very agitated. He claimed his boss had turned him into a rent boy for the pleasure of some well connected guests at private parties at a house in Clapham, south London.

'And he wasn't a rent boy before?' McCall said.

'Possibly, anyway he named two Conservative politicians who'd sexually assaulted him, one openly gay the other, a real high flyer marked out for high office, unmarried but supposedly straight.'

'What was his motive for talking?'

'He'd been fired after a big row over pay with his boss.'

'And the union's motive for allegedly pimping him to the MPs?'

'He claimed they wanted the high flyer in their pocket, in other words to have enough on him to be able to persuade him into always seeing things the union's way if he and the Tories came to power.'

'To blackmail him? That's quite a story if it's true. But how do we know this young bloke wasn't some fantasist with a persecution complex?'

'Fair point but his allegations didn't stop there. He provided information about some young girls and boys being procured for these parties, too.'

'Being sexually abused by these politicians, you mean?'

'Yes, and used in vile photographs and videos.'

'Who were these kids?'

'Most of them had troubled backgrounds, lived in care homes or lived rough so they'd been deliberately targeted for that reason and given drugs and alcohol and a few quid for their pains. If they'd complained, no one would've taken any notice because kids like them are seen as worthless anyway.'

'But Auric believed his informant?'

'He did because he signed a statement with names, dates, times and because he also agreed to talk to me - me being a lobbyist, of course.'

'Did you find him a credible witness?'

'That's it - I never got to meet him face to face. He died of a heroin overdose before we could set up a meet.'

'So the source was an aggrieved ex-employee, a drug user and a rent boy. Dead or alive, you must have seriously worried about his reliability as a witness.'

'I would've agreed with you most times but he was about to bring down some mighty powerful people.'

'You think his death could have been suspicious?'

'His body wasn't found for two months so whether it was an accidental overdose or murder couldn't be established.'

'So you were snookered?'

'Yes but the same devious politicians who'd escaped Operation Kid Glove were still at it and I was damned if they were going to get away with it a second time.'

'Not when one of them was a possible future prime minister?'

'I take it that's an educated guess?'

'Nothing more,' McCall said. 'So you knew perfectly well who Guy Inglis was when he turned up at the reservoir with those other MPs?'

'Of course... and don't think for a minute that was a random inspection. Inglis was there to sniff out anything on our Ruby enquiry.'

Before McCall could question him further or show him Ruby's drawings, they both heard a noise outside. Something heavy was knocked over. Benwick motioned McCall to stay still and quiet. He went to the window with his night sights.

'There's a guy running away... and a car, no, two cars. We've got to move, McCall.'

They grabbed their bags and hurried to the shed. Benwick unlocked a cabin-like structure in the corner and heaved out an off-road motorbike. McCall looked on, ever more intrigued by the extraordinary degree of Benwick's forward planning.

'Can you ride one of these things?'

'Years ago I could.'

'Then start remembering - and quick. My ankle isn't up to it.'

'Got everything you want out of your car?'

'There's that suitcase from the hotel in it, why?'

Benwick didn't reply but unscrewed the fuel cap, stuffed a rag inside and set it alight.

'What the hell are you doing? That's not my car and all my evidence is in it.'

'Tough shit, McCall. Just get the bloody bike started.'

Then he went to the door of the barn, took something like a grenade from his back pack and threw it towards the fireplace.

'We've got thirty seconds at most.'

McCall's survival instincts took over. He rode the bike out into the open. Benwick clambered on the pillion. They careered onto a muddy track leading across the field to the birch woods on the far side.

Less than half way there, an explosive flash turned night into day for two or three seconds. Chunks of car, metal and masonry were hurled into the air. A shock wave hit the motorbike and they almost keeled over. They skidded and swerved but made the cover of the trees as burning debris cascaded down around them.

When they stopped to look back, the ruins of the barn and implement shed were engulfed in fire which was boiling into a plume of dirty black smoke. Benwick's face had the satisfied look of a wartime saboteur. Yet again, McCall queried the wisdom of joining forces with a psychopath.

'Christ, you could've killed those guys.'

'They'd be no bloody loss.'

'But they're MI5 men. They'll never let you get away with this now.'

'You're wrong, McCall. I *am* going to get away with it - and they're *not* spooks.'

'So who the hell are they?'

'Think of them as undertakers.'

'*Undertakers*?'

'Yeah, guys who've been sent to bury the evidence.'

'Evidence of what?'

'Of what's behind Ruby's kidnapping. And if we don't get going, they'll bury us, too.'

Thirty Five

That afternoon - and against medical advice - Lexie insisted on being discharged from hospital. A young junior doctor from Australia, sun-tanned and lifeguard fit, tried to talk her round.

'Lexie, as ideas go, this one hasn't got a pulse.'

There was a time when she wouldn't have had such a man just sitting on her bed.

'If you leave us too soon, you'll be running a serious risk of possible complications.'

'If I don't, I'll be running a serious risk of going nuts,' Lexie said.

'You're suffering from a touch of post-operative depression which means you shouldn't rush to make any decision you might regret later.'

'Thanks but I can't take the deathly atmosphere in this place any more.'

Hester arrived with Ruby soon after. The child seemed even more withdrawn. She crouched on the floor staring into the middle distance as if she were somewhere else and completely alone. She was still wetting the bed at Garth, too. Hester was hardly her usual tranquil self, either. It wasn't difficult to figure out who was to blame for almost everything.

'McCall can't be up to any good,' Hester said. 'The police are after him and some guy who came to the house says he's involved with some assassin. Jeez, but I'm at my wit's end with worry about what the future holds for any of us.'

Lexie saw her looking at Ruby as she said this. If she had any doubt about discharging herself, they disappeared then. She signed a form releasing the health service from any liability before a nurse pushed her to Hester's van in a hospital wheelchair.

Ruby remained locked in her private space on the drive back. Lexie tried to ignore her own discomfort and talk to her instead. She barely got a word of reply. They might have been strangers - but what else was Ruby but a child Lexie didn't really know?

*

Hester's chicken soup could heal the sick and comfort the weary. Lexie was both and sat with a bowl of it on her lap by the Aga in the comfort and warmth of Garth Hall's old kitchen.

Hanging from nails in the beams above were bundles of herbs from Hester's physic garden - coriander, dill, thyme, oregano - drying out and giving off a faint aroma of lemons and dried earth.

Ruby had been drawing at the kitchen table but was now in bed. Before going, she'd fixed Lexie with her quizzical stare and said hospital had made her look different.

'It's like I told you, sweetie, I've had an operation,' Lexie said. 'Part of my tummy has been taken away so it'll be a little while before I can feel right again.'

'Babies come out of your tummy so that means you won't have any.'

'That's right, but I've still got you, haven't I?'

Ruby didn't react to what had just been said. She simply gave Lexie the pencil drawing she'd just finished.

This was no *mask of youth* flattery but Ruby's unforgiving take on Lexie as she'd become - face much thinner, lines more numerous, eyes darker-ringed, her hair lacking all bounce.

'You're so clever and artistic,' Lexie said. 'I'll get this framed when I'm better.'

'You look very old when you don't paint your face.'

Hester was accustomed to Ruby's disregard for the sensitivities of others. But in Lexie's fragile state, it could hurt. Yet that wasn't all that was painful. She feared McCall's continued absence seemed like a callous lack of concern for his girlfriend.

A call Hester had made to his mobile from the phone box before supper had brought no reply. She'd wanted to tell him Lexie was home and ask again when he might be joining them.

'He's been away for five days now and I'm dreading what we'll hear next.'

'Something's wrong, it has to be,' Lexie said. 'If it wasn't, I'm sure he'd have written to us or found some other way of getting in touch.'

'You've changed your tune. You were calling him a son of a bitch a few days ago.'

'I've had time to think since.'

'So have I and McCall's hardly behaving like a New Man, is he?'

'He'll never be that,' Lexie said. 'He's more of a reconditioned sort of guy, one with several careless owners... like me, for instance.'

As an admission of responsibility for anything, still less for screwing up McCall's early life, this was a first for Lexie. But Hester was too tense to notice.

'All I know is I'm picking up a really threatening vibe around here which I've never experienced before in my time at Garth.'

Lexie could do without any New Age flim flam. She was already too uncomfortably close to the other side as it was.

'I'm truly sorry the pressure's all been on you but we've got to decide which is safer for us all - to stay here or go away for a time.'

'What do you mean? Go where?'

'I'm thinking of moving to Norfolk.'

'That's the other side of England.'

'I know but my ex-husband has just bought the cottage over there where we all spent happy times years ago. He told me on the phone the other night and now he's saying I

should go there to convalesce. But I'd need you and Ruby to come with me.'

'That'd mean uprooting her again.'

'So you'd rather have her freaking out over some man following her around here and thinking she's going to be kidnapped again?'

''Course not, but what about all the responsibilities I have as housekeeper at Garth?'

'You mean where you're now scared to death every time there's a knock at the door or the phone rings?'

Hester considered the options. She'd no wish to admit her Oregon Trail spirit was failing her. Threats - implied or imagined - had wormed their way into her mind. What before had been the endearing creaks of Garth Hall's ancient oak frame or its shifting floorboards now assumed the menace of an intruder's footfall.

McCall's career always required he head towards trouble. This time, it'd come looking for him. His house was no longer a refuge for Hester. She didn't feel safe being there alone with Ruby any more.

'OK, let's go to Norfolk... if you're sure you can cope with all the travelling.'

'I can and you'll love it,' Lexie said. 'It'll be wild and stormy and we can have long walks along the beach and be miles away from everything that's worrying you.'

They were both tired and it was late. It was an effort for Lexie to climb the stairs. She paused outside the room Hester shared with Ruby.

'I'd like to ask a favour,' Lexie said. 'Don't get me wrong, but would you mind if I slept with you in your bed?'

'Would I mind? No, if that's what you'd like to do.'

'It's because I just feel... I feel like I've never been so alone in all my born days.'

So they lay together in Hester's big brass and iron bed. Lexie wanted to be held, needed the warmth of another human being, someone who would stroke her hair and kiss away the tears which came again like those of a child frightened in the night.

Thirty Six

Benwick snored from the top bunk in the flat where he and McCall were now holed up. If the sin starts with the thought not the deed, Benwick must have done a deal of thinking of late. No one should lay money on him ever getting into heaven.

Something else was clear to McCall. Whatever Benwick's game, he wasn't acting alone. His fall-back arrangements to out-run those who would catch and kill him required not just savvy trade craft but a covert support network. So why put its security at risk by letting a hack in on the secret?

Young Ronnie Stansfield had part of the answer. He'd seen an engine on the weapons factory railway hit someone - *the one who couldn't run away.*

This was Benwick's female accomplice, the mysterious Mrs Boland. Whatever they'd been trying to pull off went disastrously wrong. Benwick, resourceful as ever, had a Plan B. But it needed two people to carry it out - and he was crocked with a sprained ankle. And all the while, those he feared most were closing in. Then McCall arrived, a useful idiot willing to play get-away driver in exchange for bits of background on Ruby's case.

From the law's perspective, McCall was guilty of assisting a fugitive to endanger life and fire-bomb two buildings. He could still quit before the crap closed over his head. If he did, he'd have a chance to chase up Benwick's leads about the paedophile politicians and the sabotaged police investigation.

The newspapers would devour that, even if it gave every libel lawyer in Fleet Street the vapours. And if McCall got arrested, he'd get the sort of heroic publicity hacks crave, maybe a book or even a *Panorama* special.

Against this, he hadn't anything like the full story yet, not according to Benwick. But underlying all, McCall was no less addicted to risk-taking than him. He was strapped in on the scariest ride of his life and nothing could tempt him to jump off yet.

For the moment, he'd too much brain-whizz to rest. He made himself tea in the flat's small kitchenette then brought his notes up to date.

M/bike from big bang through birch woods. Side roads only to Roundhay, Leeds. Arrived red brick semi, early hours. House number 33, street name not seen. M/bike hidden under tarp in garage.

Benwick known to male occupier, me not introduced. They spoke only in Russian. Man looked fit, sixties, balding, lean, five feet ten, wary eyes. Dished up salt beef, dark brown bread, vodka.

Kitchen like a landfill, no female? Slept in easy chairs, untidy front room, woke late afternoon. Washed at kitchen sink, had coffee, biscuits.

Man came back with two sets workmen's outfits, second hand donkey jackets, jeans, caps, industrial rubber gloves, boots. Our clothes left behind. Man put back seats down in Volvo estate, silver, 'E' reg. We lay under blankets. Drove east about ninety minutes. Arrived Barton, little town on Humber estuary, in darkness.

Man parked near pub, White Swan, went off, returned with small bag of groceries and keys to flat over empty shop in Fleetgate then left. What the hell next? Port of Hull just across river. Russian timber ships dock there.

Is Benwick going to defect on one? If so, why do I need to be dressed like a docker, as well as him?

*

Dawn wouldn't be long coming, presaged by a late autumn mist from the North Sea, unfurling like a white silk scarf over the tiled roofs of Barton's quiet streets. Curtains were still drawn and cats kept watch from the walls of gardens where they weren't welcome. Some shops had been boarded up, others appeared shabby and in need of paint and custom.

It looked like a place having a lean time, a place probably best seen in a rear view mirror on the way to somewhere else.

Standing at the window of the meanly furnished room, McCall was acutely aware of the drama taking uncertain form around him. Across the street, those soon to wake into that miserable morning could eventually read about them in their papers, the strangers who stole in during the night to hide where nothing exciting ever happened.

McCall heard the loo flush then Benwick refilling the kettle at the kitchen sink. He joined him. Benwick asked why he couldn't sleep.

'Not knowing what the bloody hell's happening could be something to do with it.'

'Soon, McCall, soon. What would you like for breakfast?'

'Smoked salmon, scrambled eggs, lightly done toast and my grapes peeled.'

'That'll be bread and jam for two, then. You make the tea and I'll do the rest then we should talk.'

*

About one hundred miles south, the same North Sea waves humped and broke on the beach by Staithe End. The fog which came with them slowly evaporated leaving a nacreous sheen across the watery sweep of sand beyond the dunes.

Hester had been looking out of a window, too. How strange, how different it seemed to be staying in such a doll's house of a cottage. Its entire footprint would fit in the panelled drawing room at Garth Hall with space to spare.

But immediately Hester stepped inside, she'd heard *its* voices - the words of the long dead, lingering where they'd been uttered and audible only to those wise enough to listen. Yet amid these murmurs was a whisper from deep within her own self, the idea that now was the right time to leave the hills and find the sea.

She felt easier in her mind at Staithe End, sensed no shadows darkening its whitened walls and rough-sawn beams as they had at Garth.

Those who'd once dwelt here were humbler, too - land workers, fishermen, families far removed from the intrigues of their day. They'd lived by toil and sweat, weathered storms and been as content as ever those hard times allowed such people to be.

Lexie was still resting in bed. The journey from the Welsh Marches had been more arduous than she'd predicted. But nearing Staithe End and the sound of the sea, her face eased with relief and happiness as if she had truly come home.

For Ruby, what was supposed to be a holiday meant only disruption to the ordered routines she imposed on her life. She retreated further from the grown-ups, sullen and refusing to eat. But she'd brought her pads and pencils and Hester felt sure she could talk her round in a day or two.

It still worried her that Ruby displayed no concern for the pain Lexie was in. It wasn't clear if this lack of empathy was part of Ruby's psychological condition or simply revealed a dislike of her aunt.

Hester checked the weather again. Norfolk was all sky and luffing clouds. Rain might yet pluck at the waves and empty the beach of its walkers. But when Hester took up her breakfast, that's exactly how Lexie said she'd love it to be.

'I want to go out in a storm and gather armfuls of driftwood,' she said. 'Then we can carry it back and sit and watch it burn in the hearth.'

*

McCall was tetchy from lack of sleep, a workhouse breakfast and the growing certainty of spending time in those parts of a police station where the windows didn't open. Benwick must soon deliver on his promise to make this coming unpleasantness worthwhile.

'When Ruby first went missing, why did you suspect her mother?'

'Because I knew Etta was involved in a very black economy.'

'You mean she was a hooker?'

Benwick shook his head.

'Not just that though I'm sure she was at that, too. No, unbelievable as it sounds, some of the kids being abused by the paedophile ring I was scoping had been rented out by their mothers to be filmed or photographed by the half hour.'

'You're saying Etta was doing this?'

'Holding picture sessions in her flat, yes. Ruby Ross was one of the kids' names the rent boy picked up while flying the flag for his union, so to speak.'

'What could possibly make any woman do that?'

'Money, great wads of it,' Benwick said. 'There's an international trade in such images and if a mother is desperate enough for whatever reason, she'll be blind to the harm being done.'

'But you only had the rent boy telling you this?'

'Yep, in his statement to the dirty tricks guy.'

'His word alone couldn't be trusted, could it? You'd need independent corroboration.'

Benwick agreed. But when a child called Ruby Ross went missing, Benwick called in a favour and was transferred back to CID to take over the investigation.

'I went to Etta's flat and showed her the surveillance pictures of the men who'd figured in Operation Kid Glove. She'd let at least one of these perverts photograph her own child for money. She never broke down completely but I knew damn well she was covering up something.'

'Like her killing Ruby, you mean?'

'Think about it, McCall. Here's a little girl who doesn't know how to tell lies, not even social ones. At some point, she'll let the cat out of the bag to a teacher or a doctor then Etta loses her daughter, her home, liberty, everything.'

'But a motive for murder turned out to be a motive for suicide.'

'I know, that was never in my script but it pointed to a wider conspiracy.'

McCall reached into his rucksack. He took out some of Ruby's artwork and put the drawing of the birth mark man on the table between them.

'Did that conspiracy involve this particular individual?'

'Good God, Ray Gillespie. Who drew this?'

'Ruby, she's an amazingly talented kid. She's drawn quite a few faces of the men who might've abused her but this one really scares her. She thinks he follows her.'

'Gillespie was the one who took pictures of Ruby,' Benwick said. 'Etta was terrified when I showed her the sneaky photographs of him.'

'Was it Gillespie who kidnapped Ruby?'

'I'd be hard pushed to prove it in court but as night follows day, yes... he did it.'

'But why run such a huge risk if Etta was already letting pictures be taken of Ruby?'

'Try to understand how quickly paedophiles get desensitised. They always need bigger and better kicks, more depravity to meet their deviant sexual demands so abusing a kid with a handicap would be a new high. Gillespie knew about Ruby's condition and I think he wanted to take it a stage further and give Inglis the heightened thrill of actually sexually assaulting a child like her. But Etta refused to play along this time so he kidnapped her.'

This confirmed what McCall already believed. Gillespie had to be *Mr Ginger,* the threat Etta had tried to freeze out of her life.

'Why didn't you bring Gillespie in for questioning like you did Etta?'

'It wasn't that simple, not with his connections,' Benwick said. 'Besides, I'd wanted to stick it to the bosses at Scotland Yard by rolling up the entire network of abusers they'd let off during Kid Glove, those hypocrite lawyers, show-biz people and bloody politicians like Guy Inglis.'

McCall took out one of the photographs he'd shot of Gillespie in Birmingham.

'Do you recognise anyone apart from Gillespie?'

'Of course. That's your chum, Roly Vickers.'

'But what's he doing with Gillespie?'

'For Christ's sake keep up, McCall. I've told you - Vickers is an MI5 asset. He runs Gillespie at arm's length but on their behalf, has done for years.'

'But Gillespie is a dyed-in-the-wool old Trotskyite.'

'Who's on wages from Vickers for giving him the inside track about every strike in every critical area of the economy before it's even declared.'

'But with his politics, why would he subvert his own union?'

'Vickers and the spooks have him over a barrel.'

'Why's that?'

'Because of all the kids he procures for the likes of Inglis and who he abuses himself. When you've got a snout by the balls like this, his heart and mind usually follow.'

'So the spooks connive at the criminal abuse of these kids because it gives them an early warning system about strikes but better still, leverage over a politician who may one day run the country?'

'And all thanks to Roly Vickers. Make no mistake, McCall - he's not on the side of the good guys, not on this or in much else.'

But herein was McCall's problem. Vickers had to be a major target in any media exposé. Yet he had equal dirt on McCall. Vickers could portray him as a willing stooge of the security services, rewarded with stories and privileged information. McCall would never be trusted by the liberal media ever again. To move against Vickers was to court mutually assured destruction. But he'd no choice.

He asked Benwick what led to his rescue of Ruby.

'I kept getting the gypsy's warning from upstairs at Scotland Yard. You're treading on toes, back off. It was Operation Kid Glove all over again so I guess I snapped.'

He put a tracking device in Gillespie's car, followed him to a house in Clapham in south London then kicked the door in.

'Ruby was locked in a bedroom, windows boarded over. I carried her out, shouting and screaming and we drove away. Everyone heard about it - my bosses, the spooks, Gillespie, Inglis. They all knew I'd not be going quietly, not after this.'

'I still don't understand,' McCall said. 'Why risk your entire career on this one point of principle? You could've leaked the cover-up to the newspapers or an MP.'

'Sorry, I don't have much faith in either and if I left Ruby where she was, she'd not get out of there alive.'

'You're not saying they'd kill her, surely to God?'

'She knew their faces so her abusers had everything to lose,' Benwick said. 'I'd already picked up a rumour of one kid being disappeared forever and he wasn't the first, either.'

'Are you serious... this is what would've happened to Ruby?'

'Just imagine what was at stake, the enormity of what these men were gambling.'

'But murder - '

'We're getting deep in now, McCall. Try to fix it in your head that governments and spy agencies are no more monolithic than huge corporations. There are factions and power groups fighting for influence in the shadows, all with ambitions and agendas of their own... just like your friend, Vickers.'

'OK, I understand all that but who are the people who would've killed Ruby?'

'The same guys who're following us to make damn sure their man gets in to Downing Street and his dirty little secret doesn't get out.'

Thirty Seven

Next morning, alone and crossing the Humber Bridge on a bus from Barton to Hull, McCall felt no clearer about Benwick's motives, still less his long term intentions. This unease wasn't misplaced. He'd seen Benwick turn a car into a bomb to demolish two buildings for them to escape the men tracking them. He carried a gun and Vickers linked him - maliciously or not - to the assassination of a Canadian weapons scientist working for Iraq.

He could almost be playing out a Dirty Harry fantasy - the solitary good cop fighting bad guys in a corrupted world. But Benwick's sensational allegation - of police conspiring to ignore the abuse of children by high-ranking paedophiles so MI5 could honey trap a rising politician - was partly implied in Malky Hoare's notes.

But if Benwick had established where Ruby was being held, why didn't he call his bosses' bluff and raid the premises with fellow officers to arrest the kidnappers? The cops and spooks wouldn't want their dirty washing - or themselves - hung out to dry in court and would've backed off. But inexplicably, he chose to rescue Ruby himself. Maybe his schizophrenic life in S.O.10 had left him on the unstable side of reality.

As if to demonstrate this, he'd then tried to blow up a high security British arms factory with a female accomplice who'd probably been killed. So now he was on the run, fearing for his life. There had to be another narrative behind the story McCall was being offered.

*

The swelling on Benwick's sprained ankle was easing. It still gave pain if he put his full weight on it but with rest, another two days should see it right.

He lay on his bunk in the little flat where McCall had left him, unseen by people in the street below. McCall would bring food and newspapers when he returned from Hull docks. But his priority mission was to gather the intelligence on which Benwick's end game depended.

He didn't doubt McCall would come back. The hack in him was too intrigued, had too much invested not to see the affair through to the death. Benwick also detected signs of *Stockholm Syndrome* in him, an affinity with the ultimate aims of his captor making him all the more amenable as a result.

Besides, McCall seemed no stranger to the moral ambiguities imposed on those who preferred the riskier fringes of life rather than the ordeals by Garden Centre or Shopping Mall which were the penalties of a settled existence.

Benwick fixed his gaze on a small patch of damp on the ceiling, brown like a monk's cowl, and emptied his mind of all irrelevant thoughts. This was his training taking over, the ability to endure solitary confinement or hours of interrogation, focusing on a single physical feature in the cell where they would try to break him, thinking nothing, saying nothing.

In such a meditative, Zen-like state, a disciplined man can disappear deep into himself and out-manoeuvre his torturers in the end.

But the sudden, insistent ringing of a mobile phone broke his concentration. It came from inside McCall's overnight bag. Benwick hadn't realised he'd been daft enough to bring a mobile with him. They can be tracked and its user traced. He pressed the *on* button but stayed silent. The caller assumed McCall had answered.

'Listen matey, your location is known so the jig's nearly up. You're up to your bloody armpits in the solids this time but I'm told the authorities might go easy provided you get out now and co-operate about your travelling companion.'

It was Roly Vickers - the devious spook asset who'd back-scratched with McCall over the years and still had him on tap. He could yet wreck everything. Benwick thought hard but kept quiet.

'McCall? Are you still there? Say something - '

Benwick switched off the phone. He cursed McCall's stupidity and weighed up the options. Vickers could be spinning another *FUD* to jack up the pressure. They would only have a general fix so weren't yet ready to move in or set up an observation post. But Benwick couldn't gamble on unknowns at this stage. Everything would have to be brought forward. His anger at this turn of events needed to be harnessed and channelled.

He put on his donkey jacket and cap and left the flat, head down to avoid eye contact with passers-by. Ahead was the main road leading to the towering slash of concrete and steel that was the Humber Bridge in the morning mist.

He waited by the slip road near the south-side roundabout, thumb out to flag a ride. A truck from Leicester slowed down. Benwick opened the passenger door, deliberately asking the driver for a lift to Manchester.

'Sorry, mate. Wrong direction, I'm heading home.'

The lorry moved off with McCall's mobile stuffed behind the seating. Its electronic scent would now lead Roly's friends by the nose to the east midlands, if only for a day or so. It would buy Benwick a few more hours in which to regroup and change tack.

*

The King George Dock in Hull was a clamourous, chaotic spread of warehouses, fuel dumps and shipping offices beneath a low, dishwater sky liable to turn nasty. All was noise - the thunk and clank of cars driving up the ramps of ferries, grating containers being craned onto lorries, seagulls shrieking, men shouting and all this against the pulsing throb of diesel engines of ships coming, ships going.

McCall knew Benwick's wish-list but he'd a public phone box to find first. Benwick had insisted he carry nothing to help the authorities identify him if he ran into trouble.

'If they find you, they find me,' he said. 'That's not a chance I can take.'

So McCall had no wallet, driver's licence, credit cards - and no mobile. He dialled a number from a kiosk. A man answered and McCall asked if Ronnie was there.

'No, he's out playing. His Mum's just gone to the shop. Who's wants him?'

'Just a friend. We met at the golf club when we were watching the trains leaving the gunpowder factory.'

'That sounds about right. Loves the railways, does Ronnie.'

'Are you his Dad?'

'No, the next door neighbour. I'm just unblocking their sink.'

'Not a nice job.'

'No, but it gives me something to do till I can get back to work.'

'What do you do?'

'I'm a loco driver but they say I'm suffering from stress.'

'You don't sound stressed.'

'I'm not but they say I hit a woman on the track a few nights ago so I must be.'

'Well, you'd know if you had, wouldn't you?'

'That's right and no mistake and I know I didn't.'

'Where was this supposed to have happened?'

'Five or six miles out from the gunpowder factory.'

'That wasn't the train going to Hull that young Ronnie and I watched, was it?'

'Probably was but I've been ordered to say nothing about anything so sorry, but you'll have to call again to talk to the lad.'

Some days, a hack can dig in the dark for no reward. Other times, he gets lucky. The weapons factory, a train guarded by soldiers, a body on the line - these had to be part of Benwick's bigger picture.

The figure young Ronnie saw struck by the shunter might have looked male but wasn't. It could only have been Benwick's accomplice, Emily Jane Boland - the phoney pensioner whose theatrical disguises McCall took from the golf club hotel.

If he was right, it was her body that'd been taken from the factory complex and placed near the main line to fake an accident or a suicide.

Even as a corpse, the mysterious lady had been required to continue acting. But who had the motive, capability and nerve to cover up what happened on that, the oddest of nights?

*

It was looking up and suddenly being confronted by troops pointing automatic rifles at him which spun McCall back to Africa. If only for that instant, he wasn't on a wet quayside any more but in that desolate kraal again, blood on his shoes and ice in his heart.

High in the fierce blue sky, the blackest of birds circled the disarrayed limbs and flops of purple-blue offal far below. The silence, the emptiness, the desperate futility of it all swept through him like a gale of despair - and then of fear.

The crowbar men might return before his contact, the priest. McCall could yet lie amid those they'd already dealt with, bellies unzipped and darkening the sand.

The mind's instinctive defence to such threat took over. It's called de-realisation - the ears hear nothing, the eyes see nothing and the body shuts down to try and save itself.

Without knowing how, McCall found himself cowering in the cesspit, his place in the stalls when the massacre began.

But that was then, this was now.

The two soldiers who had him against a wall were Brits, rain running down their unsmiling faces and dripping from the muzzles of their guns.

'Who the fuck are you and what are you doing here?'

Thirty Eight

McCall reached into his plastic carrier bag and took out a can of strong lager from a supermarket pack of six.

'Want a drink?'

'Don't be funny, shit face. What's your name?'

He fumbled with the ring pull then took a slow swig to give himself time to think and retrieve his wits from Africa. His fake driving licence was in his mind's eye and he was straining to remember the name of who he was supposed to be.

'Are you going to tell us or do we have to insert that can somewhere painful to help you remember?'

'No, sorry... Brian Sydenham.'

'Good, got any ID?'

'All my stuff was stolen the other night.'

'Can't trust anyone these days. So what's your business on the docks?'

'I like watching the boats.'

'And getting pissed, by the state of you.'

McCall took another long drink and let some of it dribble down his unshaven chin and onto his donkey jacket. The second soldier joined in.

'Nah, he doesn't drink much. Looks like he spills most of it.'

His oppo put his face closer to McCall's. He'd had a curry the previous night.

'We've been eye-balling you mooching around so I'll ask you again, what you up to?'

'I said, I like the boats.'

'You're pushing your luck, chum. Where do you live?'

McCall knew this question was next and dreaded it. For the life of him, he couldn't summon up the address on his moody licence.

'I'm just bumming around... don't have a place at the moment.'

'OK, you're coming with us while we check you out.'

'I can't, I've got to be at the Sally Army hostel soon.'

'Not till we've given your story a spin then we'll take it from there.'

'But I've done nothing wrong. You can't arrest me.'

'You'd be fucking surprised what we can do, Brian. Now, get your arse in gear. A bit of a march might sober you up.'

*

McCall swore at himself for not going for the bus back to Barton when he'd the chance an hour before. He had seen everything he needed to by then - all except the soldiers spying on him. But he'd been too intrigued to leave. Benwick's conspiracy was starting to emerge through the mist and drizzle.

Once near the docks, McCall had found the café where dockers took breaks. He'd sat reading a paper and eavesdropping on their chat about the highly unusual consignment being loaded from the King George Dock. Then he got talking to a widower walking a dog on the jetty where his son was a crane driver.

This was how he knew the train which left the weapons factory and supposedly hit and killed Benwick's accomplice, had to be the one on the quayside - forty-two wagons tight packed with armour-piercing shells, anti-tank missiles, bombs, high explosives. The port authority claimed they carried only a general cargo of ironmongery like nuts, bolts and drainage pipes.

So why the need for warning notices all around? *Danger. Explosives. No smoking, lighters, matches or boots with metal heels or tips.* The truth was, one stray spark and they'd run out of body bags.

McCall got close enough to see crates labelled *G.H.Q. Jordan Armed Forces, Planning and Organisation, Amman* and others marked *UK Military Explosives.*

According to what McCall overheard, five-hundred tonnes of military hardware was being lowered into the MV Arta, a cargo ship newly arrived from Antwerp. It was due to leave for the Jordanian port of Aqaba on the Red Sea that coming Saturday. Benwick must have known about this shipment to a British ally in the Middle East.

Yet he'd still tasked McCall to find out its sailing schedule, the name of the vessel's agents - and to assess the general level of security. Through his own carelessness, he would now experience that at first hand.

*

'As I see it, Brian, you either tell me why you've been snooping about the docks or we charge you under the Official Secrets Act.'

McCall restrained the urge to corpse before the bacon-faced jobsworth across the desk. The plastic ID badge pinned to his lapel said he was Charles Aldridge, deputy security manager. Dockers in the café called him *Pinky*. McCall saw how well it suited the officious little drone trying to put the frighteners on him.

'I like looking at the boats.'

'Do you know what I think, Brian?'

McCall shrugged, knowing the range of Pinky's intellectual skills would take a finely calibrated instrument to measure.

'You're a PIRA man, that's what... sent to case the docks for an attack.'

First a spy, now a terrorist. It promised to be a hell of a court case. McCall tipped back his can of lager and barely suppressed a belch.

'But you've been expected. That's why we've got soldiers guarding the train.'

Then the door swung open. The man who strode in unannounced as if this were his office not Pinky's, was Larry Benwick. He wore a well cut city suit, white shirt, red tie bearing a crested Parachute Regiment motif and carried a metallic brief case.

'You must be Charlie Aldridge,' he said. 'I'm Ed Richfield, Special Branch.'

Charlie immediately stood up in deference to authority. McCall tried to hide his amazement - and immense relief - by swigging the remains of his lager. Benwick took a warrant card from his wallet so Charlie could see he was dealing with a detective chief inspector from London. They shook hands and Benwick's jacket fell open as if by chance. And there was his Makarov, pouched in a black shoulder holster.

'Hope my sergeant's not been causing you too much trouble.'

Benwick and McCall exchange grins. Charlie's face became even more pink, like the slapped arse he knew he'd made of himself.

'OK, we've not much time, Charlie. I've got to brief you but not here, some place where we're not being clocked.'

'Should I go and get my boss?'

'No, on no account do that. My instructions are to talk only to you.'

Charlie must have thought about asking why but rolled with the compliment. It would not be the last.

'The people above me rate you, Charlie... the funny people, do you understand?'

'You mean - '

'Yes, them. A job's going down here very soon and only guys we can trust can be brought into the loop. Are you with me, Charlie?'

'Yes, of course.'

A good con man intuits his mark's most unreachable desire then suckers them into a scheme by revealing a way it can be achieved. But as night follows day, there will be strings - and barbed wire - attached.

Charlie hadn't a moment's doubt he was being recruited by SB. And the more McCall witnessed Benwick's acting, the greater his doubts over who really was on stage - Larry

Benwick of S.O.10, Ed Richfield of Special Branch or even some as yet unknown third party.

'I take it you've got your car here, Charlie?'

'Out at the back, yes.'

'Good, and I'm told you still live alone.'

'Since my wife cleared off.'

'Join the club. OK, let's make our way to your billet then we'll talk there.'

*

Beneath Charlie's desire to please was the discontent of a man who believed himself undervalued, never given the chance to shine to his full potential. It hadn't been him who'd brought the undercover sergeant in for questioning. Those squaddies did that. He only acted on their information.

But now, vindication. Two Special Branch officers - the arms and legs of MI5 - were drinking Scotch in his maisonette and discussing a covert operation for which he'd been hand-picked to play a role. Equally satisfying to Charlie was being right about the threat from the Provisional IRA.

'The Provos have a man working somewhere on the docks,' Benwick said. 'Trouble is, we don't know if he's a white collar asset or a docker so that's why you mustn't say a word about us or what you hear tonight to another living soul, whatever job they do around here. You understand, don't you?'

'Totally, absolutely, on my life.'

'We'd rather it didn't to come to that, Charlie.'

Charlie cleared his throat and asked what was wanted of him.

'Keep an especially close watch on everybody and everything tomorrow. If we hit any trouble, we'll need your contacts and local knowledge.'

'What's the job we're on?'

'Right, you obviously know what's being unloaded from that train on the dock.'

'Indeed, all very secret is that so I had to be told.'

'OK, it's not certain yet but we think the Provos are working on something nasty before the ship sails so we'll have a little surprise waiting for them if they do.'

'So the SAS are here as well, then?'

'You wouldn't see them even if I told you where to look, Charlie.'

'And is that all you want me to be, eyes and ears?'

'No, there's something far more important.'

Benwick reached inside his jacket for a sealed padded envelope.

'If the Provos haven't shown by four tomorrow afternoon, the raid's being put back twenty-four hours, according to our source. In that case, I need you to get down to London before eight and go to a pub in Soho called the John Snow. It's in Broadwick Street and I want you to give this to a guy about my age and build, dark hair who'll be sitting at the bar doing the Evening Standard crossword. Just say *the rich man wants you to have this* but don't hang about, just leave.'

'Why, what's in it?'

'On a need-to-know basis, it's best you don't but a lot's riding on it, maybe even the lives of a few good men. Can we trust you to do this for us, Charlie?'

'I'm keen to help but why me for this part of the job?'

'Because certain people will be taking a closer look at you, watching how you handle yourself under our sort of pressure. I'm not a betting man but I'd put a few quid on you being in a different job in a few weeks from now.'

Too damn right, McCall thought. He felt a twinge of pity for the gowk - but nothing more. Then again, if Charlie didn't know what was going on, neither did McCall.

For the moment, Charlie fixed them up with blankets and pillows to bed down in his sitting room. Morning would soon be upon them then they'd each discover how loudly God was laughing.

Thirty Nine

Benwick was still method-acting his role as an operational DCI with Special Branch when he gave Charlie his orders after toast and coffee early next day.

'Don't be moving your bowels at noon. That's when we'll be coming to your office.'

'You can rely on me, but what happens after that?

'We'll still have work for you,' Benwick said. 'Now drop us in town and go to the docks like this is a normal, boring day.'

They watched Charlie drive off then found a café. Benwick wore a donkey jacket over his suit and gave McCall enough money to buy himself a complete new outfit.

'Make yourself look like a detective sergeant, get a decent haircut then dump your old clothes in a charity shop.'

'What will you be doing?'

'I've got things to see to and phone calls to make so I'll meet you outside the Maritime Museum in three hours, no later.'

*

They walked to the King George Dock in a chill wind coming off the sea. McCall sensed the imminent end of whatever Benwick had been planning for weeks, maybe months.

McCall no longer had the benefit of time. He couldn't be anything less than direct, to provoke a reaction and maybe find out how the illusionist was doing his tricks.

'What's all that fanny about the spooks and Charlie's envelope yesterday?'

'I need him out of the way tonight in case anyone starts asking questions and he comes over all talkative.'

'Do you con everyone like you've conned Charlie?'

'What you're really asking is if I've I conned *you*.'

'Possibly, but libel lawyers will tell you it's unwise to ever think you know the true motivation of anyone.'

'I agree. I'm always intrigued by people's reasoning.'

'So what's yours for throwing away your career and maybe even your liberty?'

'It's inevitable that we takes sides in this world, McCall, reach our own conclusions about what's right and what's wrong and if we've a chance to influence the course of events, then some of us take it.'

'Whatever the dangers and even if it means lying to people?'

'Factors you must have considered when carrying out all those missions for Vickers.'

'Deceit is sometimes required for a greater good.'

'Ah, so there was a higher purpose in what you did for Queen and country?'

'Patriotism always sounds like a scoundrel's defence but for all its faults, there are aspects of life in the old place which are still worth defending.'

'That's the gospel according to Saint Roly,' Benwick said. 'But the same can be said of some newer countries, surely?'

'To explain that, you'll need to spell out what events you're trying to influence.'

He didn't reply at once. Huge container lorries pounded by and seagulls called and cried in the moist air. Yet McCall could almost hear Benwick's actuarial brain calculating risk and probability.

'Bearing in mind what we're about to do, you've a right to know,' he said. 'But wait till we're safe out of here. Then, follow my lead and let me do the spieling.'

Beyond the dock gates, soldiers patrolled in pairs, scanning the faces of all who passed, assault rifles cradled and ready.

Benwick got back in character and McCall's mouth went a little dryer.

*

Charlie was in his office as instructed, looking even more inflated now he'd gained entry to the magic circle. He brought them weak tea in plastic beakers from a machine in the corridor outside and was anxious to give his sit-rep.

'Nothing obviously suspicious so far,' he said. 'The loading of the Arta is more or less complete and everything seems set for her to leave tomorrow morning as scheduled.'

'Good, now I'd like you to take us aboard,' Benwick said. 'I want to see the captain.'

'Right, can do. Who shall I say you are?'

'Special Branch, of course. We've had him checked via London and he's definitely not the Provo's snout.'

The MV Arta was a five-thousand tonne general cargo vessel registered in Zagreb and chartered by the Jordanian National Line for this massive arms run.

Its two deck cranes loomed above a black and red hull and the long rake of freight wagons on the quay which had transported so lethal a load across England.

Charlie led Benwick and McCall up to the bridge and introduced them to the captain. He was a prematurely grey, leathery-faced Croat who'd not shaved for days. His English was limited so he mistakenly thought his paperwork was being inspected again. Benwick didn't disabuse him.

He shuffled through a stack of end-user certificates confirming all the munitions were bound for Jordan. Charlie wanted to stay around but Benwick reminded him of the need to keep vigilant - from his office, not the ship.

Benwick turned to the captain with a knowing smile and opened his briefcase. From where he stood, McCall glimpsed an unopened bottle of Scotch and a blue plastic thermos flask. The reason for one was readily understood - and Benwick took it out. The captain found three glasses and the first of many fraternal toasts were made.

McCall wondered what Benwick's next move would be. He soon gestured at his guts with a look of constipated pain. The captain understood and Benwick went below - with his briefcase.

McCall didn't need telling what he now had to do. He refilled his host's glass and began a diverting conversation about Croatia's suffering in the endless bloody history of the Balkans.

*

It took Benwick several moments to adjust to the gloom below deck. All was quiet save for a generator keeping essential services going. The engine noise would be deafening down there when they set sail next day.

He found the loo and locked himself in a nauseous metal box stinking of diesel, piss and shit. Breathing in wasn't pleasant. He gripped a small torch between his teeth, opened his brief case then took out the thermos. With the top unscrewed, he began to set the timing mechanism inside.

As he did, the cubicle door was thumped by a crewman speaking Serbo Croat. He was most likely demanding to know how long he'd have to wait. Benwick answered in Russian and said he needed another minute. The man left.

Benwick screwed the cap back onto the flask then flushed the loo. He checked that no other seamen were on the walkway outside. Then he made for a door leading through the bulkhead to the hold on the other side.

The weather-proof steel hatches above were already clamped in place and it was dark.

But in the torch light, he could see scores of wooden pallets containing bombs, missiles, explosives, stacked at least fifteen feet high.

Benwick reached into a tight space between the crates and the ship's curved sides. He placed the thermos in one packed with anti-tank missiles. Each contained highly inflammable rocket propellant. Within the next twenty-four hours, just how inflammable would become exceedingly apparent.

He mounted the metal steps back up to the bridge. He'd been away barely four minutes. The hooch was making the captain less morose and he wanted them to stay to eat with him. Benwick apologised and said they were already late but would have one last drink to toast the enduring friendship between their two nations.

*

McCall and Benwick hurried across the greasy steel rails where the emptied freight wagons waited to be shunted away. They headed towards the dock gates. It was drizzling steadily, enough to drain the colour out of everywhere and everything. All seemed grey - the sea, the sky and the drab brick buildings around the quay.

Through it strode Benwick, aka DCI Richfield of Special Branch, his face energised with that saboteur's smile again. But for what reason? Nothing McCall witnessed him doing on the ship warranted any such apparent satisfaction. The weaponry's end-user certificates couldn't have thrown up anything new. Whatever action Benwick took must have been in the few minutes he was away at the loo.

Of more immediate concern to McCall was where they were going now and what would happen next. The initial buzz of covering whatever this story was from the inside was giving way to nagging worry. He was starting to feel strung along, used for reasons as unclear as the mystery Benwick kept promising to reveal but still hadn't.

McCall's eye was caught by a group of four or five men emerging from the portable cabins used as offices and mess rooms by the dock's security team. They began running towards the MV Arta. And there was Pinkie Aldridge, trying to keep up.

'Christ, we've been rumbled,' McCall said. 'Look who's got to Charlie.'

Right at the front was Roly Vickers. He stopped to dragoon two patrolling squaddies to join his advance towards the ship.

'We can still make it,' Benwick said. 'And don't forget, Vickers has about as much legal authority here as we do.'

Without quickening his pace, Benwick led the way onto the busy road beyond the port gates to a pub called The Sportsman. The bar was crowded with seafarers and dock workers. Sitting in the corner was the stocky Russian they'd stayed with in Leeds and who'd driven them to the safe-house in Barton.

He looked up, saw Benwick then left his beer. Not a word was spoken. They followed him out to a nearby street where he'd parked his Volvo. He opened the tailgate and Benwick gestured to McCall to climb in and lie under the blankets as before. But something didn't feel right this time.

'I'm not doing this,' McCall said. 'I've taken too much on trust. I want to know what the hell I'm involved in and where it's all leading.'

'You'll know everything soon enough. Don't waste time, we've got to move.'

'No, I've had enough of being kept in the dark.'

The Russian's arms dropped by his sides, fingers twitching. Benwick fixed his eyes on McCall's. He took a very deep breath and the faint outline of the Makarov became visible beneath his tightened jacket.

'I've enjoyed your company till now,' he said. 'But if you don't get in the car, we'll kill you where you stand.'

Forty

Coming downstairs to prepare breakfast, Hester could still smell the sage she had burned to purify the cottage sitting room the night before. She'd wanted to create an atmosphere without stress or anxiety for Lexie to envision her spiritual, mental and even cellular being with greater clarity and thereby connect to nature and the cosmos. By this, she might also come to understand the healing power of positive thinking and surrender to other dimensions beyond those which are scientifically proven.

This was Hester as shaman, ministering to Lexie in these early days of her uncertain journey towards recovery. But the move to Staithe End and life by the sea was already having benefits, not least for Ruby. This was in contrast to Garth Hall which had begun to show its darker face to hypersensitive Hester.

Its many rooms and narrow landings had come to appear sunless and oppressive, inexplicably lacking that sense of enfolding welcome she'd previously known.

It was as if all the benign ghosts of Garth had been overwhelmed by the inrush of those evil influences which always attended McCall's work but now laid siege to his home.

She still worried about his safety and hated leaving the old house locked and silent and her garden to run wild. But his absence at such a threatening time suggested a selfish lack of concern about Lexie's well-being and did him no credit.

Lexie and Ruby had to be her primary responsibility now. They had need of her whilst McCall appeared to have need of no one.

*

By late that Saturday morning, the weather improved enough for Hester to suggest making a fire on the beach to cook the sea trout she'd bought from a fisherman's shed on the harbour. They took overcoats and scarves and set up a coloured plastic wind break around them. Hester and Lexie gathered driftwood from the wrack line and Ruby ran up and down from the water's edge, carrying big pebbles to make a hearth.

'I don't think we've seen her as content as this before,' Lexie said.

'We're giving her back her childhood, that's why.'

'She's not wetting her bed any more and even the cat's settled in nicely.'

'I know. And doesn't Ruby seem fascinated by the sea? That's all she's drawing now.'

'Which is why I need to say something to you, Hester.'

'What's that, honey?'

'Look, if it doesn't work out for me, I want you to take care of Ruby... properly, I mean... legally become her guardian.'

'Of course, if that's what you want but you mustn't give in to negative thoughts.'

'We have to, same as we've got to sort out her schooling and a doctor and a dentist.'

'Around here, in Norfolk?'

'Yes, because once my place in Bristol is sold, I'll set up a trust fund for her with some of my profit and all of Etta's money.'

Hester was very tempted to ask where - and if - McCall fitted into her plan. But Lexie had said all she wanted to and it was best left there. They lapsed into silence. Each recognised the improbable mother-daughter bond developing between them, nurtured by more than just the warmth of a shared bed.

Ruby asked if she could light the fire and managed to do it with the third match. She clapped her hands and added more small branches then some pine cones and dried-out pieces of salty grey wood.

After this, she helped Hester wrap three trout in separate sheets of silver foil with lemon juice and herbs, ready to place in the embers when the fire got hot.

Lexie watched them contentedly, lying back on a softly rising sand dune where they'd made camp. She shielded her eyes from the late autumn sun which broke on the waves in countless crystal shards whenever the restless clouds blew apart. How normal it all seemed, how natural and timeless. She could almost forget something was wrong, someone was missing.

Far out to sea, container ships, trawlers, yachts, cruisers, all inched their way across the watery arc of the world. Whoever would know that in the depths beneath, mammoths once roamed and men had hunted across a land long since drowned and lost to sight?

The sun caught the twin white derricks of a cargo vessel steaming south. Lexie paid it no more attention than any of the others. Their fish were nearly ready. Ruby spooned out salad onto paper plates then filled their glasses with home-made elderflower cordial.

'Come on, let's eat,' Hester said. 'And let us drink to those we have loved.'

*

Lexie went upstairs early that evening, exhausted by the trek to the salt marshes she insisted they made after their al fresco lunch. Ruby was already in bed with Ludo on guard by her feet. Hester sat alone before the dying fire, unable to stop going over the implications of Lexie's offer if she lost out to her disease.

She'd already committed herself to look after Ruby. She was genuinely fond of the   child. The abuse she'd suffered so saddened and appalled Hester that the urge to protect her from any more harm was palpable. But being legally responsible for her upbringing imposed obligations she might not always be able to meet, however much she might want to.

What if she had to return to the States? She had relations in Oregon and friends in California and beyond. How would Ruby react to even a holiday in such distant places? More immediately, Hester was just about nearer seventy than sixty. Who would care for Ruby when she no longer could?

These were questions in search of answers. But she must hold to the still calm centre of her inner self. She pulled on a waterproof coat and walking boots then headed out under the night sky with a sleeping bag.

Being in the littoral peace of Staithe End was getting her circadian rhythms back in balance. After the disorientating menace she'd endured in recent weeks, she needed them re-set in tune with the oscillations of the tides. Benevolent nature would do the rest then she might return to the path she was meant to travel, wherever it led.

For now, she lay on the dunes amid the spiky tufts of marram grass and stared at the hierophany of the heavens which came and went between the ruffling clouds. At such times, she remembered what Einstein said about a spirit being manifest in the laws of the universe - *a spirit vastly superior to that of man.*

Was that who or what we called God? But what purpose did our feeble, eye-blink of existence serve? How could we explain our role in a harmony of parts so complex that no one had yet to fully comprehend it - and may never do so?

Not for the first time, Hester was asking herself about matters of divinity to which she still had no adequate responses.

But at last this spark of life lit from the dust of stars slept - slept with the sound of the sea in her ears and her old hippie mind blown yet again by the sacrality of it all.

Forty One

'What do you believe in, McCall?'

'Far less than I did years ago.'

'Why do you think that is?'

'How much time have you got?'

'Put like that, not a lot,' Benwick said. 'Best leave it for another day.'

McCall wasn't convinced there would be one. They were drinking coffee in the cabin of a thirty-foot motor cruiser off the East Anglian coast, keeping the MV Arta in view but from distance.

When it came to it, McCall had clambered into the silent Russian's Volvo as ordered. From then on, he felt like their hostage - and a readily disposable one, too.

He recalled the old Soviet proverb *the less you know, the better you sleep.* But McCall already had enough on Benwick to put him behind bars - not that he ever would, even if offered a deal by the police over his own criminal involvement. But Benwick wasn't to know that.

They sat across a table from each other. Neither was dressed for sailing. They wore the same suit and tie disguises - slept-in and crumpled now - in which they'd conned Charlie Aldridge. Only the Russian, in a roll-neck sweater and thick navy jacket, looked like a seafarer and held their course at the wheel.

Whatever might yet play out in the unfolding drama of Benwick's secret life, McCall blamed himself for getting too close. He'd always taken risks on stories but based on facts he could establish, people he could judge.

This time, he'd been cut off by the tide of his own personal connection to Ruby. He should have quit long before. He'd enough exclusive material and pictures then for a colour supplement spread about the kidnapping and her amazing artistic talents. But his curiosity won out. And everyone knew what that did for the cat.

After McCall and Benwick hid in the back of the Volvo, the Russian had driven them the fifteen miles or so up the coast to Bridlington and the motor cruiser he'd hired. All three slept aboard on Friday night, anchored out in the bay. Escape wasn't an option. They set sail next day to arrive astern of the Arta just after she left Hull to begin her long voyage to Aqaba.

A North Sea fog took a while to clear as both vessels progressed by the wolds of Lincolnshire then the landmark stump of Boston's parish church, towering above the pan-flat fields. Glossy grey seals lay like river-rolled stones on the mud banks of The Wash and above them, deckled clouds of wading birds yawed between their marshy feeding grounds.

Then came the coast of north Norfolk. And somewhere amid its dunes and misty pine woods would be Staithe End - McCall's own little corner of Arcadia where he had adored the woman who would never truly be his.

This much he'd always known in his heart and in his head. Here was what the shrink in Oxford would've called *cognitive dissonance* had McCall stayed long enough to have his ills given names.

For now, he stared back through time, back into all he held in amber for when his days lengthened into night. And he saw again how once she had been - that quizzical turn of her head, a glance half hidden behind wheaten hair, those eyes... conspiring, promising, treacherous.

But the one who willed him such memories, the one he lay with all those years ago, was no more. Life and circumstance take from us all. What he loved was but a ghost from an irretrievable past. We cannot return, only ever drift further away.

*

'We'll be parting company, soon,' Benwick said. 'I know you've got a lot of questions and I'll be straight with you where I can but don't expect answers to everything. OK?'

McCall held Benwick's gaze, unsure if he'd just been offered the equivalent of a condemned man's last meal. The sea looked very cold, very deep.

'I hardly know where to begin. Each day is crazier than the last with you.'

'Because we live in times of unprecedented corruption and intrigue, McCall. Even wicked old Harry Lime would find it hard to believe so we've no choice but to fight dirty and fight hard.'

'Who's "we"?'

'No comment.'

'OK, tell me what you were doing inside the weapons factory.'

'Trying to plant an explosive device in one of the underground arms dumps.'

'There's honest, if nothing else,' McCall said. 'Why were you doing that?'

'Because they hadn't taken notice of any of the warnings they'd been given.'

'What were you warning them about and why?'

'The warnings were given to those who develop or sell missiles and equipment to Saddam Hussein, the maniac who's building up a chemical and nuclear capability to threaten the whole Middle East.'

'But the Arta's cargo is not for Iraq, it's for Jordan... a western ally.'

'The end user paperwork is bullshit. The arms are for Saddam and the British government knows that Jordan is Iraq's back door because that's how Saddam gets hold of all his weaponry, whatever the international bans against him.'

'And what did our government do about it?'

'The answer is heading south at about ten knots,' Benwick said.

'But it's carrying no nuclear weapons, surely?'

'Not as such but Saddam's slowly putting the means together to make and deliver them. This piece of kit from here, that piece of kit from there, labelled yarn or agricultural implements by the complicit governments and the arms dealers whose only god is profit.'

'So the British are by-passing the sanctions on Iraq?'

'Wise up, McCall. Billions are being made so there isn't a man or a politician alive who's beyond bribing or who's unwilling to turn a blind eye for a decent kick-back.'

Benwick said Saddam spent thirty five billion dollars on weaponry in the 1980s. The munitions on the Arta alone were worth almost five hundred million.

'If the Brits don't supply Saddam just because the West suddenly doesn't like him any more, you can bet your life that others will so we just do it through quieter channels.'

'Let's go back a bit. What happened to the woman you were with at the factory?'

McCall saw from the hard look in Benwick's eyes that he wasn't supposed to know the accomplice was female. Maybe because he did, the reply was blunt and factual.

'She was hit by a shunting engine on the site and killed then her body was dumped by a main line near the factory to make it look like a suicide or an accident.'

'Who was she?'

'No comment.'

'Who covered up her death?'

'The same team which picked up Malky Hoare pretending to be spooks and who've followed us right across the country and will kill me if they get half a chance.'

'Yes, but *who* are they?'

Benwick stood up as if exasperated at so dumb a question. He went through to the Russian and cadged a cigarette. McCall didn't know he smoked. When he came back, he kept looking at his watch. There was a nervous intensity about him which he'd not shown before.

'Let me mark your card very simply,' Benwick said. 'The British economy has been ramped up by huge overt and covert weapons deals under Margaret Thatcher. Behind her are the same money men, arms dealers, spies and business interests who brought her to power and who drive her foreign policy in line with America's but telling the truth about this situation is a luxury our politicians can't afford so they surround it in double speak and weasel words. If that fails, their lawyers deem it not in the public interest allowing them all to wash their hands in the blood of others.'

McCall thought it a speech worthy of one of Hester's hippie rants against the military industrial complex.

'OK, I hear all that,' he said. 'But who are the men who want to kill you?'

'Ex-special services, ex-spooks, hired hands doing the deniable dirty work for the suits in offices who profit from the deaths of thousands of people in places where they've never been and wouldn't ever dare to go.'

'What else have you done to make them grumpy enough to want you dead?'

'No comment.'

'Look, you're not some damn peacenik on a one-man crusade, you're a cop - '

' - *was* a cop.'

'OK, but there's obviously an organisation with resources behind you, so who is it, who are you doing all this for?'

'You've asked me this already and the answer's still no comment.'

'As you wish but we're not going to get very far at this rate,' McCall said. 'Let's try it another way. What's all this got to do with the abduction of little Ruby?'

Benwick checked that the Arta was still visible then threw the stub of his cigarette into the sea. An easterly wind was taking the tops off the swelling waves. There could be rain soon. McCall understood his dilemma. The kidnap of Ruby was only one conspiracy in a cellar full of others. He couldn't shine light on one without McCall inevitably seeing the rest.

'The key to most of it is Inglis,' he said.

'Now there's a surprise.'

'He's always been of interest to MI5. They talent-spotted him at Oxford and have kept a close eye on him every since.'

'But why?'

'Because he was a pony who could win the race, McCall. Politics is about backing winners and if your winner has a weakness, that's to be exploited.'

'And Guy Inglis's weakness was sexually abusing children?'

'Exactly.'

'That's utterly wicked.'

'Maybe but great men aren't necessarily good men. Just you wait, soon after Inglis makes his triumphant entry into Downing Street, some urbane gent will take him aside and get out a few pictures from Clapham, just so he remembers what the *real* party line is.'

'And what's that?'

'Doing what the Yanks tell us and cutting any crap about disarmament or scaling back selling weapons to regimes we're not supposed to do business with.'

'And Gillespie?'

'The spooks blackmail him on the same kiddie-fiddling rap as Inglis but at arm's length, through Roly Vickers,' Benwick said. 'They're happy for Gillespie to think he's serving up little girls and boys for Inglis's photographic sessions to screw favours for his union.'

'And if anything goes wrong, it's a union conspiracy, not MI5's?'

'Neat, isn't it?'

'So why did you move against Gillespie and rescue Ruby when you did?'

'Because we'd got a bead on the Arta's cargo and I was assigned to deal with it. But I wasn't leaving Ruby in danger after I knew I'd have to disappear.'

Before Benwick could be asked any of the obvious questions his last statement provoked, the Russian shouted for him. Something was coming in over the radio. Benwick scanned the Arta with binoculars and saw a thin curl of smoke rising from where the bridge met the deck.

Within minutes, it became a billowing black cloud. Then a quick series of explosions ripped from the bridge to the bow in a rolling firestorm, vivid orange and crimson, till the ship looked like it was being hit by volley after volley of missiles.

McCall grabbed Benwick's arm and demanded to know what he'd hidden on the Arta.

'Thermate, the stuff they put in incendiary grenades. Does a decent job, doesn't it?'

'What about the poor bloody crew? Those guys are gonna die.'

'They'll get off but even if they don't, do the maths, McCall. Six or seven dead against the thousands their cargo would've killed.'

'Who the hell are you to play God with anyone's life?'

'Even Jesus Christ would agree the world's a bit safer now that lot's going to the bottom.'

'And that's supposed to make me feel better about you duping me, is it?'

'I told you, they always get warnings to change their ways.'

'Like that Canadian scientist did?'

'Especially him. He was given two choices and he made the wrong one.'

'And what choices did the Arta's crew have?'

'Listen, get it into your head, Saddam's end game is mass murder and another fucking holocaust with chemical weapons or nuclear weapons. Do you understand?'

A final thundering explosion tore through the Arta. The ship tipped backwards then slid beneath the boiling sea in a haze of steam and smoke.

McCall turned to confront Benwick again. But the man he'd helped to escape and flee from justice had been joined by the Russian. And he had his own Makarov.

'OK, show's over, McCall,' Benwick said. 'Time to get you below.'

They forced him into a storage locker beneath one of the bunks then barricaded him in. It was barely the size of a coffin. McCall began to scream in the darkness. He'd suffered a blind terror of confined spaces since childhood. The air was hot and reeked of diesel fumes and he could feel the vibrations of the revving engine through the hull as they sped away.

McCall couldn't breathe, couldn't escape. It was like being buried alive.

Forty Two

How long had those bastards locked him in that floating oubliette - ten hours, fifteen, more? He didn't know. Maybe he'd passed out. Feelings of savage anger, hatred, revenge took hold of him. The cruiser was no longer moving. They must have moored up. But where - and why? He heard voices. Benwick and the Russian. And something else, faint at first.

Waf, waf, waf, waf, waf, waf. A helicopter. Getting closer.

Waf, waf, waf, waf, waf, waf. Almost above the boat.

It drowned out all other sounds. Then the pitch of the chopper's engine changed. It was lifting off. The down draught rocked the boat from side to side.

McCall felt even more sick. That total shit, Benwick, was leaving him to die. He started shouting and thumped and kicked against the walls of his tomb.

Amazingly, the locker door gave way. He couldn't believe it. He'd finally dislodged whatever had wedged it shut - or someone had. McCall crawled out, shaking and screwing his eyes against the sudden light. All his joints hurt, his knees, neck, elbows, the small of his back. He'd survived car crashes with less discomfort.

He stank of vomit and piss and the clammy sweat of fear. There was something else in the air, too - something smelling like hard boiled eggs. It was probable the marshy creek outside.

He began to walk unsteadily along the gangway between the sleeping quarters and the galley. His mouth and tongue were gummed up with thirst. At the top of the steps to the rear deck was a puddle of rainwater. He licked at it like a dog till there was nothing left.

It was still early, maybe not long after dawn. His watch was broken so he didn't know the right time. He couldn't see anybody about. The masts of a few sailing dinghies bobbed at anchor like fishermen's floats. But Benwick's yacht scraped against the quay as he'd not bothered to put any fenders out.

McCall stood on the guard rail then clambered up the stones of the harbour wall, slippy and green with algae. It took a moment to recover his breath. A fair distance behind the boathouse and chandler's store he made out a church, a huddle of houses and cottages and further on, sand dunes and the start of a pine forest.

He looked again, unsure if he was seeing correctly. Such was his fragile physical and mental state, he might be hallucinating to escape the nightmare of confinement. Either that or he'd died and gone to whatever vale of delusion lay beyond the grave. What he saw around him was familiar. He knew this place, however dream-like his euphoric presence in it.

But his hurts weren't imagined or the gathering certainty that by accident or design, the fates had delivered him back to this spot.

Here was Jung's principle of synchronicity at work, suggesting again that coincidental events had meaning. Yet even as this student memory forced its bizarre way into his consciousness, reality exploded behind him - literally.

Something like a bomb erupted within the cruiser in a violent purple flash, breaking its back in an instant and hurling a plume of debris into the air. A jagged lump hit McCall's head and felled him.

Fire quickly engulfed the boat's crippled superstructure. Melting plastic floated on the water like hot wax and a great cloud of noxious smoke burst above him. Blood poured from the right side of McCall's face, into his eye, down his collar. He tried to get up but stumbled into the dirt once more, concussed.

He had to get away from danger - that and the police who would soon arrive in a swirl of flashing blue lights.

McCall's instinctive fears had been right. He'd never been more than a convenient substitute for Benwick's female accomplice who'd out-lived his usefulness. Why else would he make so free with such sensitive information? McCall was never going to be around to use it.

He ran between the beach and the marsh in panic - stooping, panting, falling again and again. In his mind, he could see the place where he needed to be. If only he could find his way back, he might yet be safe... and all would be well.

*

Late that Sunday afternoon, the Eastern Daily Press's district reporter filed her piece for Monday morning's paper from a phone box beyond the police cordon around the harbour. If it remained a thinnish day for news, she might make the splash.

Police were last night hunting a man seen escaping from a luxury cabin cruiser destroyed in an explosion which rocked Brancaster Staithe harbour early yesterday.

Norfolk Police wouldn't comment on rumours it had been abandoned by drug smugglers or that a helicopter was heard landing nearby minutes before.

But they confirmed a man injured in the blast is being sought. He was seen by Anna Verity, 42, who said: "I thought a bomb had gone off. I woke up and looked out of my bedroom window and saw a man in dark clothes lying on the ground. He just about managed to get up and stumble towards the beach."

In a statement, Police said: "We would ask this man to come forward urgently to be eliminated from our inquires. Officers are checking with local hospitals and any GP should contact us immediately if a man seeks treatment for what could be serious head, facial or back injuries."

The cabin cruiser - the Ellie Rosee - was rented by a foreign-sounding man last Thursday, according to a boat hire firm in Bridlington, East Yorkshire. He said he was planning a four day fishing excursion in the North Sea.

The firm's spokesman told the EDP: "He had all his tickets, including a coastal skipper's certificate and a VHF communications licence so he knew what he was doing."

He left a substantial cash deposit and gave an address in Leeds which West Yorkshire Police have since discovered is false.

In another intriguing link to northern England, a pair of black, size 8 brogue-type shoes found near the quay, contained a price label inside one of them marked "Oxfam, Hull". Police think they might have belonged to the injured man and inquiries are being made by detectives on Humberside.

Three fire appliances attended the blaze following the explosion which smashed windows in a nearby chandlery and slightly damaged other two boats in the harbour. Initial reports suggest a faulty butane gas cylinder was the most probable cause. A forensics team will examine the wreckage once a salvage company has lifted it out of the harbour.

*

This story will dominate the EDP's front page next day under the headline *Mystery Man Sought After 'Drugs' Cruiser Explosion* with a photograph across four columns showing police examining the shattered remains of the Ellie Rosee. Smaller pictures of the eye witness and the 'Oxfam shoes' will appear alongside a graphic of the east coast with Bridlington marked in relation to Brancaster Staithe.

On page five will be a brief account of an abortive air and sea search for a missing cargo ship captain. The MV Arta was carrying building materials and iron goods from Hull to Jordan but sank just before entering the English Channel after a fire on Saturday night.

Six east European crewmen were rescued from their life boat by a trawler and treated in hospital in Dover for smoke inhalation but not detained.

*

The helicopter had materialised out of a sea mist just as Hester was making a small fire near where she'd slept on the beach. It dropped down somewhere by the harbour but less than a minute later, flew back the way it'd come, fast and low. Hester had more personal matters to concern her so took little notice.

She'd not brought any food so the fire was for comfort, not breakfast. Gathering an armful of dry sticks from under the pine trees allowed her waking mind to continue processing its overnight thoughts. These were inevitably all about Lexie. Hester didn't link the helicopter to the explosion which happened a few minutes later. The sound rumbled across the fields then died away, just another unwanted interruption to the isolation her spirit craved for a few moments more.

She sat by the bright fire, cross-legged, eyes closed, till all but the sea was quiet. There was a need for her to enter into a meditative compact with nature before getting back to Staithe End. Talking to Lexie about what might happen if she died was not a conversation she relished.

It wasn't quite moral blackmail but a tiny, selfish part of her felt Lexie hadn't given her much choice. Hester was to re-configure her own remaining days, move from the Welsh borders to Norfolk and raise Ruby.

But ever charitable, Hester began to wonder if this wasn't her destiny after all. She stood up to go but some two hundred yards away, noticed a man tottering along the tide line. He was not a jogger. His arms flapped like broken wings, his legs looked ready to buckle. Then they did and he fell headlong at the water's edge.

But still he managed to crawl across the wet sand on his hands and knees. He kept looking back over his shoulder as if scared and wanting to make sure he wasn't being followed. With great effort, he tried to stand but hadn't the strength and collapsed, groaning and exhausted.

Hester hurried to him with a strange sense of foreboding. She saw blood seeping through matted hair to redden the sea around his gashed head. He'd neither shoes nor socks and the soles of his feet were lacerated and bleeding. There was a long scorch mark on the back of his jacket and his torn trousers could have been those of a tramp. But even before she rolled him over on his back, Hester knew whose distraught face was about to stare up into hers.

Forty Three

The hunt for McCall quickly gathered pace. Whatever he'd done, wherever he'd been, the police wanted to question him. Uniformed officers carrying clipboards were going house to house in Brancaster. They'd soon be knocking at Staithe End. Lexie was given a script to learn by Hester. She herself was back on the beach, heaping a big green wheelbarrow with driftwood and sticks to explain away the tell-tale tracks she'd made when pushing McCall back in it earlier.

Hester couldn't have borne his dead weight to the cottage on her own and Lexie was too weak to help. Ruby, tuning in to the grown-ups as always, provided an answer.

'Give him a ride in the wheelbarrow.'

McCall flopped in it like a corpse. He didn't make much sense and kept repeating the same words - *they wanted me dead.* Hester stripped off his wet clothes and Lexie bathed and bandaged his head. Once he was in bed, she dosed him with two of her own sleeping tablets.

A policewoman now came across the sands as Hester pushed another load of fallen pine branches to the barrow.

'Sorry to trouble you but did you hear that big explosion early this morning?'

'Yes, it interrupted my meditation. What was it?'

'A cabin cruiser going up in smoke in the harbour.'

'No one hurt, I hope?'

'Yes, a man who might have been aboard. Did you notice anyone who looked injured pass this way... slim build, dark hair going grey, dark clothes?'

'I was here on the beach all last night, star-gazing,' Hester said. 'But I didn't see any stranger pass this way after the explosion.'

Her statement was entirely factual if disingenuous. She prayed it bought time to work out their next move. Fortunately for Hester, that chalice passed from her when Lexie's ex-husband turned up at Staithe End half an hour later, unannounced and unexpected.

*

Hester thought Evan Dunne the sort of languid Englishman who only populated post-war films - wearily cynical and superior as if by right of birth.

She wasn't to know he was acting, too. He looked in his mid fifties, wispy fair hair and a tailored tweed jacket, well-worn but expensive when new.

Evan made sure he answered the door to the policeman asking questions about the wanted man.

'I'm sorry, but the lady living here is only just out of hospital,' he said. 'She's still in bed and isn't very well. She's not been outside for several days.'

'Anyone else in the house?'

'Only a friend of hers. She was on the beach early on but she's already been interviewed by one of your colleagues, a police woman, I think.'

'And you, Sir, might you have seen the man we're after?'

'No, I haven't long since arrived from Cambridge.'

'Another family friend, are you?'

'Divorced husband actually, but we try to keep everything civilised.'

Chilly smiles were exchanged then the door was shut. Ruby watched Evan from a chair in the corner, swinging her thin legs back and forth.

'You tell lies,' she said. 'Mac's in the house, and me.'

'Yes, but don't worry Ruby, I will tell them but not today.'

'People shouldn't tell lies.'

'No, they shouldn't but this time we can because Mac's not very well and we don't want him to get any more upset, do we?'

*

The suspicious coincidence of Evan's arrival in mid-crisis intrigued Hester and confirmed he knew far more than he let on. He seemed aware of what'd happened in Lexie's recent life - her operation, the tragic death of Ruby's mother, McCall going missing. She and Evan must keep in touch. Not many ex-husbands would want that, not once they'd a decree from a man-eater like Lexie. Yet there was still that easy warmth between them, the comfortable understanding old lovers share. Hester also noted Evan's concern about McCall. It was almost brotherly.

Lunch was a hurried affair of cold meat and salad. Ruby went to draw pictures of Ludo in her bedroom afterwards, but only on condition she didn't wake McCall. Evan appeared to have a plan for which Hester was quietly grateful. The drift of events piling up around Staithe End that day threatened all within.

'It's probably safer for Mac to stay out of sight here for a while,' he said. 'He looks a bit grey around the gills and that head wound's a worry but if you keep it clean and dressed, it'll most likely heal naturally.'

'What sort of trouble is he in?' Lexie said. 'Say it's not drugs or anything criminal.'

'No, it's all about politics.'

'But you haven't seen him for ages. How do you know?'

'By asking around, old thing.'

'He was supposed to be investigating Ruby's kidnap,' Hester said. 'He told us there was a lot more behind it and she still wasn't out of danger.'

'If that's what he said, that must be the case.'

'Then he ends up delirious and covered in blood on a beach in Norfolk.'

'Indeed. I'm sure we all look forward to his explanation. But I have to go now. There are things to do if we're to help Mac out of this spot of bother.'

*

McCall owed his claustrophobia to an ineradicable fragment of memory from early childhood - an image of two long boxes of pale wood being carried on the shoulders of grown-ups dressed in black. A bell tolling, people singing, a man in a white smock talking. Women's faces bent towards his, eyes soft with pity, powdered cheeks veined from tears.

It all seemed dreamlike and unreal. Yet he somehow knew his Mummy and Daddy were nailed inside the boxes and would never get out. Fear consumed him at this realisation. He was terrified that a box had been prepared for him as well. So he ran and hid behind the slabs of stone outside, carved with the names of the dead whose bones decayed beneath his feet.

He was found eventually and pacified - if only for that moment - then taken away for his life to be fashioned afresh.

But trapped in the cabin cruiser, the premonition of one day being enclosed in a small, airless space had finally come to pass as he always dreaded it would. If he'd perished in the explosion, it would have been a mercy for the alternative was surely madness.

Yet he didn't die - though how his escape was brought about remained beyond his understanding. But for now, he ghosted in and out of consciousness, vaguely aware of voices coming to him from far away and long ago.

*

Evan arrived back at Staithe End late next day with a suitcase of McCall's clothes. They could only have come from Garth Hall. He asked Hester if McCall had revealed anything new about what'd happened to him.

'No, he's mostly been asleep,' she said. 'I haven't been able to get him to eat much either, just a little soup and a piece of toast.'

'How's Lexie bearing up?'

'Far from back to her old self, I'm afraid. Seems tired and a bit withdrawn.'

'But the police haven't called round again?'

'No, thank God. Have you heard any more?'

'I've talked to some people but McCall's running out of friends in the right places.'

*

The two men walked along the beach beneath the bright autumn moon, feathering in and out of restless clouds to put a sheen across the flat calm sea. Neither wanted to be the first to break the silence. Yet both knew they needed to talk. Evan was concerned about McCall's weakened state.

'I'm OK,' he said. 'I've been cooped up long enough so a mooch will do me good.'

'You've had a pretty rough time of it.'

'Only because of my own stupidity. I've been a fool.'

'To trust Larry Benwick?'

'Yes... but I suppose you'll know why I should never have done so.'

'Possibly, but even had you come to me, I couldn't have told you anything, not then.'

'Why the hell not? He planned to kill me all along.'

'There's a bigger picture, Mac... there always is.'

'Then please tell me what it is and who Benwick's working for.'

Evan didn't reply but guided McCall towards the shelter of the dunes and their fringe of stunted gorse bushes. Far in the distance, the gloom was pin-pricked by the lights of passing ships. Evan fumbled in his waxed jacket for a handkerchief to blow his nose. He was gathering his thoughts.

'I've always believed that what someone knows is important, Mac, but not as important as what they do with what they know.'

It was difficult for McCall to interpret the thinking on Evan's shadowed face.

'Should I take that to mean you won't be helping me uncover this cesspit of a story?'

'Depends on who you're planning to chuck in.'

'Benwick, for starters.'

'Anybody else?'

'Let me see now... there's Inglis, the pervert who would be prime minister, the trade union mole who kidnapped Ruby for Inglis's pleasure, the spooks who ran a honey trap for paedophiles and the police who let them carry on abusing kids, then whoever covered up the death of Benwick's accomplice then tried to kill him - '

'Slow down, Mac. Much of this is lost on me but let's think about the wisdom of going public on all this.'

'Fuck wisdom, this is journalism.'

'But your targets are the most influential of people, powerful people who could yet destroy you.'

McCall said nothing but was tired of having the strings on his back pulled by different hands. A fresh north easterly began to keen across the North Sea. McCall shivered. Evan insisted they return to Staithe End.

The cottage was quiet but the embers of the fire which had warmed Hester and Lexie before bedtime still glowed in the open hearth. Evan resurrected it with sticks and brushwood then poured two glasses of Scotch.

'Can't have you getting ill,' he said. 'Your guardian angel's overworked as it is.'

McCall smiled bleakly and Evan settled in the armchair opposite.

'So, can we play twenty questions on this story or not?'

'I'll do my best, Mac.'

'Where and when was Larry Benwick born?'

'Dagenham in Essex in 1950.'

'Is that his real name?'

'Yes, his father was a British soldier who married a German woman after the war.'

'Is Benwick some kind of a spook or an agent?'

'Yes.'

'Who's he working for?'

'A foreign power.'

'Obviously, but which bloody one?'

'Patience, Mac. I know he was recruited from the Young Communist League the year before he won a place at Manchester University.'

'To read what?'

'Linguistics, got a 2.1.'

'He told me he joined the Foreign Office for a while.'

'Yes, he did.'

'Why did he quit the Foreign Office and join the police?'

'Because the people running him wanted a sleeper in Scotland Yard, ideally in Special Branch but when he was drafted into undercover work, that suited them, too.'

McCall was trying - and mostly failing - to keep his hack's excitement under control.

'So he was spying for the Soviets?'

'Not for Moscow, no.'

'But he spoke Russian and his accomplice on the cruiser did, too.'

'Maybe, but Benwick was spying for one of our notional allies.'

'For Christ's sake, stop jerking me around. Which one?'

'Israel.'

'Israel? You've got to be kidding.'

'I'm not, no. Back in his Young Communist days, he was what's called a *sayan* or a helper for the Israeli intelligence service.'

'That's pretty hard to believe.'

'Maybe but it's known he was involved in at least three surveillance operations in London back then and has used multiple identities since.'

'But why would a supremely professional outfit like the Mossad want, need or trust a young outsider to do anything?'

'Why not? A teenage boy is just a tree in the forest. Being invisible can be useful.'

'So what was his motive? He's not Jewish, is he?'

'No, but *sayanim* don't have to be. In Benwick's case, it's all about guilt and anger.'

'In what way?'

'His mother was a Nazi concentration camp guard at Ravensbruck.'

'Christ. Really?'

'Yes, and one who derived particular pleasure in her sadistic work, apparently.'

'And he ends up working for Israeli' intelligence. That's amazing.'

After the war, she escaped capture then met Benwick's father. They married and settled in England. When Benwick was fourteen - and unaware of his mother's past - German prosecutors sought her extradition to stand trial for war crimes.

'But rather than face that very public ordeal, she hanged herself,' Evan said. 'Benwick came home from school one day and found her... had to cut her body down. You can imagine the effect that had on a young boy.'

'Absolutely. So is working for the Israelis his way of making up for her crimes?'

'Could be. Whoever was talent-spotting for them saw the potential of harnessing his mixed-up feelings by showing him the appalling evidence against her.'

'And that's how he ultimately comes to blow up the arms shipment?'

'Yes, but view this in the context of present-day politics,' Evan said. 'Iraq is threatening Israel with attack in order to draw them into the coalition of Western and Arab powers he's fighting. Saddam's banking on no Arab state being willing to be on the same side as Israel so if Tel Aviv joined the coalition, the pro-West Arabs would quit the war and leave Saddam that much stronger.'

'You're saying he's trying to provoke the Israelis into getting their retaliation in first?'

'Yes and it's created a God-awful battle behind the scenes in London.'

'Why is that?'

Evan heaped more brushwood on the fire which spat out sparks as it flared up.

'Those were British arms on the Arta but the Cabinet and the spooks were split on whether the original contract with Saddam should be honoured on not.'

'Because those weapons could be turned on our troops now he's our enemy?'

'Exactly, but the arms lobby and their Arabist friends in the security services have other considerations, not least the unbelievable profits they make.'

'Where does Guy Inglis stand in all this?'

'With the hawks, as always,' Evan said. 'It was Inglis who notionally held the balance of power in the end.'

'In what way?'

'The hardliners in the spooks like Roly Vickers had Inglis threaten a leadership challenge to Margaret Thatcher if Saddam didn't receive the weaponry on the Arta and by then, her people didn't dare run that risk.'

'Why ever not? I'd have thought if anyone could hold her ground, it'd be her.'

'In earlier times, maybe. Now, it's different... she's almost out of road politically and Inglis knows this and has his own ambitious reasons to willingly undermine her at every twist and turn.'

'Wow. So the Israelis find this out and send Benwick into action... unofficially?'

'Right, then the arms traders send their goons in to stop him... equally unofficially.'

'And if this all comes out in the media?'

'Then the sky will fall in, not least on you,' Evan said. 'For the sake of your health, I think we need to get you out of the country - and quickly, too.'

Forty Four

McCall fought against accepting the truth of it but his subconscious self suspected that Lexie's kiss two nights before signalled the end of their renewed affair as surely as the first embrace had marked the beginning.

Lexie gave and Lexie took away. But this time, she appeared different. He detected a rare humility in her, maybe a desire to atone for past hurts and to make the harder of two choices now and thereby save him from the pain she feared her illness would ultimately cause.

'Let me come with you,' she said. 'I can easily make it to the harbour.'

Lexie couldn't bear the idea of saying farewell at Staithe End. She hadn't wanted the moment shared with Hester or Ruby or to have his memories of such a place despoiled by what she had to do.

This was their last mile together. They walked it alone, hand in hand, and made their way along the opalescent shore towards where Evan said he'd wait with a car. How neat for all three of them to be on stage for this final act.

'I'm sorry, Mac... sorry for everything I wasn't able to be for you.'

'Please, don't say that. It's what you are that I loved.'

'Funny old business, life... isn't it? I don't know what it's all been for.'

'Nor me but listen, you'll get better before long, you'll be all right soon.'

'Will I, Mac?'

'You're sure to, yes.'

'We'll see... anyway, Evan's got me an appointment with a specialist he knows in Cambridge and Hester can always take care of Ruby so I have nothing to worry about,

not really. Only you.'

'Then you mustn't,' McCall said. 'Evan says I've just got to keep a low profile for a few weeks, just till he's sorted out all this fuss then I'll be back with you. I promise.'

Lexie looked into his face, afraid he still hadn't understood. A single flash of headlights came from by the harbour causeway. Evan had seen them. They would have to part.

She took McCall to herself with great tenderness. Her hair smelled of wood smoke and the damp sea-saltiness from their walk along the sands. In the half light, her face was so grey, those once beautiful features so lightly pencilled in and leached of all natural colour.

She kissed his lips and his eyes and clung to him as if he were her son going off to war. But the battle was hers and victory far from assured.

Then Lexie broke free and turned away before any tears weakened her further. She headed back to Staithe End. He watched till she was gone. She didn't look over her shoulder.

The moon and stars lit the emptiness of the beach and the sea would soon wash away their footprints. No one would ever know who had passed that way that night.

*

McCall stared down from his window seat at the baking Namibian bush, ten thousand feet below. Somewhere in that vast sweep of desolation were jackals and lions, scorpions and snakes, all fighting to survive.

But these creatures only killed to eat, like the desert tribesmen still hunting with bows and arrows and spears. Theirs was the timeless order of things.

Yet other killers had also stalked their prey here - the *crowbar men*, assassins who murdered in the name of anti-terrorism to shore up the weakening influence of South Africa's cruel apartheid regime.

But the war was over. Namibians had won their independence, albeit the land beneath their feet was sown with skulls.

For McCall, there was no choice but to go back, to make an act of contrition on that seared patch of earth where he'd seen the crowbar men at work - and himself for what he'd become.

He wondered if Benwick might ever get the redemption he also craved. Evan had told him he wasn't the assassin who'd shot Saddam's Canadian weapons scientist in Brussels earlier that year.

Whatever else Benwick had done, Evan said that hit was the work of three killers who'd rented an apartment in the same building.

'Their appearance suggested they were Moroccans.'

'And were they?'

'Who knows, but wherever they called home, they were from the Mossad, operating in a unit called *Kidon*.'

'What's that?'

'Kidon means "bayonet" in Hebrew.'

'Yes, but what is it?'

'The Mossad wouldn't call it a death squad but that's what it is,' Evan said. 'Kidon targets and kills those enemies of Israel who pose the greatest long term threat.'

'So was Benwick in Kidon?'

'Think about it. Here's a man who's clever, highly resourceful, psychologically strong, utterly single-minded and as ruthless as blazes so what's your guess?'

McCall told Evan all that'd happened after he'd found Benwick hiding in woods near the weapons factory when his attempt to bomb it went wrong and his female accomplice was killed.

'He'd sprained his ankle badly and was stymied then I came along, only too willing to take her place.'

'What a dangerously rash course of action for you to take.'

'There speaks an academic. I don't know any hack who wouldn't have sold their birthright to get ringside at that guy's fight.'

'But with what you now know is at stake, do you think our lords and masters will sit idly by while you traduce their schemes and reputations in the media?'

'No, probably not.'

'And who've you got on your side?' Evan said. 'From what you've told me, Benwick's your only source and all your supporting evidence was lost when he blew up your car. That won't give a libel lawyer much confidence, will it?'

Evan was only pointing out the blindingly obvious - but he didn't stop there.

'Have you considered that Benwick himself would want you kept quiet, too?'

'You seriously think he'd come back and finish the job?'

'You should ask yourself why he told you so many secrets, especially since there's a Mossad curse which goes something like *may we read about you in the newspapers.*'

'So I was right. He told me things he shouldn't because I was never intended to live long enough to reveal them.'

'Correct, and now you're a risk to his security and the Mossad's,' Evan said. 'And I doubt that many wake up from the sort of silence they impose.'

*

'Welcome to independent Namibia, Mr McCall. What is the purpose of your visit?'

'I'm planning to go to Etosha to photograph the wild life up there.'

'Your passport says you are a para-legal. What is that profession?'

'It means I undertake inquiries for solicitors, lawyers.'

'Well, enjoy your holiday but take care in the north. It can be a dangerous place.'

'Thanks, I'll watch my step.'

His first hurdle was overcome. He'd flown via Geneva then Portugal to get a direct connection from Lisbon to Windhoek.

This route avoided Jan Smuts Airport in Johannesburg where the South African Bureau of State Security kept records on journalists whose credits appeared on British current affairs shows. They already had McCall on file after his near miss with Koevoet so he'd rather not make it easy for them this time.

During the long cab ride into town, he thought yet again about the enigmatic Evan. It wasn't ever mentioned directly but he'd always believed him to be a spook asset. Maybe he talent-spotted in Cambridge or his academic status allowed him freer travel behind the Iron Curtain. McCall never tapped him up for sensitive information. Roly Vickers was always on hand for that.

But why had the funny people cleared Evan to mark McCall's card so fully on Benwick? Maybe it was just as simple as he'd said. Not all the spooks were hawks about what should happen over the MV Arta and its deathly cargo.

*

Next day, McCall hired a car through the receptionist at his hotel in central Windhoek. He drove north through the capital's colonial facades from German rule, houses with tin roofs painted pink and a few office blocks to suggest progress towards modernity.

Ahead was a six-hour drive through bush and dusty dorp towards Ovamboland and the Angolan border.

Out of Windhoek, the tarred road gradually swept down several thousand feet from a high plain to the desert, a blistering, rock-strewn panorama of grass bleached brown and stunted trees, hung with the pouch-like nests of weaver birds.

Signs warned motorists to look out for elephants. Wildebeest and impala were hazards, too - but not as great as local drivers. The wrecks of their cars and trucks lay upended amid the litter of scree and boulders at the roadside.

McCall stopped in a small town around mid-day and found a place to eat. It was cool and dark inside. Three heavily built white men, slouched on chairs and drinking beer from bottles, stopped talking as they heard him speak. Suspicion seemed to carry on the smoke from their cigarettes.

A bull of a bartender raised his eyebrows a fraction by way of asking what McCall wanted. He asked for steak and French fries. The order was shouted through to a back kitchen in harshly accented Afrikaans. Then the eyebrows went on the move again.

'And a Tafel Lager, please.'

'You from England?'

'Yes, on holiday.'

'To Etosha, the wildlife?'

'That's right. I'm an amateur photographer.'

'Then watch out for the blecks,' he said. 'Steal your cameras and the fillings from your fucking teeth, they will. Think they own the goddam place.'

Well, they did now. They'd more than paid for it in blood and bodies. But McCall simply nodded and went to a corner table. It was best not to get into the rights and wrongs of the independence war, not with those who'd yet to adjust to losing.

When McCall finished eating, he crossed the street to the post office to use its public phone. It'd be marginally more secure than the one in his hotel room. The number he called took a while to answer.

'Father Steffen, hello.'

'Father, it's Mac... from London. Remember?'

'Of course. Where are you?'

'Coming up country. Can we meet?'

'Yes, why not? But where?'

'Where you rescued me... remember? I'll be there before sundown.'

*

The massacre McCall witnessed was beyond evil, albeit random and chaotic in the arbitrary way death so often was in Africa. This was little consolation for he had been responsible for it, however unwittingly. Amends had to be made.

He arrived at the stockaded kraal earlier than expected. It had been abandoned to its evil spirits. The three thatched huts he remembered were already starting to collapse, their stores robbed out by rats, walls weakened by gunfire.

Beyond was a slight bump of dun-coloured soil marked by six crosses made from twigs bound with twine. For McCall, the smell of death still hung in the clammy air, as sickly as a slaughterhouse and enough for a guilty soul to turn away and retch.

Within the compound, he saw darker patches of earth where lives had drained away. He paused, his godless head bowed, envious of anyone with faith who would have had prayers to offer those who lay beneath him.

Next month, the seasonal storms would come - massed clouds firing down the first fat drops of rain to ricochet in the dust. Then turbid rills will form to swill away the haunting signs of atrocity for ever.

Inside one of the huts, three wooden beds had been stripped bare. Their brightly patterned blankets would've been used to wrap bodies for burial. In another corner lay a simple home-made toy - coat hanger wire bent into the rough outline of a car with working wheels and a long handle so it might be pushed along.

It could only have belonged to the boy. How precious it must have been - a magic car to drive away from his world of poverty and war. McCall lifted it up with great care. This symbol of life and hope should be in his office, not the bullet casings which seeded the earth on that appalling day.

But the toy wasn't his to take. Then again, neither was the child's life.

McCall turned and walked into the brief but dramatic African sunset, a sky the colour of blood soon to fold into a blue-black night.

Out of this gathering darkness stepped McCall's priest, ready to hear his confession.

Forty Five

Father Steffen Kohler was German, the grandson of a colonial administrator from the Kaiser's time when cries for freedom were silenced by the hangman in the land which would become Namibia. Though he'd no personal responsibility for his family's past sins, Father Steffen made the ultimate act of contrition following his ordination forty years before.

He was sent to Namibia and opted to stay among the voiceless dispossessed, sharing their marginal existence and the dangers which went with it.

His gentle grey eyes and deep-lined face, buffed brown by the African sun, suggested an inner serenity derived from an unwavering conviction that he was doing God's work. He would live - or die - as the Lord saw fit.

But appearances were misleading. Father Steffen was a troublesome priest, long since committed to undermining South Africa's occupation of Namibia and the cruelty of its inhumane racial laws. Pretoria's secret police suspected he helped terrorists. Koevoet might have killed him but for the bad publicity the assassination of a respected white priest would generate.

'So you've returned, Mac. Welcome, you are most welcome.'

They hugged warmly. The priest seemed more bony and stooped than ever.

'What has brought you to us this time?'

'I'm on a sort of holiday,' McCall said. 'I thought it'd be good to meet up again.'

'Of course, but tell me, why did you never send me the story I helped you with?'

'I'm sorry but there wasn't one.'

'But why not, Mac? That story almost cost you your life.'

McCall looked away, looked up to where skittering bats hunted moths in the satin glow of starlight.

'I think that's the point, Father. The debt was mine but it was paid by others. I couldn't bring myself to write it.'

'I see, so you blame yourself for what happened at the kraal?'

'There is no one else.'

'No, you are wrong. It was me who brought you here. If you are guilty, I am more so.'

'You weren't to know Koevoet were looking for me so actively.'

'Do you think I wasn't aware of their methods or what they were capable of?'

'But the women here... that little boy. They died because I was amongst them.'

'And I should've realised how great the risks were to them.'

'So we're both guilty, priest and penitent?'

'I'm afraid we are and I pray every night for the forgiveness of those I had to bury.'

From somewhere in the distant bush, they heard a sudden squeal as the jaws of one creature closed over another. Then all went quiet again.

'So what am I to do with the guilt I feel?'

'Mac, I am a priest but I cannot offer you absolution any more than I can give it to myself. I must believe God brought you to me for reasons beyond my understanding and that the deaths of these poor people have some purpose in His plan.'

'That doesn't quite relieve me of what I feel inside,' McCall said.

'Then tell your story... tell the story of the people you saw die and how they didn't die in vain. You may feel bad about it but what you write could be their memorial.'

'And that'll do it, will it... make me feel better?'

'In the worst of times here, I would tell people what another priest once said... that when everything has been taken from you, you'll still have two hands. Put them together in prayer and you'll be the stronger for it.'

'Yes, but they believed, Father. They had a god.'

*

They could have eaten at a new hotel nearby, styled on a traditional Namibian roundhouse with thatched lodges waiting for much-needed tourism and set amid camphor bushes, bougainvillaea and white pan lilies.

But Father Steffen preferred humbler surroundings - his rooms within the plain brick and plank church built by German missionaries almost a century before.

They drove to it in reflective silence. It'd been a long day. McCall was physically and emotionally emptied out - all the travelling, returning to the scene of the massacre, subconsciously worrying about Lexie.

The head injury sustained when Benwick's yacht blew up was also giving him periodic double vision. Even worse were the nightmare flashbacks to his buried-alive ordeal, leaving him incoherent with fear and afraid to go back to sleep.

Father Steffen's quarters were simple and book-lined, sparsely furnished but offering monastic calm. McCall washed and changed into a pale linen suit before sitting down to supper of chicken and rice.

When they finished, he pushed a package across the table to Father Steffen.

'What is this?'

'A gift.'

'A gift for me? But why?'

'Because I want to make a practical contribution to your work.'

Inside was a wad of traveller's cheques with a value of ten thousand US dollars.

'I can't possibly accept this, Mac.'

'Please, you must. Use it for the benefit of the kids around here, buy some equipment for your school, some toys, books, medicines. I don't mind. Whatever you see fit.'

McCall was only too aware of how shallow his motives were.

'This is very generous but it isn't necessary for you to do this.'

'You think I'm trying to buy forgiveness, don't you... that this is blood money?'

'I didn't say that nor would I.'

'No, but I can't deny it. The truth is I don't know what else to do to even start to make up for what I did.'

'I thought you to be a good man when we first met, Mac. Nothing that's happened changes my view. I will use this money as you suggest so some good might come of the wickedness which moved amongst us.'

*

Apologists for regimes - invariably communist - appalled McCall when rationalising the slaughter of political opponents as a necessary evil for a greater good. Thus mass murder became the cliché of eggs being broken to make an omelette.

In no sense was Father Steffen inured to violent death, the waste and stink and pity of it. But he'd enough political awareness to fit the massacre McCall witnessed into the context of a long bush war on the march to independence. They were both free to draw whatever comfort they could from this.

Father Steffen invited McCall to stay for a while, perhaps sensing a deeper malaise beneath his evident remorse.

It was now October. The township where Father Steffen lived was hot and dry and in urgent need of the coming rains. Discarded plastic bags swirled in the desert wind gusting through the stalls of the open market. Inscrutably beautiful women bought vegetables as exotically coloured as their full length dresses while their excited children pointed at McCall's white face then ran away, giggling.

Next morning, he was invited into their school's cinderblock classroom and answered innumerable questions about London, Princess Diana and the Queen of England. Father Steffen found him later in the cool of his church, sitting beneath a cross on which a tortured black Jesus hung in agony.

'Are you all right, Mac? You look troubled.'

'No, I'm not really. Well, maybe I am... just a little.'

'It's not still something to do with the kraal, is it?'

McCall thought for a moment. Morality was the preserve of priests. Maybe now more than ever, he needed guiding counsel.

He began telling Father Steffen about the sensational story he'd uncovered in London, of the links between Ruby's kidnapper, a paedophile MP who might yet become Prime Minister, and a cabal of spies and profiteers from the arms industry.

'How very intriguing, Mac. Even I would read that.'

'I'm sure you would but there's a serious complication.'

'The laws of libel in England?'

'No, I know my way round them,' McCall said. 'The problem is more ethical than legal. I fear that if I wrote this story, an untold number of people could suffer and I'd have even more deaths on my conscience.'

McCall explained how a huge consignment of munitions secretly intended for Iraq had been blown up on a ship in the North Sea. The politically sensitive question of whether Saddam Hussein received these weapons or not - and the conspiracy to destroy them - were indivisible parts of Ruby's story.

'So who sank the vessel?'

'The Mossad.'

'Ah, I see. Have the Israelis made threats against you if you reveal what you know?'

'They don't have to, not directly,' McCall said.

He laid out Saddam's end game - according to Evan - and how, if it became public that Israel had sunk the arms shipment, he'd seize on that as an act of war.

'He would use this to justify an attack on Tel Aviv, maybe with chemical weapons but then Israel would retaliate even harder and the conflict would just get deadlier.'

'So you're struggling between your professional instincts to satisfy the public's right to know and your heightened sense of guilt because of those deaths in the kraal.'

'Yes, it weighs heavy having blood on my hands.'

'The question is simple, Mac. It doesn't need a theologian or a philosopher and I suspect you know the answer already.'

'Tell me, anyway.'

'All conspiracies unravel, in my experience,' Father Steffen said. 'From what you tell me, too many people already know about this one for what you've uncovered to stay secret for long. Therefore, I believe you should write this story as well. Tell the truth, Mac, and if that offends any government or any wrong-doers, so be it.'

'So publish and be damned?'

'Yes, I suppose so,' Father Steffen said. 'But when you do, I shall offer prayers for the day to come when men no longer live in a state of perpetual conflict and condemn themselves to die with weapons in their hands.'

*

The phone message waiting for McCall in reception at his hotel in Windhoek simply said *Ring Evan soonest.* It'd been received three days before. An international operator connected him to Evan's direct line in Cambridge. A female student answered and said she was his research assistant.

'He's in a meeting but he left me a note if you called,' she said. 'You should get back to the UK as quickly as possible because Lexie's had to have another operation.'

'Oh God, she hasn't, has she? Do you know how it went?'

'Not really but Evan says she keeps asking for you, no one else.'

'OK, tell him I'll somehow shmooze my way onto a flight home,' McCall said. 'And say to give Lexie my love, will you?'

It was suddenly difficult for him to breathe. The unthinkable demanded to be thought. His guts were like slush and he felt very far from all he knew and all he wanted.

Forty Six

McCall crossed the concourse at Lisbon Airport to await a connection to London. He couldn't stop picturing Lexie, re-attached to tubes and drips and being too tender to touch. Why was she asking for him? There could only be one reason. He had to get back before it was too late.

A boy of about fifteen, olive skin, dark hair and dressed in jeans and a yellow T-shirt, walked across to McCall.

'Here, you dropped something,' he said.

He spoke English with an accent, possibly Spanish. McCall looked at him, puzzled.

'No, I haven't dropped anything.'

'You did, over there, by the newspaper kiosk.'

He pushed a white envelope into McCall's hand then turned and was lost in the crush. The envelope wasn't creased so couldn't have been in his pocket or rucksack. This had to be a very personal delivery.

Inside were a photograph and two press cuttings. The first story came from the Daily Mail's diary page and was published while McCall had been in Namibia.

Would-be Tory prime minister, Guy Inglis, 48, unexpectedly married his trade unionist sweetheart, Kaye Simon at a discreet register office ceremony in central London yesterday. They then hosted a friends-only reception at Bramshill, the Jacobean mansion and police staff training college in Hampshire.

Kaye, 37, works in human resources at the Association of Federated Trades in Birmingham but will relocate to their London office - and live in Mr Inglis's elegant Georgian house in Highgate - when they return from honeymoon in Barbados.

A close colleague said: "We never thought this day would come. Guy's always been the archetypal bachelor about town but maybe with his eyes set on Number 10, getting spliced was the inevitable price he's had to pay."

I bet it damn well was, McCall thought. Where better to hide his sexual proclivities than behind the skirts of a tactically acquired wife?

The second cutting was from the communist Morning Star. It reported another extremely convenient event - that of Ray Gillespie's death. The piece carried a single column mug shot taken from the right hand side so his birth mark wasn't revealed.

We regret to report the passing of Ray Gillespie, a great socialist and supporter of progressive politics the world over.

Ray worked tirelessly for workers and the wider trade union movement through his role within the leadership of the Association of Federated Trades at its headquarters in Birmingham and in branches across Britain. He was a forceful and amusing speaker at the TUC, always joking that he was married to the AFT because no woman would have him.

It's understood he had been off work recently with health problems. Funeral arrangements have yet to be announced.

McCall knew now he was being covertly observed. He stared at the faces of those leaning over the balconies above him or riding the escalators to the duty free shops. He saw only strangers but knew he was standing centre stage in a little drama being put on for his benefit. Only one person had the incentive and capability to do this. If McCall had any doubts, they were dispelled by the photograph.

It had been taken around dawn. The early morning light caught the sheer stone walls of a bleak, castle-like structure in the background. He recognised the location immediately. This was the pumping station at Manor Hill where Ruby once played and her mother had died.

And floating face down at the edge of the reservoir was a man's naked body.

McCall looked more closely. On the left side of his neck was a dark stain. So this was how the tireless old socialist ended his treacherous days. Ray Gillespie - black arts merchant, pimp to the powerful and the spy in their camp.

On the back of the picture were the words *you win some, you lose some* typed on a square of white paper. Here was Kidon justice - Benwick's justice - natural not legal and with not a fingerprint to be found. Ruby had finally been avenged.

The London flight was called. McCall, desperate to leave now, gathered his belongings and made for the departure gate. Lexie had gone from his mind. All that concerned him was how to fly Ruby's incredible story by the lawyers then splash it across the papers and television. The picture of

Gillespie surely meant Guy Inglis was as good as dead in the water, too.

A security guard checked his boarding card and nodded him air side. McCall then heard his name being shouted from the noisy concourse behind him.

He turned slowly, knowing full well who'd be there - and maybe always would be. Larry Benwick stood watching him, dressed Miami cop-style in white slacks, his arms folded across a blue jacket. He could have been seeing his kid brother off on a foreign jaunt.

'You take great care, Mac... always watch your step,' he said. There was no obvious menace in Benwick's voice, only meaning.

'And don't go doing anything I wouldn't do.'

Then the fraternal smile died on his lips as he seemed to pass a forefinger across his throat. The gesture took but a moment and then he was also gone into the crowd.

THE END

Acknowledgements

Many people gave freely of their time and knowledge, some preferring to do so anonymously. I am most grateful to them all. Any errors are mine, not theirs.

Adrian Bradshaw deserves special mention for his endless patience in answering questions about railways, locations and much else.

For insights into Asperger's syndrome, I thank Helen McConachie, Samantha and Lee Coates and their children, Lucie, John and Cameron; also Jackie Stamp, Cheryl Powell and Libby Jones of New Pathways, Merthyr.

I was also helped by library staff in Hull, Cambridge and Blackrod; Anton Antonowicz; Judy Bryan; Paul Calverley; Ted Childs; Suzanne Doherty; Fred Goulding; the Rev Graham Hellier; Paul Hetherington; Ted Hynds; Gerald James; Dr Peter Jones; Professor Ian Linden; Jane Linden; Anne and Jack Loader; Hugh MacDougall; my friend and mentor, Patrick Malahide, who gave me constant encouragement; Lieutenant Colonel Kearn Malin MIExpE; Sue and George Miller; Anthea Morton-Saner; Keith Pedder; Mike Petty; Gaynor Richfield; Andrew Rosthorn; Sally Ryan; Richard Scorer; Ex Detective Chief Superintendent Laurie Sherwood QPM; Jack Smith; Matt Taylor; Harriet Taylor Seed; Stephen Walters and his late wife, Elaine; Commodore Simon Whalley CBE RN rtd. Finally, to my wife, Ann de Stratford, for support and forbearance beyond the call of any reasonable duty.

Credits

The rhyme, *Six Little Mice,* used in the Prologue and Chapter 19, is traditional.

The poem referenced in Chapter 2 is *Welsh Landscape* by R.S. Thomas.

The words quoted in Chapter 18 are from Allegri's *Miserere.*

10261671R00210

Printed in Great Britain
by Amazon.co.uk, Ltd.,
Marston Gate.